BARELY BREATHING

URBAN FANTASY ROMANCE

MERELY MORTAL
BOOK THREE

MICHELLE M. PILLOW

MICHELLEPILLOW.COM

ABOUT THE BOOK

Merely Mortal 3

Book three in the spellbinding first-person POV romantic urban fantasy series by NY Times & USA Today bestselling author Michelle M. Pillow

I never asked for this life.

Being the only mortal in a family of supernatural powerhouses was hard enough. Now, I have a master vampire who won't let me go, a dragon's magic that won't stay quiet, and another damn prophecy hanging over my head like a guillotine.

And the werewolves? They've kidnapped an innocent child—along with her father—for a ritual that will either destroy the supernatural world... or twist it into something far worse.

I can't save them. Not alone.

To stop the ritual, I'll have to risk everything—my family, my friends, my humanity. Costin, the dangerously seductive vampire, wants to protect me, but even he can't shield me from the choices I have to make. And Paul, the man who once gave me hope for a normal life? He's caught at the heart of it all.

I've survived dragons, labyrinths, and betrayals. But this time, the stakes are higher than ever. Blood and moonlight are calling, and if I don't fight with everything I have, I'll lose more than just my soul.

How much am I willing to sacrifice to save the ones I love?

I'm barely breathing. And the worst is yet to come.

Perfect for fans of Ilona Andrews, Patricia Briggs, and Jeaniene Frost, Barely Breathing blends high-stakes action, supernatural mystery, steamy romance, and forbidden love in a thrilling urban fantasy world. If you crave enemies-to-lovers tension, power struggles, and heart-stopping twists, this is a must-read.

MAILING LIST

To stay informed about when a new book in the series installments is released, sign up for updates:

Sign up for Michelle's Newsletter

michellepillow.com/author-updates

To John, my foreverything

FROM THE AUTHOR

Though this book can be read as a standalone if you really want to, the author recommends reading this series in the order of publication.

CHAPTER
ONE

This is not my bed.

It's the only clear thought I can manage. It pierces through the haze, settling like an anchor in the swirling chaos of fragmented images. An invisible force makes my limbs feel heavy, and every breath pulls in the smell of wood polish and incense mixed with something darker and masculine that quickens my pulse despite my confusion.

This is not my bed.

The realization keeps surfacing. If I chase the broken whispers of nightmares too closely, they threaten to pull me into a darkness I'm too afraid to face.

I am alone, and this is not my bed.

My skin tingles, making me think of the energy residue left behind by magic. The sensation is wrong. It's not the protective warmth of my amulet but something darker, more primal. The air feels charged, like the calm before a supernatural storm.

But I don't have magic. I'm a mortal born into a supernatural family. I know about magic, but I don't have—

Fuck.

A sharp pain stabs my temple, and I'm forced into a memory.

I feel as if I'm floating above my past, watching it from above like staring into the depths of a deep well. I see myself entering a rock troll's cave home with the vampire, Costin. I hear the gemstones hanging from the ceiling jingle with angry vibrations as if they can feel my intrusion, but I can't see them.

Morvok's rock body blends with his surroundings, and I only see the troll because I know where to look. He pushes to his feet, and the low, guttural sound of his breathing fills the cave. He looks tired as he ambles to the worktable where my broken amulet awaits. I cannot understand the strange show playing out in front of me, or why it's even happening. The moment feels real, but I know this is from the past. I know I lived it, but I can't recall what happened next.

"Costin and pet." Morvok turns to face us. Well, past us. He doesn't seem to notice me above them watching. "Morvok did not expect you to return."

Suddenly, I'm back in my body, standing on the cave floor. I remember wondering why everyone in my life always underestimates me.

"Fix it." My raspy voice comes forced from my throat, and I hold out my hand. I need the troll to fix the amulet. My weakened body needs its protection. "We don't have much time."

What kind of magic is this? I try to pull out of the fragmented memory, blinking hard to determine what is real and what is the past. It doesn't work.

"You are too late. Draakmar is awake," the troll says.

Fear fills me just like it did the first time. Draakmar, the ancient dragon who will rain fire down on the world. The prophecy is clear.

One second, I'm in a cave. The next, I get a flash of a different memory, watching a river of lava make its way down Manhattan. Heat swallows everything.

My eyes focus on the orange glow, and the lava is replaced by firelight gleaming in the troll's eyes. I'm back in the cave, standing before Morvok's worktable as he repairs the amulet. The air in the troll's home is warm, too warm. "If you have failed, we cannot try again."

He's talking about the labyrinth. I endured the trials to earn enough magic to fix the stone and stop Draakmar. Time freezes, and Morvok doesn't move. Before I can wonder what's wrong, time skips forward like a stone across the surface of a pond—skittering before finally settling to ripple over us.

I don't want to be in this dream, filled with anxiety and nausea. My body aches.

Morvok examines one of the amulet's broken shards in the light. It looks like a gem, but it's really a fragment of Draakmar's scale.

"It was forged long ago, a piece of his very essence—his fire, his soul, his power. Only that power can stop him," Morvok says.

The dragon could only be tamed by a piece of himself, but that piece needs to be fixed. The troll uses my blood to mend it. Fixing the amulet brought back its protective magic and stopped the apocalypse.

The past just stops like we hit the end of a recording. I'm now back in the bed. Alone.

This is not my bed.

I touch the amulet hanging around my neck. The stone is too warm to be from body heat. It pulses in time with my heartbeat. A low hum, so subtle I might be imagining it, reminds me of the distant echo of a dragon's growl. My fingertips tingle from the magical connection I have to Draakmar.

The amulet is repaired. It's a powerful magical artifact that connects me to Draakmar and helps me to tame the beast. Now, I control a dragon, an ancient and destructive fire dragon that sleeps deep within the earth. At least, I think I control him. It might be wishful thinking on my part. The deep connection is new, so I'm unsure how this works. Sometimes, his consciousness brushes against mine like he's trying to tell me something, but the meaning stays out of reach.

I shut my eyes, trying to get my bearings. Is this moment real, or am I drifting into another fragment?

"Open it."

I open my eyes at the familiar voice to see my grandfather sitting on the edge of my hospital bed. This delusion is so vivid that a lump forms in my throat. I know this isn't right. He died from Covid. And yet, here he is, smiling at me expectantly. I want to tell him I miss him, but that's not what happened. Instead, I open a jewelry box to find the amulet. My hand looks small, too small. I was young when this happened. One of my arms is in a cast after my brother Conrad pushed me from a balcony at the country estate.

The smooth stone of time comes skipping along, stuttering the moment when I would have it linger. I feel safe with my grandfather, even though I'm in the hospital. He loves me and wants me to feel protected.

When time rights itself, his hands are in the air. A swarm of magical butterflies flutters around us. It's a simple glamour spell, but their delicate beauty looks real. One lands on my cast and then bursts like a bubble. The spell ends.

"The world needs butterflies, Tamara, as much as it needs dragons. Probably more. We all have our place." He kisses the tip of his finger and then presses it against my forehead. Before he makes contact, I'm back in the bedroom alone.

What the fuck is this insanity? Am I having a fever dream? Am I under a spell? Why am I reliving snippets of my life?

Fuck. Am I dead?

I'm holding the amulet in my fist. My grandfather told me it would protect me. And it has. The magic connected to the stone has saved my life multiple times, shielding me from supernatural threats. Then Conrad broke it when he tried to steal it, causing chaos and disrupting the balance of power in the paranormal world. That's when Morvok helped me fix it.

I've since repaired the amulet's magic, which has given me a degree of control over the sleeping Draakmar. However, the full extent of the amulet's power and my link to the dragon are still not fully understood. A sense of uncertainty and danger haunts me.

My fingers continue to trace the amulet. It's a familiar weight trying to remind me of something. I feel a sharp cut against my finger and immediately lift it to see. It's okay, but the sensation reminds me of the stone shattering around Conrad's neck, killing him and resetting the timeline of those around me like pieces shuffled on a game board.

The amulet pulses faintly, like the ancient heart-beat it belongs to. I see Draakmar's face. I don't want to drift, so I stare up at the bedposts, trying to anchor myself in the fog of my thoughts.

This is not my bed, and these are not my clothes.

The bed swallows me whole in crimson sheets that shimmer faintly in the quivering light. My hand brushes the cool fabric, soft as water against my fingertips. The intimacy feels intrusive, and I sit up. An ache in my limbs is a dull reminder of the recent chaos.

Costin's bedroom.

I take a closer look around me. The intricate carvings on the bedposts rise toward the ceiling like sentinels. Ornate in a way that borders on overindulgence, each post is etched with twisting ivy and perched ravens. I don't remember seeing them before, but then last time I was conscious in here I wasn't focused on the vampire's interior decorating skills.

Like everything about Costin, this room displays a power that should intimidate me. Instead, it sends an unwanted thrill down my spine. I've spent my life avoiding supernatural seduction, yet here I am, surrounded by evidence of Costin's otherworldly allure.

A draft caresses my cheek, carrying that faint scent of floral incense and wood polish. Beneath that is an unmistakable essence that is purely Costin—dangerous and achingly familiar. My body remembers his touch even if my thoughts are murky.

The idea of him draws my attention back to the present. Somewhere around me, a faint creak echoes. It's the groan of old wood adjusting to pressure. The scent haunting me mixes with something more profound—musty and metallic, like old blood lingering in the air.

The room stretches into darkness as heavy velvet curtains swallow the light. The flicker of candelabra flames casts shadows in motion, alive and restless. Silence feels deliberate as if the walls are holding their breath.

Thick, dark wood furniture looms like guardians of another era—heavy wardrobes and an intricately carved four-poster bed. I detect small details in the polished wood. There are faint scratches, like claw marks, and faded spots where countless hands have rested.

The fireplace across the room is dormant. The mantel is cluttered with centuries' worth of trinkets —goblets, rings, and curiosities whose stories are lost to time. Their arrangement hints of melancholy as if they are mementos of lives Costin has outlived. I wonder what meaning they carry for an immortal vampire. Costin doesn't strike me as the sentimental type, but I can well imagine there are swirling depths beneath his calm surface that I haven't seen.

This is not my...

"*I will take care of everything.*" Costin's voice echoes through me. I look around, but he's not there.

I'm dating Costin. I'm dating a vampire.

It occurs to me that words like dating and boyfriend don't fit when you're with a powerful, immortal supernatural creature. Flashes of Costin appear before me—holding my burned hand in a dark forest, standing over me in the driveway when I broke my arm, following me in the labyrinth, fingers stretching toward my face before he kisses me.

I blink and look for another anchor to keep me in reality.

A sword hangs above the hearth, its hilt encrusted with rubies that match the deep, rich hues of the room. It perfectly reflects the vampire. It's elegant, timeless, and unnervingly precise.

"Beautiful," I whisper, testing my groggy voice. "Dangerous."

"*I will take care of everything.*"

The echo of his words doesn't make sense. Maybe it's not even a real memory.

It's not just the amulet protecting me. Costin has

saved me more times than I can count. He was there with Morvok. Together, we stopped the destruction of the paranormal hub beneath New York City. He pulled me from the wreckage of my mortal life and stood by me in the depths of supernatural conflict. But I worry there is a calculation behind his protection, something I can't quite name.

Maybe that's just how vampires are—always playing the long game. Or maybe I'm afraid to acknowledge the heat in his gaze when he looks at me, the possessive way his hands linger whenever he touches me. It would be easier if it were just supernatural manipulation instead of a dangerous connection between us.

But I faced Draakmar alone. I'm a freaking hero. Take that, supernatural elitists! A mortal saved your sorry asses from a lava apocalypse.

My smile is short-lived.

I push the thick blanket off my body and swing my legs over the side of the bed. My bare feet brush the cold floor, and I suppress a shiver as I remember how Costin's touch feels against my skin. Even when angry at him, I can't stop my thoughts from straying in more pleasurable directions.

This needs to stop. I need to regain myself. My head is still spinning with the residual haze of whatever is happening to me.

A flash of memories surfaces of Costin's voice,

low and soothing, as he tells me to rest. "*I will take care of everything. You can forget all about him.*"

His voice echoes inside me, that silky tone that makes my pulse race even in memory. I hate how I crave that sensation.

Why am I flittering between desire and rage? I know better than to fall into a supernatural fantasy. Why can't I focus?

I remind myself exactly what is going on. My vampire boyfriend mesmerized me without my permission. *That* is why my thoughts are jumbled and skipping around.

Mother fucker.

How long have I been asleep? I struggle to remember the moments leading up to being mesmerized. Something important dances along the edge of my thoughts.

I need to concentrate.

A sharp pang of guilt twists in my stomach as I remember Paul.

Paul Cannon is a mortal I met before magic turned my life upside down. He helped me when I was just a stranger to him. We drove halfway across the country together, and I fell in love with him after only a week of knowing him. He represented everything I thought I wanted—a normal human life.

Every choice I make seems to come with a price. I chose trying to be normal, and the supernatural tried to kill Paul and his daughter. I chose the super-natural world over a human life with Paul, and now he's paying for that choice. I chose to trust Costin, and he took away my free will. Even fixing the amulet had consequences I couldn't foresee. It brought back memories that should have stayed buried, drawing attention from powers that should remain dormant.

Paul.

The name comes with a flood of emotions—warmth, longing, regret. The memories of him sprinkle inside me in fragments. I remember the way he smiled, his voice when he was with his five-year-old daughter Diana, and the quiet strength that made me feel safe. He saved my life. Literally, and on several occasions. He and Diana helped me when I had no one. I owe them so much. We met at a cemetery, two lost souls looking for peace, and for a brief time, I thought we had found it in each other. Then the amulet broke, and the magic made him forget all about me. When it erased his memories, it was a mercy. Being with me was too dangerous for him and Diana.

I shouldn't be thinking of Paul. Not here in Costin's bed.

I am romantically involved with Costin, a powerful master vampire. Costin and Paul represent two very different paths—one is immortal and dangerous, the other mortal and safe. It was easy to choose between the two when Paul didn't know who I was. But I'd be lying if I didn't say I have lingering feelings for Paul. I am torn between the two men, and the situation has become complicated because Paul's memories of our time together have been restored.

I rub my forehead as if that will dislodge my thoughts. I need to remember something about Paul. He was there when the amulet broke. I was meeting my birth mother for the first time, and my adoptive brother, Conrad, had tried to kill us. I need to save Paul from Conrad.

Wait. No. That's the wrong memory. Conrad is dead.

If Conrad is no longer a threat, then what?

I press my palms hard against my temples, forcing the memory of Paul to focus. There was a flash of fur in the streetlights outside the family penthouse. Wolf.

Dread fills me. The werewolves took Paul. I remember it now.

I was waiting outside the penthouse for Costin. Paul showed up to tell me the spell that had erased his memory of our time together was reversed when I fixed the amulet. He remembered me. He remembered us.

But I had moved on. I was with Costin now. I chose the vampire.

Why didn't Costin stop the werewolves? Why were the werewolves kidnapping people off the street in Manhattan? That makes no sense. The wolf didn't act like a typical predator. He wasn't defending the alleyway because wolf territory is limited to industrial neighborhoods. He purposefully came to grab Paul.

The tall mirror framed in gold on the far wall catches my reflection. The glass wavers slightly, as though the image might shift if I blink. For a moment, I think I see the edge of a shadow dart behind me, there and gone again. It sends a chill crawling up my spine, but beneath the fear is that familiar thrill of anticipation. I've sensed Costin's presence in shadows, and my body has learned to recognize the electric charge he brings to the air.

The floor creaks with each step as I cross toward it. Candlelight from the candelabra dances over my reflection. I'm a hot mess. Wild curls tumble over my shoulders in a tangle that would take hours to tame with a hair straightener. Shadows sit heavy under my eyes, their bluish tint a stark contrast to the paleness of my skin. I trail my hands down my arms, brushing over faint scars that remind me of battles I didn't think I'd survive.

The white nightgown I'm wearing isn't mine.

The fabric clings too perfectly, the neckline dipping lower than comfort, and I feel exposed knowing the vampire chose it for me. I try not to think about his hands undressing me, putting me to bed while I was mesmerized.

I don't look right.

I remember the feel of Costin's teeth as he drank from me. The amulet protects me, but I still feel my neck and check my teeth for fangs. Everything appears normal, but something about being underground inside what feels like a pharaoh's tomb makes my skin itch. Blood and shadows—that's the currency of his world, and somehow, I've become caught up in both.

Older powers are stirring, ancient magics that make even vampires seem young. I can feel them pressing against the edges of reality, drawn by something. By me? By the amulet? By whatever the wolves are up to?

Maybe I'm being dramatic. My awareness of Draakmar is still new, and I might be picking up on his primeval fears.

The door opens before I can fully gather my scattered thoughts. The hinges barely make a sound, but the subtle whisper of air shifting as the door swings open prickles the fine hairs on my arms. Costin steps inside, and despite my anger, my body responds to his presence. The nightgown suddenly feels too thin, and I resist the urge to cross my arms over my chest as his gaze travels over me with predatory intensity.

It's not fair how he can command attention just by existing, how the very air seems to charge with electricity when he enters a room. Even after mesmerizing me against my will, part of me still wants to trace the sharp line of his jaw with my fingers, to feel if his skin is as cool as I remember. The memory of his touch ripples across my skin, and I hate how my pulse quickens in response.

Costin moves with vampiric grace. Vampires are the perfect predators, soundlessly stalking and eternally beautiful. It's not fair. What chance does a mortal woman have against a man like this?

His steps are quiet, but I hear the faint rustle of fabric. His movements' elegant, controlled rhythm reminds me of a dance we've been performing since the first time he kissed me. Every instinct tells me to back away, yet I find myself swaying toward him, drawn by that magnetic pull that's always existed between us.

Shadows carve the sharp angles of his face, from high cheekbones and a strong jaw to lips curled into their usual smirk. There's that primal energy that attracts me to him. I know there is a dark side to him. He needs human blood to live. He's killed. I used to mock women who fell for such monsters in movies and books. And, yet here I am, living the real-life version, fighting an attraction that feels as inevitable as gravity.

I'm a fucking mess. I don't know what I'm doing.

Every step deeper into this supernatural world costs me something dear—my normalcy, my independence, my ability to pretend I'm just another human. But staying away costs even more. I've tried running from what I am and who I am. All it's done is endanger others. Maybe that's the real price—knowing that someone gets hurt no matter what I choose.

The flickering light catches Costin's long black hair. His eyes, dark and fathomless, hold a flicker of crimson, a warning I've learned not to ignore. He's dressed impeccably, as always, in a tailored waistcoat and black trousers. The fabric clings to his broad shoulders and lean frame like it was tailored for him, and knowing Costin, it probably was.

He's as beautiful as he is terrifying.

A shiver works over me. There is no doubt I'm attracted to the vampire, to that darkness inside him. He represents everything I've fought so hard to distance myself from. He's a master vampire—powerful, feared, immortally beautiful, and seductive. His dark eyes meet mine, and for a moment, the silence between us is deafening.

I have questions.

He has secrets.

"You're awake." His voice rolls through the room like smoke. There's an irresistible pull in his tone that wraps around me and tightens before I realize I'm holding my breath. "Good."

"How long?" I ask, my throat dry.

"A week."

The air changes and becomes heavy with unspoken tension. My pulse quickens as I search his face for answers, but his expression is as unreadable as ever, and I'm left guessing what he's thinking.

"You needed rest," he says, stepping closer. "Your human body needed time to recover from—"

"Where's Paul?" I demand, my voice firm despite the tightness in my chest. "Why did the werewolves take him? I need to find him. A week? That's far too long."

I shake my head.

Clearly annoyed, Costin's lips tighten into a thin line. "What's your plan, Tamara? Storm the were-wolves' territory and demand their Alpha return Paul to you?"

"I have to try," I snap, the guilt and desperation rising. "I owe it to him."

I think of his daughter, Diana, and my heart beats faster with worry. She's with her grandparents in Kansas City, and Paul said she doesn't remember me. I have to believe she's safe for now.

Costin's gaze narrows. I wonder if he can read

my thoughts. I don't think so, but there are rumors about just how much power vampires have. He doesn't speak, but the silence feels heavier than any argument.

He moves in a blur to close the distance between us until he stands before me. The proximity sends my pulse to racing. His nearness is intoxicating and dangerous. My body instinctively knows what my mind refuses to acknowledge. This man could kill me with little effort.

I step back but bump into the mirror. Now trapped, all I can do is glare up at him.

He reaches for my neck as if examining the quickened beat of my heart. The light scrape of his nail moves along my jaw. I know I have the amulet, but a thrill of fear still courses through me.

"Did you know the werewolves were coming for him?" I whisper.

"I thought you said it was over with him." Costin withdraws his hand. I see the accusation in his gaze, as if he senses I still have feelings for Paul. I get the impression he knows more than he'll tell me.

"It's complicated." Guilt fills me at the admission. I don't expect him to understand. He's been a vampire since the medieval period. He can't remember what it's like to be human.

I could say that things have changed. Paul

remembers me now. It was easy to decide when I didn't have a choice.

But Costin has been with me through some of the most challenging moments of my life. He's always been there, lurking in my shadows, protecting me.

Fuck. I'm *that* girl—the indecisive one torn between two lovers. I don't know if I'm pathetic or just a cliché.

When I look at Costin, I can see a life with him filled with danger and magic. He's a master vampire who controls all vampiric North America. Supernaturals bow to him. It doesn't hurt that he has the body of a god and more than a bit of a bad-boy ego. Being with him is like dangling over the side of a skyscraper, trying to catch my breath.

With Paul, I feel safe and normal. Paul's affection is like being held close, wrapped in a thick blanket while being hand-fed carbs. I will always know where I stand with him. If he says he loves me, I'll believe him, and I know he'd spend his life proving it —his *mortal* life.

"Costin, I owe Paul. He saved my life." I think of Diana, the girl who's already lost her mother. She can't lose her father, too. "Paul's only in this mess because of me. It's my fault he's in trouble. I'm the reason he came to Manhattan. He's confused by his returning memories. I have to help him make sense of them."

"You're wasting time chasing something that will only bring you pain." Costin's eyes begin to swirl in an attempt to draw me in.

I lift my hand, turning away. "No. Don't even try it."

I look for my clothes and cell phone but don't see them.

"Where are my things?" I ask. "I should call my brother. Anthony will be worried about me."

"Anthony knows you're safe. Rest. Stay here," he whispers.

The hypnotic words carry a deep undercurrent that makes my knees weak. The walls seem to press in, and I find breathing difficult. The surrounding shadows darken until all I can focus on is him. His eyes lure me into his will like a siren's call, and I feel my resolve waver. The worst part isn't his supernatural power over me. It's how much I want to give in to it, to let him wrap me in his arms and keep me safe from everything, including myself.

Stay here.

The words hang in the air like a command.

I force my feet to step aside and move toward the door. "I can't. Anthony..."

The space between us is electric with mounting tension. Every step away from him feels like I'm fighting the earth's gravitational pull. My body remembers too well how it feels to be held in those arms, to surrender to that otherworldly spell.

Yes, my brother might be worried, but that's not why I need to call him. Anthony's childhood friend Peter is a werewolf. He might know something that can help me.

"Stay," he insists.

"Or what? You'll make me?" I haven't forgotten he mesmerized me for a week against my will. It pisses me off. Still, it's hard to scream at a master vampire when every cell is hyperaware of his nearness. I'm in his home, surrounded by his power, and he can stop me if he wants. The thought of his control sends an inappropriate thrill through me that I desperately try to ignore.

What in the hell is wrong with me? I'm stronger than this.

I hurry from the bedroom into a wide hallway. More artifacts line the walls like his personal vampiric museum. The metallic smell of blood becomes stronger, and the temperature drops. Light from behind a cracked door catches my attention, and I see a young man resting in a chair, his arm hanging over the side as blood drips from a bite on his wrist down his fingertips.

A naked figure appears between us as a blonde vampire stares out from the cracked door. He looks familiar, and I realize in the erased timeline he'd been with Costin's sister when they tried to kill me. He won't remember it but seeing him causes me to shiver in fear. Now, he simply smiles at me before pushing the door closed.

"Tamara," Costin insists.

I see my clothes folded on a small table by a door with my phone on top of the pile. It's next to an elevator. I don't stop as I grab them on my way past to push the call button.

His soft voice follows me as I step into the elevator. "You'll regret this."

Costin's underground home is disorientating. I see hallways and doors stretching into shadows but have never explored them. I'm too afraid to look. It is based underneath Manhattan to keep him safe from daylight, but it doesn't feel like it.

The last time I was here, I found electric lights behind the curtains, mimicking peeks of daylight. I can't imagine what it would be like never to see the sun. The mirage must feed his nostalgia, even if it's not real.

Perhaps there is a part of him that longs for the humanity he lost long ago. Or maybe it's just another form of control—creating artificial day and night at his whim.

Maybe I keep trying to ascribe human emotions and motivations to a master vampire.

After feeling his cold touch and seeing how he looks at me... I'm not sure what's more dangerous, believing he feels nothing or believing he feels too much.

The elevator has one direction: up. It opens to a marble foyer that reminds me of the inside of a large mausoleum with cold stone and soft light. I pause long enough to change out of the nightgown into my clothes. I open the elevator and toss the nightgown into the corner.

The silence is so deafening that my shoes sound too loud as I cross toward an oak door. As I pull the heavy door open, I'm surprised to see bright daylight. I would have guessed it was the middle of the night since the vampires downstairs are awake.

My mind is cloudy from being mesmerized for so long. I'm not sure what to feel. Costin should not have done that, but I'm used to supernaturals living by different rules and doing what they want. They don't see things the same way humans do. My entire life, I've been forced to flow in the direction of others' whims. My parents claim it's for my protection because my family has a lot of supernatural enemies.

My family's legacy is a web of magic and expectation, one I've never been able to untangle myself from. My father's power is legendary, but my human birth mother was one of his many affairs. I take after Lorelai.

They say all families have issues.

My brother Anthony inherited their magic, and even my adopted human brother Conrad—*as flawed as he was*—had found ways to harness it before his death. And me? I'm the mortal afterthought.

Until recently.

Ever since I subdued Draakmar and faced the labyrinth challenge, I think they'll look at me differently.

My adoptive brother Conrad betrayed me in the worst way by trying to set me up for multiple murders. Though Conrad is dead, his angry spirit still lingers—literally. He has been haunting me, appearing to give me threats as a constant reminder of his treachery.

No, that's not right. *Lingered*. Past tense. A necromancer's magic now imprisons Conrad's angry spirit.

The heavy oak door of Costin's home closes behind me with a decisive thud that seems to echo into eternity. I pinch the bridge of my nose and remind myself to breathe. My brain is still skipping around. Being mesmerized for a week has taken a toll.

I feel as if I've surfaced from a dream. Around

me, the city is alive, and people pass without a clue as to what is happening beneath them. I think of Costin's home, of the paranormal creatures hiding in the supernatural city below, infesting caverns and old subway tunnels.

I go toward the sound of traffic under the shadows of skyscrapers that make the morning feel earlier than it is. Even the familiar commotion of Manhattan feels different today. A street vendor's coffee cart provides momentary cover as I pause to get my bearings. Anxiety gnaws at my stomach. I feel like someone is watching me, but I don't see them.

Each step pulls me further from Costin's intoxicating presence and deeper into a pit of doubt. I want to tell myself I'm crazy, that I'm okay, but I know better.

I shouldn't feel safer alone on the streets, but I do. Or at least, I want to. I touch the amulet at my neck for comfort. I can be injured, but no one can kill me. Don't ask me to explain why vampires can't bite me, even if they don't intend to kill me. I'm not going to question it too closely. I can assume it's because their bite is death or some such reason. It's not like my education covered these details. My tutor focused more on the just-don't-get-bit-or-you'll-be-dead lessons.

Draakmar stirs restlessly through the stone as if

death isn't the worst fate I should fear. I hope the creature can't feel my annoyance with his constant interruptions. I mean, he is keeping me alive.

Costin's distant voice lingers in my mind. *"You're safer with me, Tamara. You know that."*

When Costin's home is no longer in sight, I lift my phone to call for a car. I wait near the side of a building, trying not to draw attention to myself. A man passes with some kind of hybrid fluffy poodle, and all I can think of is werewolves. I stare at the dog until they disappear from view.

My ride pulls up, and the driver says nothing as I slip into the backseat. I rest my forehead against the window to watch the scenery as we pass through traffic. The sounds of car horns and squeaking brakes are so familiar they're comforting. Even the half-dressed lady shouting obscenities into the street feels normal in the city.

My mind drifts, and I have no idea how long it takes us to arrive at the Devine penthouse. My thoughts loop between Paul and Costin. Paul, whose warmth feels like safety. Costin, whose darkness feels like an inevitability.

The driver stops in front of my building. Seconds after stepping out of the car, I can't remember if I thanked him. The doorman holds open the door. I hear him saying my name, and I try to give an automatic answer. By the time I cross the penthouse lobby to step inside the elevator, my mind prickles with the weight of too many unanswered questions.

Why did the werewolves take Paul?

Why did Costin mesmerize me for so long?

Why didn't Costin stop them? He's a master vampire. Surely, he could have tracked and subdued werewolves.

What the hell am I going to do about it all?

The elevator's soft chime as it opens feels like a death knell. I don't get off until I see the doors starting to close, which prompts me into action. I reach between them, letting the doors bounce off my arm to reopen.

The penthouse is high above the city, with a wall of windows that display the many lights. At night, I like to stare down and imagine I'm looking at stars instead of streetlights and windows. There is a feeling of being removed from those below.

The house smells like cotton candy. I find it odd. My mother, Astrid, likes things a particular way. Our homes are always pristine. The paintings and sculptures are always in the same place. The furniture is unchanging. Since childhood, the only thing different in the penthouse has been the kitchen, which is modernized for our family's chefs. I think Astrid likes the sense of control the sameness gives her.

Lorelei is my birth mother, but Astrid is married

to my father and the only mother I've known. That makes Astrid Anthony's mother by birth and mine by... well. Force? What do you call it when a man forces you to take care of his lovechild bastard? For me, Astrid is the woman I thought was my mother until I recently learned the truth.

I see the gray skyline muted by tinted windows. Costin's eyes flash in my mind, and I hear his voice say, "*I will take care of you, Tamara.*"

The promise lingers, but so does the question. Why?

Anthony appears from the kitchen holding a tall glass filled with pink liquid. At twenty-nine, he's a year older than me. His suit is as immaculate as ever, and there's a looseness to his posture. My brother is all charms and smiles, even when he's stressed. He's learned to play his part in this family well. Everything is appearances and duty. It gleams on us like shiny varnish, lacquered over our smiling portraits to hide the canvas underneath. As the magical and legal heir, he hides more than I do. Expectations of the family mortal have always been low in comparison.

Anthony's face lights up with relief as he approaches me through the living room. He gives me a once-over and smirks. "Nice hair."

"What are you drinking? Unicorn piss?" I counter

with a grimace. The smell of cotton candy is more pungent now that he's near.

Anthony takes a sip and laughs. "The new chef had an emergency, so she sent a friend to stand in. Lady Astrid is going to lose her shit when she sees the kitchen. This new guy is making candy smoothies, candy chicken, candy I-don't-know-what. Apparently, processed sugar is his food niche."

"So, where have you been hiding, Tam-tam?" Anthony takes another sip of his drink.

"Nowhere." I try to brush past him, but he blocks my path.

"Costin keeping you chained in his dungeon?" His smile never wavers, but that's Anthony. Rarely do I see behind his façade.

I force myself to meet his gaze and keep my voice steady. "I've been recovering from all that happened."

Anthony snorts. "Is *recovering* what they call kinky vampire action these days?"

I think of spending the week in bed, mesmerized. It's not exactly the exciting time my brother is hinting at.

"Ah, come on, don't look at me like that. If I had a hot boyfriend who looked like Costin, I'd never get out of bed."

I arch a brow.

"I'm teasing," he says with a wave of his hand. "Here, try this monstrosity."

He thrusts the unicorn piss into my hand. I don't want it. My stomach feels nauseous as it is.

"Honestly, where have you been?" he asks.

"I didn't realize I was expected to report my every move." I brush past him toward an end table to put the drink down.

"Oh, you're not. But Astrid was worried." The lie rolls out of him, but I know it for what it is. "You know how she gets when she's worried. I, for one, enjoy having my head attached to my neck."

I give him a bemused look. I highly doubt Astrid was worried about me.

"Fine. I was worried. You weren't answering my calls," he admits. "I thought maybe you got trapped underground in the supernatural city or got in a fight with Costin, and he left you stranded on top of the Eiffel Tower or something."

"Eiffel Tower?" I shake my head at the absurdity. "Anthony, be—"

"Speaking of drama," he interrupts. His tone softens, the humor slipping just enough to reveal the concern beneath. "The Freemonts want a hearing before the council of elders. Apparently, you broke poor Chester's heart when you called off your engagement. To hear them tell it, he's inconsolable."

I flinch to hear his name. Chester Freemont is a

gross toad of a man. He only wanted to marry me to be connected to the Devine family.

"I'm sure the multitude of prostitutes he engages will bring him some comfort," I grumble. "The only thing I broke of Chester's is his pride, and that will quickly recover."

Mabel Freemont carries a constant look of disdain, conveying a perpetual sense of superiority and ignorance. At the same time, Francis Freemont dominates conversations with loud, self-important bluster, recounting his wealth and business exploits that are only of interest to him. They made it clear they were doing me a favor by allowing me to marry their son. They announced it before the contracts were finalized.

"Though," I continue, "I probably did break Uncle Mortimer's heart. He had his sights set on the arranged marriage panning out."

Uncle Mortimer has been pushing me toward Chester since I was a teenager.

Anthony laughs. "The look on Mortimer's face when he heard you were with Costin was priceless. I doubt we see him at family dinner for a while. He'll be too busy pouting about a master vampire dating a member of the elite Devine family. Oh, how the gossips have enjoyed spreading this one around."

Anthony laughs harder.

I'm almost scared to ask. "What gossips?"

"You really have been chained in a basement. The supernatural underground is buzzing. Everyone is talking about how you helped him defeat Draakmar—"

"Helped?" I interrupt, annoyed. Of course everyone thinks I couldn't do it on my own.

"—and now, with the alliance between Lord Constantine and our family, they speculate what this will mean for supernatural hierarchies. Astrid has been receiving visitors all week trying to get into her good graces in case this alliance becomes permanent."

Permanent? For fuck's sake, we just started dating. And I'm not sure I would call him a boyfriend right now.

"Elf bookies have laid odds on when Costin will turn you. Want to give me a heads up before I place—"

I hit his arm. Hard. He suppresses a laugh and pretends like it hurts. "I'll never agree to that. Lay odds on never in a million years."

"Ow! You're broody today. Care to share what's going on in that head of yours? I was teasing. You're not seriously considering a sunlight allergy, are you?" He reaches to push my hair out of the way to look at my neck for bites.

I swat him away.

"If that is the immortality you want, I'll support

35

you," Anthony says. I see his serious eyes behind his fallen smile.

He looks like he wants to say more but doesn't. Long ago, he'd promised me he would figure out a way to cure my mortality. It was a sweet gesture to make his little sister feel better at the time, but I think that promise has grown to mean something deeper. Conrad is dead. There are only the two of us Devine siblings left. Anthony doesn't want to be left alone in our family for an eternity, and he knows I have an expiration date.

The expectations of Anthony as the oldest son and the only one to inherit the family magic must weigh upon him like an anchor pulling him deep into the abyss.

I know. I swim in that abyss.

I hesitate, my thoughts a tangled mess of Paul's memory, Costin's cryptic promises, and my spiraling doubts. "No. I don't want to be a vampire."

The idea of drinking blood for an eternity repulses me. Or at least it should. I tell myself it does.

He bumps my shoulder lightly. "Come on, Tam-tam. Give me something. You've got that 'end of the world' look again. What's going on? Please tell me we don't have to fight another dragon. I'm still a little stiff from the last battle."

I touch my amulet. I sense Draakmar is resting.

The even fall of his breathing calms me and makes me feel safe. It's a strange sensation being tied to the ancient beast, and knowing any magic I have is not my own.

I let out a breath, trying to keep my voice steady. "It's just... everything. The Freemonts, Costin, Draakmar and the prophecy, Conrad and the fire—"

Anthony holds up a hand. "All the ingredients for a migraine. Got it."

I feel the pressure closing in and imagine being back in the car with Paul, driving across the country, watching the hypnotic lines on the road. It had been easy to fall into a human routine and pretend this world didn't exist.

"Let's take a breath." Anthony squeezes my arm in comfort. "Freemonts can kiss our asses. I, for one, am happy our families aren't connected. The prophecy has been defeated. Thanks to you, Draakmar is again asleep, and the world is safe. No apocalypse. Conrad is dead, and after what he did, it's normal to have mixed feelings about our brother. I loved him, too, but he tried to kill us and our parents. The important thing is that his angry spirit won't hurt anyone ever again. You saw Leviathan intervene. The necromancer will keep our brother locked up tight. You need to put the past out of your head, or it will drive you insane. We have to focus on the present."

I still feel the lingering fear of Conrad's ghost watching me. That's the thing about ghosts—you don't always know when they're around.

"You're right," I say. "It doesn't matter. I'm just having a mortality moment. We've been through a lot, you know?"

He studies me. "You don't have to carry all this alone. I know you're used to being treated like the delicate human in the family, and you think we don't listen to your problems, but you're still my sister. And you're stuck with me, whether you like it or not. If there is a new problem, we'll figure it out together. I know I haven't always been there for you, but I'm here. Nothing is insolvable."

His words loosen the knot in my chest, and for a fleeting moment, I'm grateful for his relentlessness. "Thanks."

His grin returns full force. "Now, let's figure out how to deal with the Freemonts without starting a supernatural war."

I frown. "Do we need to do anything? They'll bitch and moan, and then something else will come along to distract them. Zephronis withdrew his blessing. Do they really think the council will go against a great wizard's decision?"

Even as I say it, I know that the pompous family probably does think they have a case.

"I don't think we need to worry about the

council right now. But if the Freemonts stir enough rumors and trouble, it will become a problem. Supernaturals can be gossipy bitches."

"I'm sure our mother has a plan for fighting gossip," I say.

"That does seem to be in Lady Astrid's wheelhouse," Anthony agrees. "We'll table that problem. What else is going on?"

I am all too willing to stop talking about the Freemonts and change the subject. "I could use your help with—"

The elevator dings, and our mother glides into the penthouse. The click of Astrid's diamond-studded heels announces her presence. "Tamara, there you are."

Her clipped tone doesn't reek of motherly concern. I don't answer as I wait for her to continue.

"Is the thing with Costin still happening?" she asks before sniffing the sickly sweet air and wrinkling her nose. She waves her hand in front of her face as if to brush away the offensive odor. "You're not eating candy, are you?"

She looks pointedly at me.

"No," I say.

"No, you're not seeing Constantine?" she demands.

I can tell she hopes I got the vampire out of my system. Telling her my relationship status is *"it's complicated"* isn't a good option. Besides, it's not like I'd go to Astrid for relationship advice. So I simply answer, "Yes, I'm seeing Costin. No, I'm not eating candy."

I look at Anthony's pink drink. My brother never gets interrogated about his diet. That honor is all mine.

"Very well. I suppose we need to have Costin and his sister over sometime soon." She talks more to herself than to us, her fingers tracing the edge of her book. "We'll need a new blood supply sent to the country estate. I hate dealing with the New York blood banks, but it can't be helped." She pauses, studying me. "There are eight million people in this city, and the banks act like they can't just go out and get more blood."

"I hear the homeless population doesn't mind donating for cash and a meal," Anthony suggests, suppressing his grin to hide the fact he's teasing her. "Want me to invite—?"

"We can't serve a master vampire hobo blood from a back alley." Astrid misses the joke.

"I'll call the banks for you," Anthony offers.

Astrid starts to nod before frowning. "No. The last time you ordered enchanted blood, I had vampire bats sleeping in every dark corner of the house for a month. I'll take care of it."

I share a smirk with my brother. It wasn't an accident. He thought it was hilarious.

"What is your hair?" Astrid furrows her brow.

I automatically lift my hands to touch the wayward curls.

"Fix," Astrid waves her hands to encompass me, "all of this."

"That's the newest trend," Anthony comes to my defense. "You don't like it? It's been in all the magazines."

Astrid frowns at him but, instead of answering, asks me, "Is Costin currently speaking to his sister, Elizabeth?"

I give a light shrug. Not that anyone would remember since the amulet's magic had erased and reset that timeline, but Elizabeth had tried to kill me in that version of events. I can still feel her cold hands on my body and see the death in her gaze. She's not like Costin. I felt an evil in her that I don't feel with her brother. "I don't think you need to invite her."

"Find out for sure," Astrid says. "There is a fine etiquette to these things. We must handle ourselves above reproach. Everyone is watching after that Freemont debacle. Francis and Mabel are spreading their venom to anyone who will listen."

"What now?" Anthony asks.

"According to Mabel, they are now the ones who

called it off because we're socially deficient. They're accusing us of everything from sabotage, unpaid debts, whispering during the opera." Astrid's smile is all teeth. "They want us bleeding from all angles."

The weight in my chest tightens. More Devine drama. More pressure. "Let them talk. It's all lies. They can't prove anything."

Astrid chuckles wryly. "This isn't just idle gossip. All eyes are on us. We need to be at our best."

I nod, as expected. "Of course."

"Just talk to your vampire. I need a guest list," she says.

I nod again.

"Now, why does my home smell like a carnival's unwashed backside?" She saunters off toward the kitchen without another word.

"Bye, mom," I mumble sarcastically after her. "Thanks for the pep talk."

Anthony lifts his hand and counts down with his fingers. Before he gets to one, we hear Astrid screech in horror. She starts screaming at the chef about the candy concoctions.

Anthony laughs and hooks his arm around my shoulder, quickly leading me away from the scene. "Don't worry about our mother. She's only happy when she's unhappy."

"I think she's sad." I don't know what makes me say it. No one would agree with that opinion. Astrid is one of the strongest people I know, but her cold demeanor contrasts with subtle moments of vulnerability... *real subtle moments*. She believes in duty and tradition over emotions. I've come to realize that isn't to say she doesn't have emotions. They're just buried under centuries of repression.

"I think your boyfriend drained too much blood. You're delusional." Anthony pulls me faster as Astrid's yelling about dietary plans becomes more intense. We move through the penthouse toward our bedrooms. "You were starting to say you needed my help with something before we were interrupted."

"Oh, I was just going to ask if Peter was still living in the city," I answer.

"Peter?" Anthony arches a brow. "Werewolf Peter?"

I nod, trying to ignore the way Draakmar stirs at the mention of werewolves.

"Yeah, he still has an apartment here, but he's been acting strange lately. Even for a wolf. Why? Are you tired of the vampire already? Want to try a little fur coat instead?" he teases, but there's tension beneath his humor.

I think about jolting him in the stomach. "I'm not interested in dating Peter."

"I'm still not going to tell him that. Gotta leave the poor pup some hope." Anthony grins. "He had the biggest crush on you when you were in high school."

High school was a private tutor. I don't point that out.

"He practically begged to come home with me at each school break," Anthony continues.

The last thing I need in my life is another love interest. I'm full up on those.

"You're not laughing." Anthony studies me, and I can't avoid his eyes.

"I'm trying to figure out..." I look at my palm. "Do you remember when we were kids, and you let me hold that fireball?"

"You know I remember that. We were all playing that stupid game, trying to hit Peter with magic. I gave you the fireball, and you took off screaming into the forest. I was sure our parents were going to kill me when they found out. When I caught up to you, Costin had found you."

"He's always been there, lurking in the shadows," I say, still tracing my hand. I can feel the memory of his cool fingers against the burn.

"He and our grandfather were good friends. I never thought about it too much, but I guess looking back, knowing the prophecy of the amulet, it's not surprising." He pulls me closer and places his arm over my shoulders. "Who would have thought my baby sister would save the world from a fiery apocalypse? I suppose that's as good a reason as any for Costin to lurk around. Better than any alternative motives."

"He was never inappropriate when I was a kid," I assure Anthony. "I don't think he wants to like me. I get the sense he'd rather not. I think his promise to help me through the prophecy is the only reason he came around."

"Don't sell yourself short. You inherited the Devine charm. You're a catch. He's lucky you gave him the time of day."

I arch a brow at him but don't comment on his teasing. "I know Costin is dangerous, but I've never feared him until..."

"What did he do?" Magic flares around my brother's hand.

I touch Anthony's arm to calm him. "It's complicated."

"Did he hurt you?"

I shake my head. "I'm having a hard time thinking clearly."

Anthony extinguishes the magic, and I watch smoke trail up toward the ceiling like the last breath of a cigarette. "He mesmerized you?"

I nod. Out of everyone in my life, I feel like Anthony is closest to me. If you would have asked me a year ago, I would have said it was our brother Conrad. But Conrad betrayed me. His greed for power and money had been more driving than I could ever imagine.

"The whole time?"

I nod again.

"Why?"

Paul's face appears unbidden in my mind.

"Paul remembers me," I manage.

Anthony's eyes widen and he waits for me to continue.

I try to clear my mind to explain. "Paul showed up while I was waiting for Costin and said his memories were returning. But before we got too much into it, werewolves abducted him off the sidewalk. Costin appeared right after and acted like he gave pursuit but then said he couldn't track them." I force a deep breath. "I think he is lying to me. I get this feeling he knows more. Before I could do something to help Paul, Costin mesmerized me for a week without asking my permission first."

Anthony stares at me, giving a small nod to indicate he's listening.

"I'm not accusing Costin of having something to do with the kidnapping, but I don't think he was helping either. I don't think he tried to find Paul."

"Political balances between the werewolves and vampires are tenuous. I'm sure he's just being cautious," Anthony puts forth. It feels like he's defending Costin, and I don't like it.

"I think he might have mesmerized me out of jealousy to keep me from looking." I try not to hang my head as I try to shake this last statement away. "Not that I think Costin would be jealous of me."

Anthony smirks. "You don't think?"

He's making fun of me again. I cross my arms over my chest and grimace at him.

"You don't think a master vampire will get jealous?" He starts laughing, and I force myself to keep frowning. "Tam, what do you think happens when a powerful, immortal king, who reigns over dark armies, believes Sir Human Lancelot is making eyes at his woman? You might not call that jealousy, but it's definitely a sister emotion, and that family—"

I hold up my hand in front of his face to stop him. My foggy brain is not functioning at one hundred percent. "That example had a lot of metaphors and words in it, but I think I get your point."

"All vampires have a little narcissism in them," he explains, like it's actually news. "They're undead predators needing blood to live. They're used to taking what they want without permission, and if they don't take what they want, nature will force them to take what they need. Of course he will be possessive of what he claims to be his. Of course he's not going to ask permission. Vampires don't ask permission, especially not from humans."

"I was raised in this family, but you all act like you think I'm two paces behind," I mutter.

Anthony ignores my surliness. "That's my point. You chose a vampire, Tam. A *master* vampire. You can't pretend to be surprised when he acts like a vampire."

He does have a point. I don't like it.

"Now, tell me about Paul..." My brother smiles, and I hear the need for drama in his tone. "All of his memories are back?"

"When we fixed the amulet, it reversed the spell. He remembers both timelines, like me. His daughter doesn't, as far as I know. She's in Kansas City with her grandparents."

Anthony frowns. "Who's looking after their dog?"

After their memories were erased, Paul bought a dog for his daughter. I'm a little ashamed I didn't think of the animal before now. I shake my head. "I don't know."

"I'll send someone to check," Anthony says. "Poor little guy."

"You don't know where Paul lives," I answer.

"I don't?" He gives a small laugh.

"You do?"

His grin widens. "I was curious after I heard what happened between the two of you. I might have looked him up."

"Thank you. Yes." I run my fingers into my hair, and they tangle. "I should take a shower."

"What about Peter? Want me to set up a date—I mean, meeting?"

"Yes, please. I need to see if he knows anything about who took Paul and why." I don't want to get my hopes up. Peter isn't exactly in the top echelon of his werewolf pack, but he's the only werewolf I've met who doesn't scare the shit out of me. He's my only lead in this supernatural mess and possibly my only chance to find answers about Paul's disappearance.

"On it, Tam-tam." Anthony gives a slight bow as he steps backward down the hall. "You can count on me."

I retreat to my bedroom, the frustration of drifting for the last week still clings to my thoughts. I lock the door and lean against it, slowly exhaling. It's daylight. Costin won't show up until after dark —if he is going to show. He didn't stop me from leaving.

Stay here.

I hear his voice whispering in my head as if, even now, he's influencing my thoughts.

Costin is hiding something. I feel it. He's always been secretive and too controlled. He says the right things, but what's behind those words?

My hand drifts to my neck, where the amulet

feels like both a curse and a blessing. Its protection has come at a tremendous personal cost. Part of me wants to take it off and smash it again, but I worry that will cause Draakmar to wake up. I can't go through all of that again.

I take a deep breath and begin to undress. I've chosen Costin—*or so I keep telling myself*—but why can't I shake the feeling that Paul isn't exactly a thing of the past?

THREE

Peter's retro coffee shop choice is so unremarkably normal that it feels strange that we'd be talking werewolf kidnappings amongst a sea of writers absorbed in their projects. The clack of keyboards underlies the indie rock pumped through old speakers and the sound of grinders. The smell of espresso is so intense that I feel jittery just breathing it in like my body will absorb the caffeine-filled air through my lungs and skin.

The golden sunlight of evening streams through large windows, casting hazy rectangles across the wooden tables. Anthony sits beside me, radiating protective older brother energy. He refused to let me come alone, even though I don't think there is anything to fear from Peter. I've known the werewolf forever, at least from the peripheral of his friendship with my brother.

Anthony stirs a third packet of sugar into his coffee as he tries to appear casual, but I notice how his eyes track every movement in the café. I can well imagine the magic humming beneath his skin, ready for an attack.

"Relax," I whisper. "We're only meeting Peter."

"I am relaxed." He takes a sip and grimaces. "This isn't nearly as good as the candy chef's."

"You just like watching our mother get riled."

Anthony grins. "Guilty."

Seeing several people on their phones, I feel compelled to check mine. There are no messages from Costin. I'm not sure if I'm relieved or disappointed.

Then again, he's not one for texting. He usually just appears out of the shadows.

I recheck the sunlight, seeing the subtle shift in color as the evening approaches. Where is Peter? I had hoped this meeting would be over before sunset.

The bell above the door chimes, drawing my attention. Peter is exactly as I remember him. He's lanky and tall with messy brown hair that falls into his eyes. The years haven't changed him physically, but there's now a wariness that wasn't there when we were younger. I suppose age does that to us all. It takes away our innocence and replaces it with a more cynical shell.

His smile, however, is the same goofy boyish grin. "Tamara!" Peter's voice carries more than he probably realizes. Or maybe he doesn't care. He spreads his arms wide, like entering the coffee shop is part of a performance and he's the star. "Darling, you look as beautiful as ever." He glances at Anthony and laughs. "Can't say the same for you, old chap."

Several patrons glance our way and then quickly return to their devices.

To look at Peter, you wouldn't think werewolf. It's a stereotype, but I always picture big, beefy shoulders and hairy lumberjacks.

I stand to hug him, and he squeezes me so tight my ribs protest. The scent of pine needles and earth is faint under a layer of cologne. I don't know where he'd run through pine trees in the city. The familiar scent brings back memories of childhood games in the forest behind the estate.

"You look well," he says, pulling back to study me. His nose twitches slightly. "Though, I guess the rumors are true. You smell like a vampire."

I lean down to sniff my shirt, but I don't smell anything beyond the lingering of my soap.

Anthony kicks out a chair. "Sit down before your loud mouth says something that draws the wrong attention."

Peter drops into the seat, still grinning. He lowers his volume. "Please. These tech addicts wouldn't notice a supernatural if we danced naked on their table. Speaking of naked, remember when we—"

"No," Anthony and I say in unison.

Peter laughs. His eyes dart to the windows, then back to us. He's worried about something. Or someone.

"So," he says, lowering his voice even more. "Anthony says you need werewolf intel. That's treacherous territory these days, Tamara. Especially for someone sporting vampire cologne."

I resist touching my neck where Costin's bite has long since healed. "I don't care about the danger. I owe it to a friend to ask."

Peter's smile fades. "A mortal or vampire friend?"

"Mortal. His name is Paul," Anthony says. "We're not trying to jam you up with your pack. All we want is a conversation."

Peter glances between us and looks uncomfortably around the coffee shop before hunching forward to lean on the table. All of his playfulness fades. "I don't think I can help you."

"He was taken off the street by a werewolf about a week ago here in Manhattan," I say. "I just need to know who and why."

"A week?" Peter repeats carefully as if stalling. "I

don't need to explain how this whole thing works to you two. If a werewolf attacked your friend a week ago in the city, then you're either waiting for a dead body to float up in the Hudson or for the next full moon to pass. Either way, he's not going to be what you remember. I think you should just forget it all about—"

"You know something," I interrupt. "You're not a good liar, Peter. Just tell me."

I don't need lessons on the danger of were-wolves. And I'm sure as hell not going to just forget about Paul.

"I know lots of things." He leans back, crossing his arms. "Most of which I shouldn't tell you or anyone."

A chill runs down my spine, and I glance toward the windows. I can tell by the light that the sun has just set. For a moment, I swear I see a shadow move —fast and deliberate. Costin? The thought makes my pulse quicken.

I can't know for sure. Several creatures move like that.

"Peter," Anthony says, his tone carrying a warn-ing. "We're not asking you to betray pack secrets. But if you know something about Paul's kidnapping—"

"Kidnapping is such a harsh word." Peter's gaze fixates on my amulet.

I lean over to make him meet my gaze. "What do you want me to call it? An abduction? I was there. I saw what happened."

Peter's attention moves around the shop. "Let's call it a necessary relocation."

"Relocation for what?" Anthony persists.

Peter shakes his head. "I can't."

I reach for Peter's hand. I know it's manipulative because he likes me, but I must know. I give him a light squeeze. "You can trust us. What's going on here? What are you scared of?"

"Listen," Peter takes a deep breath. "I heard a rumor that this Paul guy is Devine protectus."

If Paul claimed Devine protectus, then he remembers more of our shared past. When we were together, before the amulet broke, I had told him that if anything supernatural tried to mess with him or Diana, he needed to tell them he was Devine protectus. It's an old Latin term for protected humans, a rare honor that isn't really used anymore. And it isn't something that I can enact as a mortal.

Anthony gives me a strange look but doesn't call me out. "If the wolves know that and they still have him, that's an affront to our family."

"You have to know this is not an attack on your family. You have to know that," Peter insists. "None of us wants to go up against the Devines. You know we have very little say in what the Alpha and his guard get up to. I mean, I barely see the guy and I kind of prefer it that way.

"If you don't want it to be open season on werewolves, you need to tell us something, buddy. Come on." Anthony's threat is veiled, but it's enough.

"There's a ritual—" Peter stops abruptly, nostrils flaring. His gaze snaps to the window, and he jerks his hand away from me. "They have been collecting pieces for years. Since that night at the shipping yard..." He cuts himself off, looking guilty. "Forget I said that."

"What ritual?" I whisper insistently. "What night?"

"I shouldn't have said that." Peter quickly stands, and his chair legs scrape against the floor. More heads turn our way in irritation at the disruption. He leans forward. "Listen, Tam, for old times' sake—stay out of this. The Alpha... He's promising things. Change. Real change."

Anthony wraps his hand around his coffee and taps his fingers.

Peter studies us and then looks around to see if anyone is listening. He lowers his voice. "You two grew up in the elite circles. You don't know what it's like for the rest of us. The vampires get their ancient estates, the magics get their ivory towers, and we get industrial wastelands and shipping yards. But Thane says that's going to change. He's found a way around the old treaties, around all the rules that keep us in our place." His eyes flick to my amulet. "Some curses run deeper than dragon fire. You don't want to mess with this. This is so much bigger than your mortal boyfriend. Bigger than any of us."

"Paul's not my boyfriend," I say automatically.

Peter's laugh is hollow. "No, you upgraded to a vampire king. How's that working out for you?"

Even though I can't see him, I feel the weight of Costin's invisible presence. I find the disappointment of broken dreams on Peter's face. There was never anything real between us beyond friendship and his boyhood crush. I know he doesn't love me, not like a man should.

Is this what a future with Costin will be like? Everyone judging me by the vampire in my life? Could I even blame them? Until recently, I imagine I had that same look of disdain when it came to vampires.

"Be careful with him, Tam, seriously. You don't know what Lord Constantine is capable of. He's not... He's not a nice guy."

"Peter, please," I start, but he's already backing away.

"I have to go. But Tam?" His expression softens. "Whatever you think you know about Paul's situation, you're wrong. And getting involved will only make things worse. For everyone."

I stand to stop him from leaving. "Peter—"

"Be careful with that vampire. You can't trust him." He avoids my hand and strides toward the door, pausing with his fingers on the handle. "Oh, and Anthony said you're wondering about Paul's dog. She's safe. We're not monsters."

He leaves. I slide back into my chair and watch Peter disappear into the crowd outside.

Anthony lets out a long breath. "Well, that's cryptic and unhelpful."

"He told us enough. The werewolves took Paul for a ritual, which means he's alive, and they're scared enough of something to risk pissing off our family."

"Ugh, I hope this isn't another prophecy," Anthony mutters, running his hands through his hair before stretching. "I can't handle another apocalypse."

"Don't go there. He didn't say anything about an apocalypse or prophecy. He said ritual."

"You say that like it's better somehow. Honestly, I kind of thought it had something to do with the Freemonts paying a wolf to take him to get back at you. Guess that would have been too easy." Anthony nods toward the window. "Speaking of boyfriends..."

I turn to see a shadow solidifying into a familiar silhouette across the street. Even at this distance, I feel Costin's eyes on me. My amulet pulses with warmth, and I get the sense the dragon is read-justing in his sleep. I wonder—*not for the first time*—just how much control I have over my life.

"You okay?" Anthony asks.

I touch the amulet, drawing comfort from it. "No. But I will be once we figure out what the hell is going on."

The problem is, I'm not sure I will like the answers.

"Want me to chase him off?" Anthony asks, sounding very much the protective big brother.

"No, don't get in the middle of us." I appreciate his caring, but my relationship drama is not his battle. "If he wants to talk to me, he'll find me. I can't run from him."

FOUR

Devine Country Estate, Twelve Years Ago...

Floating in the estate's pond, watching clouds drift across the late afternoon sky, is about as close to free as I've ever felt—free from the constant reminders of my mortality, anyway. Like everything else on the estate, the water feels charged with old magic. Something always lurks beneath the surface of our world.

When I left him, Conrad had his face deep in an old tome in the family library. I don't know what answers he thinks he'll find there, but I doubt they'll change anything. We're mortal. There is very little we can do about that. At least, that's what they keep telling us.

I guess vampire bites or werewolf attacks might do the trick. Or we could be brought back from the dead as a necromancer's plaything. Do zombies count as immortal? I mean, they're dead before they're undead. Then they rot and eventually will become dead again.

It's a gross thought, but it's where my mind wanders.

My clothes lie in a heap on the bank, hidden beneath low-hanging branches. I didn't have time to change into a swimsuit before sneaking out of the house and into the woods to hide. The water is cool against my bare skin, contrasting with the peeks of hot sun streaming through the branches. I feel weightless. It's just me, the water, and the rustle of leaves in the trees.

I'm perfectly safe. The pond on my parents' land is deep. It's protected by magic, so no one comes out here during the day without permission.

Night is a different story. That is when the monsters come out to play, and my parents force me to hide away in the protected wing of the estate.

The truth is I'm out here because I'm bored and restless. The alternative would have been staying in the house where my mother would find me and make me run off calories on the treadmill. My mother is a cold bitch who only thinks about image. I guess, in a way, it's my own fault. I wasn't careful when I stole that pan of brownies out of the kitchen.

Oh, but they were delicious.

My father is traveling. He's always traveling. Belize, Belarus, Beirut, or some other B-name place... I can't remember. I was only half listening when they mentioned it at dinner.

Anthony is away at his special paranormal private school. The golden boy is so lucky. He gets let out of the jail cells that are our family homes. I would give anything to live in a dorm away from Lady Astrid and her endless rules of etiquette.

A loud crash in the underbrush makes me flail and sink into the water to hide my nudity. I hear Anthony's laugh and an answering howl.

Shit. What is he doing at home, and who is with him?

I look at the distance between me and the willow. Crap, crap, crap. I start swimming frantically toward it. I don't make more than a few strokes before a brown wolf runs to the pond's edge and bursts under the willow's branches. My clothes scatter, some landing in the mud along the water's edge.

Fucking Peter. He's bigger than a normal wolf, but not by much—he hasn't grown into his full supernatural size yet.

I tread water, helplessly watching as he loops around the tree. Peter skids to a stop at the water's edge, tongue lolling out in a panting grin.

"Cheater!" Anthony emerges from the trees, his shirt half-unbuttoned and hair wild from the chase.

Magic sparks from his fingers like tiny fireworks. "Using four legs is grounds for—" He freezes, finally noticing me. "Oh, hey, sis."

I sink lower in the water, grateful for the pond's murkiness. "What are you doing home?"

"Someone set fire to the dorms and..." Anthony eyes me and then my clothes. He starts laughing. "Are you naked?"

"Can you get him out of here so I can get dressed?" I motion toward Peter, who's staring at me.

My legs kick frantically. I hide my chest with my arms the best I can while staying above water.

I hear a loud crack as Peter's wolf form shifts. His bones sound like they're breaking as his body morphs into his human form. I flinch at the sickening noise and have to avert my eyes. The sound reminds me of branches snapping in a storm. When the sound stops, I find my brother's gangly friend completely naked on the shoreline.

"Hey there, Tam! Want some company?" Peter laughs, still high from the chase. He stares at me like he can see through the water. In turn, he's oblivious to Anthony's focus on him.

My brother's little crush is obvious, at least to me. He hides it well, and I don't call him on it. In this family, we all need space to have our secrets.

"What are you doing out here?" Peter continues. "Lady Astrid said you were studying."

Anthony finally snaps out of his daze. "Peter, for fuck's sake, you're naked, and that's my sister."

"We used to swim naked out here all the time when we were kids." Peter stretches, utterly unself-conscious. I notice Anthony's shoulders tense. "Remember that time your dad caught us and lectured us about proper behavior for like three hours?"

"That was because we were here naked with the fairy king's virginal daughters," Anthony answers.

Peter doesn't lose any of his humor. "I hate to break it to King Sylvaran, but his daughters were not—"

"Hey, do you mind turning around so I can get out of here?" I yell, tired of trying to tread water and hide my chest at the same time.

I remember hearing our father lecturing them about that. I also remember the way Anthony watched Peter that whole summer. But Peter never notices, too caught up in his own supernatural world. It always amazes me how prudish supernaturals can be about image. They cheat, have orgies, kill people, kill each other... And they still care what their pretty portraits look like to the rest of the world as if a glossy smile can hide all the depravity and darkness.

I see that darkness, though. The rest of the world might not, but I do.

I have a theory that it has something to do with the supernaturals' need to stay hidden from the humans to protect themselves from another inquisition. It's become like some game to them, seeing how much they can hide until every conversation sounds like a game of chess.

Magic crackles more intensely around Anthony's hands—a sure sign he's trying to control his emotions. It pulls me from my thoughts. I should say something to divert attention from my brother's secret.

"I need my clothes," I say, trying to sound commanding despite my compromised position.

"I'll get them." Anthony starts toward the shoreline, but Peter is faster.

Peter bounds over to my scattered clothes, still naked. He holds up my muddy bra like a trophy. "Nice panda bears."

"Peter!" Anthony and I scold in unison.

A cold wind sweeps across the pond, making me shiver. The temperature drop is sudden and unnatural. I know that chill.

Uncle Mortimer appears at the edge of the pond. He's wearing one of his impeccable old suits. Transporting is one of the creepier magic tricks. My uncle just shows up places out of thin air. That's not what is making the summer air turn to winter. It's the disapproval radiating off him like frost. Mortimer waves his arm toward the boys.

Peter yelps and drops my bra, diving under the tree branches. Anthony's magic sputters out like a doused flame.

"I expected better from you, Anthony. You're lucky I was able to calm the headmaster down, or you'd find yourself suspended. How do you expect to lead this family with a human education because that is the only place that will have you if you are kicked out of this school?" Mortimer's voice carries the weight of generational expectations. "Then, to find you here frolicking with a werewolf like common rabble?"

"Uncle, we were just—" Anthony starts, but Mortimer holds up a hand.

"And you." His cold eyes fixate on me in the water. "Get dressed. At least pretend like your parents raised you with morals. The Freemonts will be here for dinner, and I won't have you looking like a drowned rat when Chester arrives. Your mother has laid out appropriate attire."

I resist rolling my eyes. Of course she has. After sixteen years, I'm already well-versed in being the family's mortal disappointment. I've been getting the impression that the only thing I'm good for is to be an advantageous marriage.

MICHELLE M. PILLOW

"Chester Freemont?" Peter makes a gagging sound from behind the tree. "That pompous—"

"Mr. Freemont is a family guest," Mortimer cuts him off. "Though I wouldn't expect a werewolf to understand the delicacies of high society." His gaze sweeps over my brother. "Anthony, you have responsibilities. Enough childish games. It's time for your dog to go home."

I see Anthony change under the weight of those words, like a dark cloud sinks over his features and pushes at his shoulders. Conrad might be older, but he's adopted, which doesn't count. Anthony is the Devine heir, the magical son, the one who carries all their hopes.

"The cook made brownies." I try to take the attention from my brother. "I came for a run to work off the calories and decided to take a swim before heading back."

Mortimer sighs like I'm trying his patience, but he can't be bothered to respond.

I hear Peter's bones crack as he transforms into a wolf, but I can't see him. The sound of his paws thunder along the forest path in a primal beat, taking him away.

The familiar sting of Mortimer's words makes me want to sink beneath the surface and never come up. Instead, I lift my chin. What else can I do but keep treading water in this abyss?

"Get dressed," Mortimer says. "The Freemonts arrive in three hours."

Great. An evening of Chester Freemont's wandering hands under the table while everyone pretends not to notice.

"What an asshole," Anthony grumbles. He gathers my clothes for me as I come out of the water.

I pull on the half-wet, half-muddy shirt and shorts but don't bother with undergarments. Anthony says nothing as he keeps his eyes turned away from me. When I join him on the path, we walk back toward the house in silence. Seconds later, Peter joins us in his wolf form.

We're just three kids trying to find our way in a world that's already decided our fates. And, like many others in my life, duty and expectations have ruined a beautiful day.

FIVE

"You're not actually considering going into the Alpha's territory, are you?" Anthony asks as we walk back toward the penthouse from the coffee shop. I can't shake the feeling that we're being watched and can only assume it's my stalker vampire boyfriend.

Boyfriend. That word still feels wrong. Paul is boyfriend material. Costin is...

I don't have a name yet for what he is.

I don't have a name for what we are together. Although *stupid* comes to mind.

Ill-fated. Ill-advised. Mistake.

"Tam, seriously," Anthony insists when I forget to answer.

"Of course not. Does that sound like me?" I touch the amulet for reassurance. "I'm just gathering information."

"Liar." He bumps my shoulder. "You've got that look."

"What look?"

"The same one you had right before you convinced Conrad to chase that ghost in Jersey."

I start to laugh, but then I picture Conrad's face, and all the humor in the memory leaves me. "Jersey Devil. Conrad wanted to find the Jersey Devil."

"You two drove into a cemetery and nearly got possessed," Anthony says.

"Only a little possessed," I joke. In reality, we only told our parents that because the cops picked us up for trespassing. We had to tell them something.

"I'm hurt I wasn't invited," he says.

Suddenly, the world feels like it tilts. Heat radiates from the amulet and floods through me. Anthony catches my arm when I trip on the sidewalk, but I barely feel it. I see flames engulf a nearby building. Draakmar's consciousness intrudes into mine, more urgent than ever before. Images flash, and I see blood running down stones, moonlight through glass, and wolves circling. As fast as the hallucination hits, it dissipates like smoke in the wind. But the danger whispering through me lingers.

"Blood and moonlight?" Anthony's voice sounds far away.

"What?" I blink several times to get my bearings.

The vision fades, leaving me with the lingering sensation of a sunburn.

"You said blood and moonlight," he insists.

"Did I?"

"What's wrong?"

I shake my head. "Nothing. I'm fine."

He frowns and presses his hand to my forehead. "You're not fine. You're burning up."

Before I can answer, Costin materializes from the shadows beside us, his interruption making the air thick with tension. When he looks at me, I see the predator in his eyes. The possessive gleam makes my pulse quicken. As mad as I want to be at him, there is no denying he stirs my blood.

"Planning an adventure?" the vampire asks, his tone deceptively calm.

Anthony leans close to me. "Just taking my sister home."

"Actually," Costin's gaze fixes on mine, "I can see her home. Tamara and I need to have a discussion."

"There's nothing to discuss," I tell him. "A friend needs help, and I owe it to him to help. I'm not waiting for your permission."

"So I gathered from your conversation with the wolf." His lip curls slightly. Had he been eavesdropping? "Tell me, castoff, do you think storming werewolf territory alone is the wisest course of action?"

I hate that nickname. It's so dismissive. He first

used it when he found me in the forest with a burned hand. "I wasn't going to—"

"You were." He moves closer, and even Anthony takes a step back.

"You can't know that," I say.

"No?" He arches a brow as if daring me to finish the protest.

"You need to go away." I walk faster, making both men keep up with me. Between gritted teeth, I grumble, "I'm still mad you mesmerized me for a week."

"Not cool," Anthony mutters in support.

Costin ignores him. "However, if you insist on this foolishness, you won't go alone."

I narrow my eyes. "What are you saying?"

"I'm saying," he reaches out to trace my jaw with cold fingers, "that I know where the Alpha lives. I will take you there myself for an audience."

I'm not sure I trust him, but I'm too focused on finding Paul to question why.

His touch lingers longer than necessary, and I hate how my body betrays me by leaning into it. I shiver at his proximity. His coolness calms the sunburn sensation from moments before. I get a flash of his hand holding my small one after Anthony burned me with the fireball. It feels impossible that I've known him for a lifetime, and he still looks exactly the same. Never would have I guessed as a child that I'd grow up to be his... whatever we are.

I feel him starting to pull me back in, and I jerk away from his touch. We've given up the pretense of walking.

"Like hell you will," Anthony interjects. "After what you did to her—"

"What I did was protect her." Costin's voice carries an edge of steel.

"She is a Devine. She's not yours to control." Anthony pushes past me, crossing his arms to face off the master vampire.

"Easy, boy." Costin's words are both condescending and dismissive.

"Who are you calling a boy, old man?" Anthony returns.

"The little man in front of—"

"Oh my gods, stop it!" I yell, forcing their attention back on me. "You're both acting like children."

"Werewolves are dangerous—" Costin begins.

"Nighttime is dark, Captain Obvious," Anthony interrupts.

"—and your sister insists on throwing herself into their path," Costin finishes.

"Fine, you want to help?" I step between them and face Costin. "Then tell me what you know instead of treating me like a child who needs protection."

A woman slows as she passes us, her rapt attention on our conversation.

"What are you looking at?" I yell at her.

"Keep moving," Anthony adds. The woman rushes along.

Costin keeps his gaze on me and continues as if we weren't interrupted. "You are a child compared to me, Tamara." His eyes flash crimson. "I've watched empires rise and fall. I've seen what creatures like the Alpha are capable of. Werewolves are not like the rest of us. They're…"

"Wild," Anthony finishes for him.

"Dogs," Costin says at the same time.

"I have to agree with Costin," Anthony says begrudgingly. "This is dangerous."

"I'm not scared of wild dogs. I'm not helpless," I snap. To Costin, I say, "Now, remind me because I forget. Was it you who faced down a dragon and saved the world?" I glance at Anthony. "You?"

Anthony turns his attention down the sidewalk and studies a crowd of drag queens coming out of a bar.

Costin's expression softens slightly. "No, you're not helpless. You're reckless. There's a difference."

Part of me wants to tell Costin to go to hell, that I don't need him or his misogyny. But then I see my brother. Anthony won't let me go alone, either. My brother is powerful. I trust him.

I trusted Conrad.

Anthony isn't Conrad. I need to remember that and not let Conrad's betrayal mess with my head.

"Fine, Lord Constantine," I finally agree. I can't put Anthony in danger with the werewolves. My brother is the future of the Devine empire. As much as I might hate it, that idea of familial duty is rooted deep in me. "We'll do this your way. But no more mesmerizing me. No more secrets."

His answering vampire smile is dangerous. I see the hint of fangs in his mouth.

"I'm serious, Costin," I warn. "You mesmerize me again against my will, and that's it between us."

"I won't mesmerize you." He is suddenly closer, though I didn't see him move. I gasp in surprise. "But secrets, little castoff? Secrets keep us alive."

The amulet pulses a heated warning against my chest. I still can't tell if it's warning me about Costin or the werewolves. Maybe both. Maybe neither. I haven't been able to determine if Draakmar is my friend or a beast I have to keep subdued so he doesn't spew lava over the world.

Anthony clears his throat. "If you two are done with your twisted courtship ritual, can we please get off the street? We're drawing attention."

I start to agree, but another wave of heat floods through me. This time, I hear Draakmar's growling in my head. Somehow, I am able to translate words from the ancient sounds telling me that blood will flow under the moonlight and old powers are stirring.

I shake my head, trying to get the noise to stop. I don't want to hear it. I don't want another complicated prophecy or supernatural ritual. I just want to save Paul and send him home to his daughter.

When I look up, Costin is watching me with an intensity that makes me wonder just how much he knows about what's coming. His calculating gaze reminds me of chess pieces being moved into position.

Why can't Draakmar either say what he means or just keep quiet? The distractions are not helping me stay calm.

Not for the first time in recent months, I feel as if I'm straddling a large crack in the earth. On one side is the supernatural. On the other is humans. The crack slowly spreads, and soon, I'll have to choose where to jump or fall into the dark chasm below.

"Then it is decided," he says as if coming to a decision. "I'll take you to the Alpha tomorrow night."

"Why not now?" I insist, not wanting to wait. "The night is young."

"He'll need time to request an audience for us," Anthony says, clearly expecting he'll be going too.

"You need time to consider what you want to

know," Costin adds. He strokes my cheek with the back of his hand, and I feel our connection pulling me toward him. "And remember, some questions are better left unasked. Wolves do not carry the best of men."

"That's cryptic," I mutter.

Costin's lip twitches like he's going to smile, but then he disappears. I quickly look around but can't see a trace of him.

Anthony touches my shoulder. "You certainly like them domineering."

I frown at him, and he laughs.

"Hey, no judgment," Anthony adds.

I ignore his attempt to lighten the mood. "What do you think this ritual is all about?"

"We shouldn't talk about it out here." Anthony pulls me with him down the sidewalk toward home.

I take a deep breath, trying to process everything. Draakmar seems to have calmed, but I fear it's only for a short time. The dragon's ominous message of blood and moonlight feels like a threat. I can't help but feel that I'm walking straight into another prophecy. Only this time, I'm unsure if I'm the hero or the sacrifice.

SIX

"We had a visitor to the house while you were out." Astrid's voice drifts from behind her book as I pass through the penthouse living room toward the kitchen.

I don't want to hear the end of what she has to say, so I pause just outside her view. It takes me a moment to slowly reverse my steps to face her. I've just changed my clothes after returning from the haircut appointment she foisted on me earlier in the day. Normally, I'd be annoyed, but at least I had something to pass the time. Not that Cosette's chatter took my mind off of meeting the Alpha.

The sun is setting outside the wall of windows behind her. The light paints the balcony in shades of amber and blood.

Blood and moonlight.

"Oh?" I prompt.

"Lorelai Weber has come from California." Astrid doesn't look at me. When she told me she wasn't my birth mother several months back, so many things in my life started to make sense— most significantly, my lack of magic. "She left the address where she's staying. I put it on your dresser."

I wish words would come more easily when I talk to Astrid, but our relationship has never been one of easy words. She's been my protector in many ways, raising me within the confines of the powerful Devine family, keeping me healthy, and teaching me what supernatural society expects of women. However, what little affection is shown is heavily veiled by her strictness, and I spent most of my childhood isolated and feeling like an outsider in my own family.

Sometimes, I wish Astrid would yell at me and lay voice to what has to be true on some base level. My life is the product of her husband's affair and a constant reminder of his betrayal. How can she not resent me for that? Or my father?

I tried once to tell her I was sorry for what my existence must do to her, but she didn't want to hear it.

"What...?" I search her expression for a hint of what she's feeling. I'm not surprised when I don't find it. I don't expect emotion from the woman. She's too practical for that.

"Speak up." Astrid turns a page with deliberate precision before finally lowering the book to meet my gaze. Her perfect posture is in stark contrast to my travel-ready attire. "Going out?"

I nod.

She glances at my hair. The curls are tamed, blown straight and styled. "Cosette did well."

"Are you...?" I stop short of asking if she's all right.

"She's called here multiple times looking for you, as well," Astrid states, as if she doesn't know what I'm trying to ask.

I inch closer to where she sits. I see an empty martini glass near her foot. "Did she say what she wanted?"

"To speak with you, obviously." Her diamond wedding ring catches the light behind her for the briefest of seconds, making me think of her life with my father. "The woman has become quite persistent since you fixed that amulet. You should decide what you want to do there."

She doesn't invite me, but I sit beside her anyway. The gesture seems to catch her off guard, and she closes the book. I can tell by the worn cover it is old and probably in a language I don't understand.

"Thank you," I say.

Astrid frowns. "For taking a message?"

"For raising me." I can instantly tell that my attempt at connecting makes her uncomfortable. She much prefers her mask of emotional detachment and practicality.

"Duty is duty. There is no reason to go on about it." She starts to open the book, but I put my hand on top of it to stop her.

"Are you all right with...?" I want to say the right things. They never seem to come out correctly. I take my hand back and place it in my lap. "Do you have an opinion on all of this?"

"You're asking for my advice? This is new." She keeps studying me. "Here it is. Don't let sentiment cloud your judgment. Lorelai left for a reason."

I nod. "I know. Goblins were attacking me in my crib, and she couldn't protect me."

"You can't fault a human for failing any more than you can fault a snowflake for melting. Mortals are fragile and easily exploited." She reaches to pat my hand. "I know you don't always agree with how I've raised you, but look at who you are becoming, look at what you've achieved, look at your resilience as a mortal in a supernatural world."

"But I'm human," I say. By her logic, I'm doomed to fail. I touch the amulet. All magic I have is borrowed. "Mortal."

"No, Tamara, you're a Devine. It's not the same. Mortal attachments often bring pain and vulnerability. This is why I've taught you to focus on survival and your responsibilities as part of the Devine family." If I didn't know better, I'd say there is a grudging respect in her tone. "Appreciate Lorelai's sacrifice but keep her at a distance. Her leaving might have been necessary, but those dangers she ran from when you were a child are just as real now. Reopening the old wounds will only invite vulnerability and distraction."

Like always, it is practical advice.

"If you didn't..." I take a deep breath. Part of me feels this is not a road I should go down. Still, I find myself saying, "If duty didn't come into this, would you have agreed to..."

I'm a coward. What I want to know is if she loves me.

Talk about mommy issues.

She touches her wedding ring and gives it a slight wiggle back and forth on her finger. "Don't dwell on what you can't change. Duty is a real thing, and you belong here."

"She knows I know about her now. I have to talk to her."

"Of course you do." There's something in Astrid's tone, a thread of genuine concern she can't entirely hide beneath her frost. "The things you have faced recently—the labyrinth, Draakmar, your amulet. These are all challenges."

I'm not sure what she's getting at.

"I raised you to be strong and self-reliant. You're ready for the big things life throws at you. You've proven that." She touches my hand again, and this time, her touch lingers. "It's not the big things that do us in. It's the big things that take our attention. That's when the small creeps in—a tiny little thing you're not looking at falls on top of you like an unassuming feather. It is that last straw that breaks you. You wanted my advice. There it is. Fight the big battles, but don't take your eyes off of the little things."

"I understand." I nod. At least, I hope I understand. It seems the only correct answer.

She lets go and reopens her book. "Do try not to start a war tonight. The Freemonts are causing enough trouble without adding werewolf politics to the mix."

"You know?" The question slips out in my surprise.

She scoffs and brushes off the question with a small wave of her ringed hand.

"Oh, and your father returns next week," she says as if reading the text from her book.

The mention of my father makes my stomach

tighten. I wonder if he knows Lorelai is in town. I wonder if he cares.

My birth mother and werewolves hardly seem like little things to me. I should have suspected Lorelai would show up. This means Paul's aren't the only memories to return. Lorelai was present when the amulet broke. Maybe that's the key.

Please don't let Diana remember. Let her remain safe and innocent.

"Costin is here," Astrid says as I stand from the couch.

Before I can respond, Costin materializes beside me, dressed entirely in black but for a peek of blood red lining the inside of his slim jacket. The contrast between his elegance and the fact I chose jeans, running shoes, and a T-shirt strikes me as absurd.

I mean, come on. *Werewolves.* I'm going in ready to run for my life.

"Lady Astrid." He bows slightly.

"Constantine," she acknowledges, smoothing invisible wrinkles from her silk blouse.

"Is that what you're wearing?" Costin asks me, his eyes trailing down my body in a way that makes my skin warm.

Astrid chuckles.

"Yes." I grab Costin's arm. "We're leaving."

"May I mesmerize you for the trip?" he offers, reaching for my face.

"No, we'll take the elevator." I cross the foyer and press the call button. The memory of being under his influence for a week only makes me angry. I hate feeling like I missed something crucial during that lost time.

"But I can—"

"No. I don't trust you to bring me out of it. Besides, I felt like my brain was encased in fog for hours last time." When the elevator opens, I step on. He joins me, and I push the button to the lobby.

"This way will take a long time," he says.

I don't care. I'm proving a point.

I take out my phone. "I'll order us a car."

He tries to push my hair behind my ear, but I lean to the side. "Don't be sweet. I'm mad at you."

"As you wish."

The doors open, and I stride from within. I beat the doorman and push my way outside. A blast of cool air hits me. I see a familiar car pull forward and instantly get inside the back.

"Where to?" the driver asks.

I look at Costin to answer before I begin texting. Costin gives basic directions, and we start moving into traffic.

"What are you doing?" Costin asks.

"Telling Anthony I'm sorry I didn't wait for him, but I'm not letting him put himself in danger." I lied when my brother asked me what time we were leaving.

"How long until we're there?" I ask, setting my phone on the seat beside me.

"An eternity by this carriage," Costin grumbles.

"We call them cars now," I tease.

"You're smiling. Does that mean I can be sweet now?" His hand glides over my thigh.

I try to shake him off, but it only makes his fingers explore higher. The driver's eyes meet mine through his rearview mirror. I place my hand on Costin's to still his exploration.

I give a meaningful glance forward. "Not here."

"May I mesmerize the driver?"

I push his hand off my leg.

He holds himself quiet, but I feel the weight of his presence beside me like a physical thing. I can't tell if he's mimicking me or feeling the effects of time. I find myself watching him more than where we're going. Hypnotic lights dance across his handsome face, highlighting the sharp angles of his cheekbones and the curve of his mouth, bending and moving like a living thing over his features. He doesn't need vampiric magic to mesmerize me. He's doing a good job of it just being close. But beneath his beauty, beneath his power, I see the calculating way in which he watches the city pass.

My breath catches when his hand finds mine on the seat. His thumb traces circles on my palm, each touch sending shivers up my arm.

"Your heart is racing," he whispers, too low for the driver to hear. "Are you afraid?"

"Not of you." The lie comes easily, like flirting.

His smile is treacherous. I know the power he holds. He leans closer, his cool breath ghosting across my neck where he's bitten me before. "You should be."

I'm not scared of him. I feel the tender seduction that contradicts his words. The pull between us is more potent than any supernatural power, and that's what terrifies me most.

It's not fair. I want to be mad at him. Logic tells me to, but I find myself wanting to forget the transgressions.

Fucking vampires. It's how they're made. They draw humans in. He probably can't help it any more than I can help breathing.

I gently push his face away and rub at my neck as if that will erase the memory for both of us.

My cellphone dings, pulling my attention to a text from Anthony that simply reads, "*Asshole.*" Seconds later, another comes, "*Be safe.*" Then, the third, "*I can't believe you ditched me.*"

"Stop," Costin commands the driver. I see his

finger lift and move to the side like he's casting a spell.

The car pulls over.

We get out in a sketchy neighborhood. Street-lights flicker over abandoned buildings in an industrial district. The muffled sound of heavy metal music pounds beneath the sidewalk, leaking up from grates and cracks. Each breath is filled with the taste of dust, stirred by a breeze sweeping over us. Energy hums in the air, but I don't know if it's real or my fear.

I've heard stories of werewolves. They're much worse than Hollywood movies.

We turn a corner, and I see smoke lifting from a metal grate. The scent of cooking meat and burning wood is enhanced as the primal music becomes louder. Someone howls, and the sound is followed by gruff laughter.

"Remember," Costin says as we approach a padlocked gate, "werewolves aren't like us. They're—"

"Don't say dangerous," I scold. "I'm not stupid. Everything in this world is dangerous. You're dangerous."

"I was going to say unpredictable." His hand finds the small of my back. "They live for the moment, for sensation. They don't always think. It makes them dangerous in ways vampires aren't."

As if to prove his point, another howl pierces the night. It's answered by others, creating a savage harmony that creates goosebumps on my skin. Through a gap in the fence slats, I see fires burning in old oil drums. Violent figures move around them, some human, some wolf. Several fights break out but are short-lived as they end in laughter.

I don't know what I was expecting, but seeing so many of them, knowing any one of them could tear me apart, makes me want to run.

And here I thought running shoes were going to make a difference.

"Welcome to the Pack," Costin says softly. Before he opens the gate, he turns to me, pressing me against the fence. His body shields me from the street view, and for a moment, the howls and music fade away. "Remember who you belong to in there."

"I don't belong to anyone," I whisper, but my body betrays me, leaning slightly toward his in invitation. The air is charged between us, and I'm achingly aware of every point our bodies touch. Even through my anger, I can't deny the primal pull.

He cups my face, thumb brushing my lower lip. "Don't you?"

The kiss that follows is fierce, a claim that leaves me breathless. My legs spread as he lifts me off the ground, anchoring my hips in his strong hands. The wall is cold against my back, but his body burns against mine despite his vampiric nature. Our clothes force a chastity I don't feel, becoming an exquisite torture as his hands grip me possessively. The press of his arousal against me only hints at what we both want to happen. Desire moves like hot lava through me, pulsing and all-consuming. I should push him away. We're outside a werewolf den, for goodness' sake! Instead, I find myself pulling him closer, craving more of that dangerous passion.

A fang nicks my tender lip, filling my mouth with blood. When he pulls away, his eyes have a crimson shine. My thumping heart wants to come out of my chest. I see my blood staining his bottom lip as he licks slowly.

"Mm." His pleasure moan sounds like sex.

A series of howls echo from the courtyard beyond, jolting me back to awareness. My heart hammers violently at the idea of where we're at, of the danger just beyond this flimsy barrier. I don't want to stop. Not just yet.

"Say the word and I'll take you far away from here," he offers.

It's tempting. Oh, so tempting.

"Costin, I can't," I refuse.

He lets my legs fall back to the ground. This is not the place. I'm grateful the gate supports my back and keeps me upright.

"Ready?" He doesn't wait for my nod before he pushes the gate open as if the lock doesn't matter. "Try not to stare. Wolves hate that."

SEVEN

Don't stare.

That advice becomes impossible the moment we step inside. The chaos of the werewolf courtyard is a nightmare that has come to life. Heavy metal music pounds through my bones, seeming to come from everywhere and nowhere at once. Fallen bricks and rusted scaffolding create a maze-like enclosure that feels more like the opening of a deathtrap than a party space. Every exit I spot disappears in the shifting shadows behind the fierce creatures who party here.

The smell of meat and beer mingles with the hint of wet dog. A pile of discarded, broken liquor bottles is next to a wall. I see a flash seconds before I hear glass shattering as another joins its forgotten friends.

I can't see the moon, but I know it's there by the color of the light. Bodies writhe around the burning oil drums, human, wolf, and some caught in that horrifying in between where bones crack and reshape, where skin splits to let fur push through, where human screams turn to animal howls.

Costin's hand rests possessively on my lower back, his touch both steadying and electric. My lips still tingle from our kiss, and I can taste the faint copper of my blood where his fang nicked me. The puncture is raw, but the bleeding has slowed. Even here, surrounded by danger, part of me wants him to do it again. By the way his fingers flex against me, I know he can still taste my blood too.

Blood and moonlight.

The words echo in my head like a warning. Draakmar's consciousness presses against mine with increasing urgency. The dragon knows something I don't—something about Costin, about the wolves, about all of this. But, like trying to remember a dream, the knowledge slips away whenever I reach for it.

A woman dances topless on a metal platform, her body covered in tribal tattoos that travel like living things over her skin as she moves. When she throws back her head to howl, I watch in horror as her jaw dislocates. Teeth elongate past her chin in a grotesque display of partial transformation. The crowd cheers, the sound primal and hungry, and I realize not all the meat is being cooked as some of them are feeding on raw meat torn from carcasses.

I lean into Costin. "Is this a celebration?"

"No. This debauchery is every night." Costin's touch makes me shiver despite the heat from the fires. His fingers possessively dig into my hip as he jerks me closer. "Stay close. The Alpha's protection will only extend so far, and some of them look ready for a hunt. If something happens to us, he'll claim my presence provoked it."

I notice how some of the wolves watch the vampire in their midst, their golden eyes glowing with barely contained animosity.

A motorcycle revs before tearing through the courtyard, nearly clipping several dancers. The half-naked woman leaps off the metal platform with inhuman grace, her spine cracking and reforming mid-air as she tackles the driver. They hit the ground in a tangle of limbs and partial transformations, blood and fur flying as claws emerge. The riderless motorcycle careens into a wall, exploding in a shower of sparks that illumi-nates dozens of glowing eyes in the darkness beyond.

I grab Costin's arm as the driver and the dancer start brawling in earnest. I press into him, trying to get him to walk another way. He doesn't obey.

Instead, he brushes my fingers off and tries to step in front of me. I don't let him.

A laugh draws my attention to a dark corner where a young girl plays with entrails. The sound doesn't belong here, and my first instinct is to run to protect the child. But before I can find a path toward her, she turns to reveal the face of an ancient crone. Sharpened teeth gleam as she bites into her meal. I gag and recoil in horror, but the image burns itself into my mind.

Two massive wolves break away from the crowd, deliberately padding toward us. Their fur is matted with what looks like blood, but when the men shift to human form, the red streaks appear too bright against naked flesh. It's probably paint. Glowing eyes meet mine.

"Vampire," the taller one sneers. "Your kind is not welcome here."

"I have business with your Alpha." Costin's voice carries over the music.

"Let him stay." The shorter wolf laughs, but it's not a pleasant sound. "I like an enemy who can fight back." His eyes fix on me, nostrils flaring. "And you brought a snack? How thoughtful."

Laughter rises.

Costin moves so fast that I barely see it. Suddenly, he has the wolf by the throat, his feet dangling above the ground. "She is mine. Look at her again, and I'll tear out your eyes."

The music cuts abruptly, and the silence feels heavier than the bass had been.

"Release him," someone orders.

"Kill him!" another growls.

The pack surrounds us like a fist closing. Voices erupt in roars and howls that are more animal than human. Bodies begin to shift en masse, the sound of cracking bones and tearing flesh filling the court-yard. I spin, looking for escape, but we're trapped. The gate we entered through has vanished behind a wall of transforming bodies. The smell of blood and fur is overwhelming, and I worry that maybe I'm wrong and the red spattering isn't paint.

"Costin," I manage, barely getting the word out. What was I thinking? This is too dangerous.

"Costin," repeats a burly man with fur crawling up his forearms before yelling louder, "Constantine!"

The wolves back away like a wave retracting from shore as the word circulates amongst them.

"Shall I remind you of the treaties?" Costin asks the creature he had lifted in the air.

"No," the wolf manages, the sound strangled.

Costin releases him, and he drops to his knees. I sense he could stand if he wanted, but he remains on the ground, head bowed. Heavy pants of air escape him.

"Now," Costin says pleasantly, dusting his hands. "I believe your Alpha is expecting us."

"I'll take you," the burly wolf says, his fur receding as he completely shifts back to human. He lifts his hand, and without having to ask, someone throws a pair of jeans at him. He catches it without looking. Unlike the others who remain naked, he slides on his pants. "Forgive them, Lord Constantine. They're young and are amped up with anticipation of the full moon. They do not recognize you or know what you have done for us."

Costin doesn't answer. I wonder what he's done for them. I doubt anyone will tell me.

The wolf eyes me. I pull the amulet out from under my shirt as if that might somehow make me scarier. It doesn't seem to.

"I don't expect you'll remember, but we met roughly fifty years ago at the last treaty negotiation," the wolf says to Costin.

"Good to see you again, Sully."

Sully's lip twitches up at his side.

"I'm Tamara Devine," I say when Costin doesn't introduce me.

Sully looks at me in surprise and nods his head. He gives me a seductive once-over—if you can call a giant werewolf looking like he wants to tear off your clothes and devour you *seductive*. "The mortal Devine. I have heard of your battles with Draakmar.

Impressive. I also heard you are recently single after you called off your engagement to—"

Costin grabs my arm and pulls me next to him, effectively stopping the flirtatious comment before it fully forms. Typically, I'd want to say something about women not being property and whatnot, but I'm not too stupid to admit I'm grateful he's laying claim to me. I don't think I could survive a werewolf courtship. This Sully is not Peter, that's for sure. I'm not sure the word no would stop Sully's romantic advances.

"My mistake," Sully says. "Follow me. Alpha Thane will see you now."

It is clear Sully is considered a leader by the way the others part to let him pass. He leads us through the chaotic throng to an abandoned factory building. He gives a short grunt. A metal door groans open to reveal a long corridor lit by flickering fluorescent lights. The walls are covered in claw marks, telling stories of fights and displays of dominance. They look centuries old if the edges of rust and crumbling concrete are to be believed.

The heavy metal music resumes over the court-yard, as does the partying. Someone closes the metal doors, and instantly, the music is stifled, separating this part of the werewolf enclave from the outside. Though I appreciate being away from the others, I now feel trapped.

And underdressed.

I pull at my T-shirt, glad it doesn't have some fuck-off band logo on it. Running shoes sounded smart when I put them on. Now I hear Astrid's voice in my head lecturing me about propriety and etiquette. She would have probably put me in a dress for an audience with a werewolf king.

Maybe it won't matter. This hardly seems like a palace. I also hear Astrid's voice telling me that werewolves are dirty, feral creatures and part of the lower echelon of the supernatural world. It's possible she'd have recommended a hazmat suit over a dress.

Water drips somewhere in the darkness. My shoes thump against the concrete floor, the sound heavier than the two larger men with me. I consciously try to step lighter.

I find I'm gripping the amulet like the talisman it is. Steel and concrete give way to exposed brick. I can't tell what forgotten purpose this building was initially used for, what old-fashioned products it would have spit out that the world no longer wants. There are many like it in the city, scattered pock-marks that give home to vagrants and the super-natural.

The further we go, the more the décor changes. Bricks morph into polished stone. Torches replace the fluorescent lights, casting dancing shadows that make me edgy. Costin stays close but doesn't touch me as we walk. His shoulders are stiff, and each movement seems measured.

"The Alpha likes to remind us of where we came from," our guide explains, noticing my interest in the transition. He gestures to an ornate door ahead, carved with scenes of wolves hunting under a full moon. It's not the sanitized hunting of nobility but the raw, primal chase that makes other supernaturals fear them. Even so, hunting might be too nice of a word. It looks like they're chasing humans. "He calls it progress. We are not who we once were. I personally hate the torches. They need to be replaced too often. But then these are not my decisions to make."

Costin makes a small noise of disbelief.

The guide hears it and smirks. I see a challenging light in his gaze as it fills with gold to threaten a shift. "Don't mistake progress for weakness. The treaties might force us to play nice, and they might restrict us to these industrial territories while the vampires get their mansions and the magics get their estates. But we remember what we really are."

My heart beats fast. I don't know what to expect as the door opens to reveal a throne room out of a gothic nightmare. It's not what I would expect after seeing the outside of the building.

Classic rock plays. Voices carry like a soft

murmur, nothing like the chaos outside. Couches, chairs, and tables form conversational areas. Scantily clad men and women enter carrying trays filled with food and drinks like waitstaff.

The ceiling is high as if the floors above had been cleaved out to make space. I see openings along one wall, the exposed rooms left after the cut, stacked three stories up. There is no rail to keep people from falling over the edge, but I see them moving around up there. Some sit around a poker table. Others watch television or play video games. A spiderweb of chains hangs like an industrial chandelier. Wolf sculptures that come out of their stone bases in an eternal struggle fill the walls, as beautifully detailed as any statue found in Rome.

"Jack," a voice yells. "Get up here!"

I watch a half-shifted werewolf leap from the ground up two stories to the room where they play video games. Seconds later, another jumps down to take a beer off one of the trays.

"This way." Sully takes the lead as we approach the Alpha.

Costin nudges my arm to walk. I hadn't realized I'd stopped to stare.

At the far end of the room lounges a dangerous-looking man on a throne made of welded metal and leather. He's not shifted, but his long brown hair falls wild around his naked shoulders. Tattoos cover his massive chest, only to disappear down his waist into his leather pants. His eyes are wolf-gold and unwavering, suggesting he's powerful enough to hold partial transformation indefinitely. That gaze fixes steadily upon us. I'm unsure why his bare feet suddenly hold my rapt attention, but it's better than meeting his eyes.

Thane lazily rests his head against his fist, but there's nothing lazy about the predatory focus in his gaze. As we approach, I find myself hyper-aware of Costin beside me, wanting to press closer to his familiar darkness rather than face this wild, untamed power. The memory of our kiss outside burns through me, making me wish we were anywhere but here.

"Alpha Thane," Costin says, holding out his hand to get me to stop moving. I glance upward. The Alpha shows fangs as he grins.

"Constantine," Thane rumbles. Dropping his arms to his legs, he leans forward on the throne. "Have you come to renegotiate our arrangement?"

"This isn't about that." Costin's clipped voice contrasts with Thane's boisterous tone. I feel Costin reach for my back, fingers flexing against me like a warning.

"Arrangement?" I whisper, not liking how Thane's wolfish smile widens at my question.

"The treaty between our kinds," Costin mutters

dismissively, but there's tension in his jaw that wasn't there before.

Thane laughs as if he hears us, but I don't get the joke.

"Ah yes, the treaty." Thane's eyes gleam with dark amusement.

Sully whispers in Thane's ear.

"The mortal girl who tamed a dragon and saved us all." There is something in Thane's tone that doesn't radiate gratitude. If I had to guess, he's mocking me. "I've heard interesting things about you, Miss Devine."

His massive form dominates the space, radiating a raw power that treaties and politics can't fully contain. It wouldn't surprise me to learn that he was chosen for his size alone. I've heard stories about werewolf hierarchy and how they spill blood to climb their ranks. Thane is not Alpha because he was voted in.

"Tell me," he continues, in that same smug tone, "does your vampire master let you wander far from his territory? Or does he keep you on a shorter leash than he keeps us?"

"Pleased to meet you, Alpha Thane," I say, not taking the bait.

For some reason, this causes him to laugh again.

"You are a long way from your penthouse tower,

little princess. I'm surprised Mommy and Daddy let you out to play." He slowly stands. The motion is full of power as his golden eyes gleam with savage pride. "Here, we don't pretend to be something we're not. No fancy etiquette or little niceties you elites love so much. You are not pleased to meet me, just as I am not pleased to have your escort the vampire king in my court."

I look up at Costin, who says nothing as he holds himself tense. I notice the noise has lessened, and the werewolves are watching us. The beasts are doing nothing to hide their animosity toward him. He keeps his eyes on Thane.

I'm too scared to speak. I don't know what to say to the man. Automatically, I touch the amulet to remind myself he can't kill me.

"Now, princess, what brings you to my humble abode?" He waves to encompass the throne room. It may be industrial in a scary part of the city, but it is far from humble.

Costin nods that I should speak.

"You have something that belongs to the Devines," I manage as I feel Draakmar stir again within the amulet. The dragon's agitation feels like a warning, but about what? The wolves? Or something closer to home?

"Do I?" Thane's golden gaze shifts to Costin and then back to me.

MICHELLE M. PILLOW

"The mortal man taken by your wolves a week ago," I tell him.

I catch Costin and Thane exchanging a look that makes my blood run cold. There's something passing between them, some unspoken understanding that I can't quite grasp. I wonder what would happen if they were alone and there was no treaty keeping them in line. The amulet pulses against my chest, and I wonder if Draakmar is trying to tell me what I'm missing.

I know werewolves and vampires hate each other as a rule. Is that what is causing the tension between them?

Maybe Draakmar is messing with me because he's mad I forced him back underground.

Maybe the dragon is bored.

"Paul Cannon," I clarify. "He's Devine protectus. Return him."

"Is he?" Thane studies the amulet around my neck.

"Yes," I insist. "I demand you release him to me at once."

"I think that dragon has gone to your head." Thane comes toward us. The sound of the werewolf laughter reminds me of gravel in a blender. "Your kind wrote the rules to keep us contained, but nature doesn't bow to paper laws."

Nervously, I look around. Movement along my

114

peripheral catches my attention. Peter stands partially hidden by shadows near a statue of a wolf eating a man. When our eyes meet, he subtly shakes his head in warning.

"Or what, little human? You'll start a war between magics and wolves?" He shakes his head. "Do your parents know you're here making threats?"

I am out of my comfort zone. My parents spent my life protecting me from creatures like this. There's history here, dark and dangerous.

"He's claimed as Devine protectus," I say, my tone not as brave as before.

"And why should I believe that? Let the Devine I have affronted come forward with the claim." Thane leans his face into mine. "Because we know as a mortal you don't have the authority or the power to make such a mark."

He knows I'm lying.

I feel Costin tense beside me.

"Do you have him?" I have to actively tell myself he can't kill me. But as I watch Thane and Costin exchange looks, I wonder if death is really what I should fear.

Thane gives a small nod, but it's so slight I'm unsure if it's an answer or just an acknowledgment of something passing between them that I don't understand.

Costin is being of little help, so I look at Peter, who is still watching us. My eyes then move to the others. Werewolves stand above in the alcoves, staring down. I feel as if they might leap upon us at any moment.

"Give her the mortal," Costin finally says. "We'll settle the account later between the two of us."

"The full moon approaches." Thane waves toward the ceiling like he can see the sky hidden beyond the building. His attention falls entirely on me. "But perhaps *we* can make a deal."

"What kind of deal?" I ask, trying to keep my voice steady despite Thane's proximity.

"A trade." Thane's eyes flick to Costin as if taunting the vampire. "Your mortal for another favor."

"No deals," Costin answers for me. "Return him. Find someone else."

"Or what?" Thane's darkness seeps from his every pore. His golden eyes swim with power. I get the sense they can all hear the pounding of my heart. Every instinct tells me to run. "You'll start a war over one human? That seems beneath you, old friend. Unless you want to step down and give your sister the throne. How is the beautiful Elizabeth?"

The room is tense. I feel the aggression bouncing all around us like a living thing. I notice several wolves inching closer, their bodies beginning to shift. Even the serving staff has stopped to watch.

"Perhaps the girl and I could discuss terms privately," Thane suggests, his smile predatory.

"Absolutely not," Costin states.

"No," I say at the same time.

Peter appears beside me so suddenly I jump. He bows his head in respect. "Alpha, if I may?"

Thane waves his permission, appearing amused by the entire situation.

"The ritual requires specific timing," Peter says carefully. "The moon will be full in three days. Perhaps that gives us time to..."

Peter stops talking and bows his head more.

Ritual? I take a deep breath, willing Peter to continue. "What ritual?"

"Leave it," Costin orders.

"Nothing that concerns you," Thane says, but his eyes tell a different story. "Unless..."

"Unless?" I prompt.

"Unless you're willing to make an exchange." He gestures toward a dark hallway. "Come. Let me show you something."

Costin grips my arm. "We're leaving."

"Am I to understand you're speaking for the Devine family now, vampire?" Thane's voice carries enough threat that several wolves growl. He gestures his hand as if to keep them back. "Last I checked, you were merely... what's the modern term? Dating?"

"She's mine. I forbid it," Costin says.

I pull away from him. "I'm not your chattel, Costin."

"She's not your chattel," Thane repeats. I hate the mocking in his tone. Someone needs to give the Alpha a big slap across the face to wipe the smirk off.

It's not going to be me. He's likely to rip off my arm for just thinking it.

"Show me." I want so badly to be brave. I owe it to Paul. But I feel like a fraud. I'm terrified. It's all I can do to keep my legs from shaking.

"Tamara don't—" Costin tries to stop me.

But I'm already following Thane out of the throne room. When I glance back, wolves surround Costin. I wonder if the vampire can take them in a fight. It looks like he wants to.

I shake my head slightly, trying to tell him to calm down and behave. I'm not sure the message gets across.

"Thane, I'm warning you..." Costin yells.

Thane doesn't turn around. He lifts his fingers to give a short wave before disappearing through a narrow door behind the throne.

The passage leads to a circular room that feels ancient despite its industrial trappings. Through the glass ceiling, the moon watches us, nearly full and somehow appearing larger than it should be as if the glass magnifies it. My skin crawls as if the moonlight itself is alive, searching for something. Beneath it stands what looks like an altar made of twisted metal and stone, its surface stained with old, dark marks I don't want to identify. Carved into the altar's edge are the words "*Sanguis et Lūnāria.*"

Thane touches the carving, translating words as he traces over them to make my blood run cold. "Blood and moonlight."

I take a step back. "What does that mean?"

His claw scrapes against the stone as he walks to the other side. Thane presses his hands flat against the altar. He nods toward it before rocking his hips suggestively. I can see the outline of a thick arousal beneath his light pants. "Care to take it for a spin? One minute riding my wolf, and you'll forget all about that cold popsicle."

I shake my head.

"He can't hear us in here. Unless you want him to, then I promise your vampire will hear every moan." He winks as if that's a real enticement. "Let's have some fun and get the heart pumping in that dead blood sack, shall we?"

I can't tell if he's teasing.

"No." I shake my head again. "No, thank you."

His arms flex, and he pushes up on the altar,

leaping over it to land before me. I gasp and stumble back in surprise.

"You're not what I expected." He lets his finger hover over the amulet but doesn't touch it. "I'm curious. How far will your protection let me go?"

I don't know how to answer that.

"Take it off," he urges, eyes flashing and throat rumbling. "I hear your heart beating. I know what you want. Danger. Excitement. A hard fuck. I'll give you an orgasm better than a near-death experience."

I want to be repulsed. I really do. But there is something feral and raw about the way he wants to devour me. Costin's earlier kiss already has my senses heightened.

"Why did you bring me here?" I insist.

"Straight to business, then?" Thane sighs.

"Blood and moonlight. What does it mean?"

"It's the ingredients of an ancient magic ritual."

"To do what exactly?"

"Transfer a curse." He leans closer.

I try to stay strong, but I'm terrified.

"You see," Thane's breath is hot against my ear, his closeness making me long for Costin's cool touch instead, "sometimes the old magic requires... great sacrifices."

The amulet burns against my skin like a brand as Draakmar's warning becomes clear. The dragon's rage floods through me, but it's not directed at the wolves. What am I missing?

He stares at the amulet as a claw extends from his fingertip. As if daring himself, he touches my arm lightly, dragging the claw against my skin. Right before he pulls back, he lets the tip puncture my forearm. I grimace and jerk away.

Thane lifts the claw and sniffs before licking the tip. "Mm. Interesting. So your dragon does let you play a little."

"Why are you showing me all of this? Where's Paul?" I inch away from him, wanting to run. I don't want to be in this room.

"Your heart is so fast." He closes his eyes. I ball a fist, wishing I had the nerve to hit him. My human strength would only amuse him.

"I'll make you a deal. Come back in three nights as the sun sets. I'll consider giving him to you."

"For what price?" There's always a price.

"For a choice," he says.

He thinks he's clever and enigmatic. I see it in his expression. But I have been playing word games with the supernatural my entire life. Draakmar's half-whispers, Thane's hyper-focus on my amulet and attempts at seducing me to take it off, his effort to have me return at the full moon...

The werewolves don't just want Paul. They want

me. And as the moon watches through the dome, I realize this trap was set long before I walked into it.

There's something else Draakmar is trying to tell me. I try to listen to his strange language, but all I get is vague warnings about betrayal and choices made in darkness. Too bad the dragon's riddles aren't as easy to uncover as Thane's narcissism.

EIGHT

"Some curses run deeper than dragon fire."

Peter's warning from the coffee shop echoes through my head. I didn't understand what he was trying to tell me at the time, but now it is starting to make terrible sense. They want me for their ritual, and I can't help wondering if this is why Costin tried so hard to keep me away. Is this why he mesmerized me? Why he didn't stop the wolves from kidnapping Paul?

But why didn't the wolves take me instead if I am who they want?

The amulet. They're afraid of its power. Thane hesitated before touching it as if testing its magic.

My heart pounds in time with the pulsing amulet. The stone feels like it's catching fire, hot enough to burn my skin. This isn't right. Before we fixed the amulet, it didn't act like this. For most of my life, I thought it was just a necklace my grandfather gave me. I had assumed the magic was more symbolic, like a token to remind me of familial love. But then Conrad tried to kill me, and its magic was activated. It protected me from death. That is when I knew it was more, but there was still no heat, or pulsing, or dragon warnings.

I've been trying not to panic, telling myself that my awareness of the connection to Draakmar is what's different. But I fear it's more than that.

"Sometimes, the old magic requires great sacrifices."

Thane's words swirl with Peter's in my mind as I stumble from the ritual room. They need me for their ritual, and they are leveraging Paul to make that happen. I can't prove it, but it's the only thing making sense.

Has Costin known all along?

What pieces am I missing from this puzzle?

I keep waiting for Thane to stop me from leaving. I glance back to find him watching me, smiling knowingly as if he already sees how everything will play out.

It must be nice to have answers. I'm still trying to figure out what's going on.

The throne room is a blur of bodies and classic rock. Two burly wolves are waiting at the entrance like guards. The animals look at me from either side of the door as I force myself to walk past. Their golden eyes track my movement. My heart won't stop pounding, and I hope I look braver than I feel.

The werewolf palace feels fuller than when I left it. I see some of the men who were partying outside now gathered indoors. I can't tell if they're here to prevent my escape or if they'll give me a clear path. Behind me, I hear Thane's laughter, rich and dark like aged whiskey.

"Tamara." Costin materializes in front of me, reaching for my arm. "We should go."

I dodge his grasp. "Don't touch me."

"Tam—"

"I'm not yours to command," I argue, mindful to keep my tone low. "You don't own me. This isn't the Middle Ages. You're not lord of the manor. So take your misogyny and—"

"You don't understand what's happening," Costin cuts me off.

He's too late, though. I hear some of the werewolves laughing at us. Damn supernatural hearing. Very little can be kept secret, especially in crowded rooms.

I don't care.

"Then why don't you tell me?" The amulet's weight feels heavy, and it pulls at my neck. Draakmar tries to whisper, but I ignore him. "Why did you even bring me here?"

His silence only adds to my suspicion.

"You act like you don't want me to learn what's happening. Is that why you came? To stop me?"

He moves so fast I don't see him until he stands beside me, hand gripping my elbow. "Now is not the place."

A commotion near the throne draws my attention. A familiar figure in expensive designer clothes stands with the Alpha—Chester's mother, Mabel Freemont.

"What is she doing here?" I whisper, forgetting my anger toward Costin. He looks at me annoyed like that is who he was warning me about.

The woman looks entirely too comfortable among the werewolves. And beside her, a woman I've never officially met in this timeline but whose face I'll never forget. Elizabeth. Costin's sister. She and her vampire followers had tried to kill me at a lonely gas station in the middle of Kansas. If not for the amulet, she would have. The vampiress is as beautiful and terrifying as I remember, though she's never met me in her current timeline.

The pieces are forming a picture I don't want to see. This isn't just about Paul or even about me. This is about power—vampire, werewolf, and something older whose name will taste like blood in my mouth.

"Tamara Devine." Elizabeth's voice carries across

the room like silk slicing against steel. "I've been looking forward to meeting you."

For a moment, I see her as I remember her with short dark hair framed in the moonlight with fangs bearing down on me for the bite as she pins me to the ground. I lean closer to Costin. Then, she'd been looking forward to eating me. Now, she appears like she still wants to devour me. That smile doesn't fool me.

I'm starting to miss the days when I was regulated to the protected wing of the Devine country estate while the supernaturals partied. How many hours did I dream of escaping? Staring out over the yard from the balcony, longing for a normal life?

I was such a dumbass.

Standing in the party surrounded by supernaturals is much worse, even with protection. I'm hyper-aware of their claws and fangs.

Elizabeth makes a show of gliding toward us. The tight black leather of her clothes feels a little contrived, yet she pulls the supervillain look off quite well. Her movements are too graceful and practiced. As a vampire, she could blur across the room, but instead, she walks. She likes being seen.

Mabel follows behind her, designer heels clicking against the stone. In some ways, she reminds me of Astrid. Only Astrid is pragmatic to Mabel's tedium.

The werewolves give them a wide berth.

"Elizabeth." Costin's grip tightens on my elbow. "When did you get back?"

"Hello, brother," Elizabeth says. Her gaze fixates on me, and her smile doesn't reach her eyes. "So nice to see you, too."

Mabel's expression doesn't hide her anger toward me. If anything, she wants me to see it. There is a smugness to her.

"What are you doing here, Elizabeth?" Costin's tone is far from welcoming.

"I wasn't aware you wanted approval over my travel itinerary." Elizabeth waves her hand in dismissal. "If you must know, I was invited by an old, dear friend."

Costin turns his attention to Thane as the Alpha climbs back onto his throne. The werewolf whistles, and instantly, two women appear next to him. One climbs onto his lap.

"Since when do you hang with wolves?" Costin asks.

I have to admit, it's good to know he gets that same arrogant, condescending tone with everyone. It's not just me.

"No, not by Thane," Elizabeth laughs.

I try not to watch as the Alpha begins making out with the women, kissing one as the other grinds against his hips. No one else seems to care. I find it distracting.

And a little arousing.

"You should not be here," Costin says. "The treaties are too delicate."

"The Freemonts are old friends." Elizabeth hardly appears concerned. "Besides, I found their invitation compelling. Did you know they're proposing changes to the territorial agreements?"

Mabel's lips curve. "The old ways aren't serving anyone. Power should be shared more equitably among supernatural factions. Don't you think?"

Elizabeth grins as if challenging her brother to argue.

Mabel gives me the same look. This isn't about sharing anything. It's clear the Freemonts want more power, and she's making a play to come after my family.

Annoyance floods me like a wave of nausea, and I sense Draakmar doesn't like these women.

"Careful," Costin warns, but I hear tension beneath his usual control.

"Or what?" Elizabeth is enjoying herself. Her eyes finally light up. "You'll add me to your naughty list, Santa?"

"Unlike Mr. Claus, my punishments are very real," Costin answers.

Elizabeth's attention turns to me. "I see you

brought your mortal pet. How very progressive of you. Though I suppose she's not entirely mortal anymore, is she? Not with that particular accessory."

"She's worse than mortal," Mabel puts forth. "She's a mortal who thinks she's above her station."

I hate Mabel's smug face.

"How's Chester?" I mock before I can stop myself. "Still single?"

I hear snickering at the comment. Some of the wolves are eavesdropping.

Mabel's entire body becomes stiff. This woman would suck at poker. "You're as bad as the rest of them. The Devines' stranglehold on magical resources must—"

Elizabeth holds up her hand to stop Mabel, her eyes studying me with an unsettling intensity. There's something clinical in her gaze like I'm a specimen she'd love to dissect. "Now is not the time for politics. Though I must admit, your... resistance to supernatural influence is quite fascinating."

She waves her hand around where the were-wolves watch us and instantly switches her tone as she says to Mabel, "Look where we are! We're here to have fun."

Mabel presses her lips tight. I want to tell them both to fuck off, but Costin pulls me closer to his side.

Elizabeth lifts her fingers to her mouth and

whistles. She points at two large werewolves standing on the broken floor above and motions for them to come. One has an eye patch, which makes him look all the scarier. They instantly jump down and cross to her. She studies them before murmuring, "You'll do."

"We're leaving," Costin announces as his sister starts tongue-kissing her chosen targets.

Thane's laughter carries from his throne.

Costin moves us toward the exit, his body between me and the Alpha.

A wolf howls, and others soon join her. Costin ushers me out of the throne room into the passageway leading outside. The sounds of werewolf revelry fade behind us, replaced by the echo of my racing heart pounding in my ears.

The courtyard has emptied except for a few men bound to a post. Their eyes flash golden, and I don't bother asking why they're chained. When we pass through the gate, I am finally able to take a deep breath.

"What the hell was that about?" I demand, trying to pull my arm out of his grasp. "Why is your sister there making deals with the Freemonts?"

"Not here." His voice is clipped as he tries to force me behind him as we walk. "We need to get away from here first."

"Dammit, Costin!" I jerk away from him. "Talk to

me. What is going on? I know you know more than you're telling me."

He stops so suddenly that I run into him. When he turns, his eyes hold something I've never seen before—fear. "Did Thane lay hands on you?"

Is he jealous of the Alpha? I think about his finger reaching for the amulet. "No. He just talked."

"What did he say to you?"

"Blood and moonlight," I answer. I know he wants me to say more. Well, that makes two of us. I want to know what Costin is hiding.

"I'm taking you home," he states as if coming to a decision. Before I can protest, he pulls me into a dark alcove between buildings. His body presses mine against the brick wall, one hand sliding up my spine while the other braces against the wall beside my head. The position shields me from view but also traps me against his chest. I feel every intimate detail of his body as his arousal grows against my stomach.

"What are you—"

"Shh." His finger traces my lower lip, the touch so light it makes me shiver. "Wolves are trying to follow us." His voice drops to that velvet tone that makes my knees weak. "Your scent is... intoxicating when you're afraid."

I should push him away. I want to push him away. But his cool touch soothes the lingering burn from Thane's presence, and my body betrays me by arching into his. The memory of our kiss outside the gate floods back—the taste of blood, the press of his fangs, the way he made me forget everything but the feel of his mouth on mine.

"Your heart," he murmurs against my ear, his lips brushing the sensitive skin. "It calls to me." One hand slides into my hair, tilting my head back as his mouth traces down my neck. His fangs scrape lightly over the spot where he's bitten me before, and despite everything—*despite the danger, my anger, knowing he's hiding something*—I find myself clutching his shoulders and offering my throat.

The amulet pulses once between us, hard enough to make me gasp. Heat floods me, but it's not desire this time. It's a warning.

The shock of it breaks whatever spell he's trying to wave over my senses. I press my hands against his chest, but the movement is weaker than I'd like. I can't quite make myself push him away entirely.

At this moment, I understand two things perfectly. First, Costin isn't the only one playing games with my life. And second, I'm running out of time to figure out the rules.

"No," I manage, my voice embarrassingly breathless. "Not until you tell me what's happening. No more games or mysteries, Costin. Tell me, straight up, what's going on."

He pulls back just enough to meet my eyes. The crimson bleeds into his irises, and I recognize that swirling pattern—the same one I've seen before, though I can't quite remember when.

The amulet flares with sudden heat, making us both flinch. Draakmar's consciousness slams into mine with the force of a battering ram. The dragon's presence feels different, more awake and aware. His ancient power grows restless with purpose. It triggers a memory of a dark passage, a spy hole, and the taste of terror in my throat. He warns of a change coming over me that will alter everything.

"These old passages can be dangerous..."

I stumble away from him, fragments of memory threatening to surface. "You've done something to me," I whisper. "Made me forget things."

His expression doesn't change, but something flickers in his eyes. "Tamara—"

"Don't." I press my hand against the amulet, which thumps like a second heartbeat. "I remember..."

The memory hits me like a physical blow, and I'm sixteen again, watching through a spy hole as Costin teaches someone a very permanent lesson about loyalty.

NINE

Devine Country Estate, Twelve Years Ago...

My hands shake as I press my face against the spy hole, trying to see more of the library beyond the wall. The secret passages are strictly forbidden—*especially when the supernaturals are partying like it's 1799*—but I can't stay in hiding another minute. They've locked Conrad and me away in the protected wing again, treating us like we're made of glass just because we're mortal.

Conrad is in one of his grumpy moods and being impossible. He's been ranting for hours about some spells he read to ensure people return as ghosts and how our parents and other magics keep the knowledge from us. It's like being locked in a cell with a conspiracy theorist. Seriously, who the hell wants to come back as a ghost? I barely want to be here as I am.

My hideaway is cramped and musty, making it hard to breathe. I've been told the secret passageways are here for security reasons to sneak us out of the house when under attack. Or to hide refugees. I'm not supposed to talk about the tunnels, and I'm definitely not supposed to venture around inside them.

Sweat makes my palms slip on the smooth wood around the peephole, and I press them softly against my jeans. Cobwebs catch in my hair, tickling my scalp, but I don't dare move to brush them away. One wrong sound, and they'll hear me. Several supernatural creatures have crazy-good hearing, and I don't know what I'm spying on.

Vampires in formal evening wear circulate through the library, their movements reminding me of sharks circling prey. Blood-red wine sloshes in crystal glasses, but I know it's not wine. Even from here, I can see the predatory gleam in their eyes, the way their fangs flash when they laugh.

My fingers find the amulet my grandfather gave me. I clutch it like the talisman it's supposed to be. I don't think it works, but its presence always makes me feel safer.

Mabel Freemont stands near the fireplace with a blond vampire I don't recognize, her perfectly manicured hand resting on his arm like she's marking her territory. Her smug smile is exactly how I remember it. I have no clue why she's at the party. My mother doesn't care for her. I can tell by the way Lady Astrid's eyes tighten whenever the woman laughs— that fake, tinkling sound designed to draw attention.

The blond vampire has hair that is longer than is fashionable and a too-handsome face. The sharp angles make it look as if he's sculpted of stone and Botox. All vampires have an eroticism about them, but this one looks like a graphic novel come to life. Conrad says their beauty is meant to lure their victims, namely us humans. Only a fool would fall for it.

Conrad says a lot of things. My brother has a great many opinions, and very rarely are his conclusions happy ones.

"The North American territory is too vast for one master," the blond vampire says. "Constantine's control is slipping. Even his own sister questions—"

"Careful, Robert." Costin's voice slices through the room like a blade. He appears from nowhere, making several vampires stumble back. A shiver works over me, and I try to hold my breath. My heart nearly stops as I lean to find him through the peephole. "You're speaking of matters you know little about."

"Lord Constantine." The blond traitor bows, but

his tone is defiant. "We merely suggest that perhaps it's time to discuss... changes. The Freemonts have concerns about—"

Costin moves so fast my eyes can't follow. I have to readjust against the peephole to see his hand around Robert's throat. Mabel stumbles back, white wine spilling down her designer dress. Her face drains of color, and her mouth works silently like a fish gasping for air. She takes another step back, bumping into the fireplace mantel, but doesn't dare run. I see her fingers trembling as she clutches her throat to protect her arteries.

"The Freemonts," Costin says with terrible gentleness, not looking at Mabel, "should remember their place in the hierarchy. As should you."

"The others will—" Robert's words choke off as Costin's grip tightens.

"The others will what?" Costin's smile makes me want to run, but my legs won't move. I can't let them hear me. "Rally behind you? I dare you all to question my authority. My dungeons are empty, and I do so love making examples."

I shouldn't be seeing this. I need to look away, but terror holds me frozen.

"I challenge—" Robert's words are cut short as Costin's hand plunges into the vampire's chest. The wet tearing sound makes bile rise in my throat, and I clamp my hand over my mouth to stifle a whimper.

"A heart," Costin turns to the others in the room, holding up something dark and pulsing, "is such a delicate thing." His fingers squeeze, and the organ crumbles to ash.

The vampire's body collapses into a pile of dust on Astrid's favorite rug. My mother is going to be pissed. As Costin's dust-covered fingers flex, I watch Mabel press against the wall, trying to become invisible. The room has gone so quiet I can hear my heartbeat thundering in my ears. I wonder if they can hear it, too.

I hope not.

"Anyone else think we live in a vampiric democracy?" Costin asks as casually as if he's offering a drink. "No? Then perhaps we can return to more civilized conversation. But I will leave you with a thought. Traitors will be dealt with swiftly and without mercy. If you have a problem with how I run things, I invite you to speak to the European Council. But a word of warning. They are more intolerant than I."

When Costin's gaze sweeps the room, it pauses on the wall where I hide. Just for a moment, but long enough to make my knees weak. Tears blur my vision as I back away from the peephole. I bump into the wall and gasp. Instantly, I cover my mouth with both hands, trying to take the sound back.

Oh, fuck. Oh, fuck. I shouldn't have left the protected wing.

The passage is pitch black except for the pinpoint of light coming through the spy hole. I try to move quietly away to go back to my room. My foot catches on something, and I stumble backward into what feels like a wall—until it moves.

"Careful, little castoff," Costin whispers, his cool fingers digging into my shoulders. "These old passages can be dangerous."

He twirls me around to face him. I make the mistake of looking up into his eyes.

"What are you doing out of protection, little spy?" he asks, lightly touching my cheek with the same hand I saw ripping the heart out of a chest. I stiffen in fright and feel tears burning my eyes.

"You killed him," I whisper.

He looks at the amulet around my neck as if it holds some meaning for him. "Your heart is beating so fast."

"I won't tell," I promise, terrified.

"You should not have been here," Costin answers with a frown. "This world is not for you."

I take it as a threat. I don't want to die. A scream builds in my throat, but his eyes have begun to swirl.

"Tamara?" Costin asks, his voice jerking me out of the secret tunnels. My head feels dizzy, and it takes me a moment to remember we're still inside were-wolf territory. The past is so real that the feelings of being a teenager in that house linger even as my vision clears.

This is not the information I was expecting. We're wasting precious time out here while the memory of his brutality towards vampire traitors wars with my need for his help in the present.

I'm out of my league. I'm not too stupid to realize that.

This revelation about his past violence isn't what I need. Not with Paul captive. Not with time slipping away.

"Tam—"

"Don't touch me!" I jerk away as Costin tries to steady me. The memory leaves me shaking, but anger burns hotter than fear. We need to deal with the werewolves. Instead, I'm discovering more lies. "You've been messing with my head since I was sixteen? What else have you hidden from me?"

"What do you—?"

"Don't try to deny it. I remember you finding me in the tunnels at the country house after I saw you..." I can't bring myself to say it out loud. The lingering fear of being in the secret tunnels settles inside of me. "I saw what you did."

How many other memories has he stolen? How many other secrets is he keeping?

"Let me take you somewhere safe." He reaches for me again.

"Safe?" A small laugh escapes me in disbelief. "Like your home, where you can mesmerize me into submission for another week?"

His eyes narrow. "You're making a scene."

I look around the empty road. Before I can protest, he pulls me against his chest. The world blurs into darkness. His body the only solid thing I can feel. It keeps my nausea from the teleporting at bay...barely. When my vision clears, a burst of candlelight reveals that we're in his bedroom. He doesn't immediately release me. For one heated moment, I'm aware of every point where we touch.

I wrench away from him. The covers are pulled back on the bed, and the familiar crimson sheets mock me with memories of waking up confused. I grab my dizzy head and try not to vomit. "Damn you, Costin!"

"I didn't mesmerize you," he says like he's done me a favor.

As my fist launches, I know it's stupid. I punch his jaw, and his face doesn't even move—not even to flinch. Pain radiates up my hand, but the contact sends an electric current through us both. His pupils dilate, nostrils flaring as he senses my anger, my fear, my unwanted arousal.

I'm going to ignore both the blow to my ego and how my body responds to his proximity.

"Listen to me." He catches my wrists as I try to shove him, using the momentum to pull me closer. His breath tickles my skin, and I hate how my pulse jumps in response. "Everything I've done has been to protect you."

"Liar." The amulet burns between us, and I feel Draakmar's rage mixing with mine. "None of this has been for me. You only care about your agenda. You've been controlling me, hiding things from me. Just like with Paul—"

"Stop."

"Or what? You'll make me forget him, too?"

"Don't say his name." Costin's voice dips dangerously low. His grip tightens on my wrists, and I see his careful control slipping.

"Why not? Because you let the wolves take him?" I try to pull free, wanting to strike out in my frustration, but he keeps me close. "You can't expect me to believe you couldn't catch the werewolf who took him. You're Lord Constantine, the most powerful vampire on this half of the planet."

He says nothing.

Oh, how I wish my fists could hurt him, but he's like trying to battle a steel wall. There is nothing I can do to sway him.

"Please tell me you didn't have anything to do with their taking Paul." I start to lose my fight, and I'm desperate for him to deny it.

Still, he says nothing.

"Did you arrange for them to take Paul?" I stare into his eyes, wanting to find the truth. "Is that why you mesmerized me for a week? So I wouldn't figure out your part in it?"

His jaw clenches. "You were safe here, with me."

It's not a denial.

"Tell me the truth, Costin, or we're over." I think of all the years I've known him. It's been a lifetime for me and barely a glimpse for him. I don't expect my threat to have any effect on vampire royalty. I'm merely a human with a magic charm. He's one of the most powerful people in the world.

"I feared the moment you fixed the amulet that everything would unravel, but what choice did we have? Draakmar needed to be tamed. The prophecy needed to be fulfilled. I promised George." The crimson in his eyes dissipates until there's no darkness left.

My grandfather, George, was one of the few people in my life who genuinely loved me for me. He accepted that I was human and didn't make me feel bad about it. And he was always honest with me. I feel like I'm a pawn to everybody else.

The pieces are falling into place. "You knew. You knew when we repaired the amulet that Paul would remember, and you knew he'd come for me."

"I suspected a great many possibilities." His hand slides to my throat, his thumb pressing against my pulse.

My heart stutters. "What are you saying?"

"Paul shouldn't have come back here," Costin continues. "He should have taken his daughter and stayed in Kansas."

I try to piece together the truth from what Costin is saying. "So you knew Paul's memories would return?"

"What would you have me do, Tamara?" His voice rises with each word. "I smelled him on you the night of the birthday fire. His scent, his mortality, his claim—"

"His claim?" I laugh, but it comes out breathless as he backs me against the wall. "You're jealous. The great Constantine, master vampire, is jealous of a mortal."

"I don't share what's mine." His mouth hovers close to my lips, and despite my anger, they part in anticipation.

"I don't belong to—"

His kiss cuts off my protest. The hard press of his mouth is all about possession. His hands release my wrists to slide down my sides, gripping my hips hard enough to bruise. I should push him away. Logically, I want to push him away. Instead, my fingers curl into his shirt, pulling him closer as the amulet heats between us.

A memory flash of being pressed against a different wall, fluorescent lights overhead, threatens my thoughts, but Costin's touch pulls me back to the present.

His fangs graze my lower lip, drawing blood. The metallic taste should repulse me, but it only fuels the fire building between us.

"Tell me you don't want this," he growls against my mouth. "Tell me you don't feel what is between us."

I should. By all the gods, I know I should. But instead, I lift my leg along his thigh as an invitation.

"No more lies," I demand between kisses. I keep

a fist around his shirt, torn between pushing him away and pulling him closer. "No more—"

He takes my hips and lifts me easily against the wall. I feel the length of his arousal, and the promise of what's to come rushes through me. My heart beats so fast I hear the blood rushing in my ears, and I know he can hear it, too. It's the sound of my mortality. Costin moans, the sound more monster than man, and I shiver in anticipation.

His lips slide across my cheek to my neck. Fangs lightly move over my skin, but he can't bite me when I wear the amulet. It gives me a sense of pleasure knowing I can make him lose control like this, make him fight against his nature.

"No more Paul," he whispers hotly. "I don't want to hear his name on your lips."

The possessive growl in his voice shouldn't arouse me. Heat pools low in my belly. It feels so good to be claimed by him.

He carries me to the bed, laying me across those damned crimson sheets. They're cool against my back, and I feel like a fool for being here willingly. I can't tell if it's fear or anticipation as I wait for my mind to slip into a mesmerized haze. Costin is so powerful and in control. He makes me feel helpless and yet safe at the same time. It's a dangerous combination—this trust I have in him despite everything and this need that goes deeper than physical attraction. Every time I try to pull away, we end up here, drawn together like moths to a volcano that will probably destroy us both.

"No more talk of werewolves." His mouth trails down my neck. "Just us. Nothing else exists."

There is a begging in his tone I haven't heard before.

The amulet grows hot, trying to warn me to be careful, but the sound of my heartbeat drowns out Draakmar's whispers. Costin's hands slide under my shirt, his touch making me arch in pleasure.

"Promise me," I manage, even as my fingers work to undress him from his shirt. "Promise you'll tell me everything."

He leans back just enough to meet my eyes. His expression becomes unreadable. "You don't want everything." His thumb traces my lower lip. "Some truths are better left buried."

"That's not your choice to make." I wrap my fingers around his wrist, stopping his caress. "I'm not a child anymore, Costin. I've faced Draakmar. I've survived your sister. I can handle—"

"My sister?" There's something dangerous in his tone. "What do you know about Elizabeth?"

Shit. I forgot that timeline was erased. Before I can think of how to explain, he's already pulling away, his expression closing off.

"What aren't you telling me?" he commands.

This might actually work in my favor. The fact Elizabeth is having issues doesn't seem to be new information to anyone. Things are starting to make more sense after seeing the memory Costin had erased from my past. Elizabeth was scheming even then. It's not like I have to protect her and not tell him. "You first."

"You want honesty?" Costin's mouth finds mine again, harder this time. He pulls back only long enough to say, "Here's the truth. I want you." His hands move under my shirt, making me shiver. "I've waited years for that prophecy to end and for my promise to be fulfilled."

"That's not—" My protest cuts off in a gasp as his lips move over my neck and across my collar-bone. His tongue traces patterns on my skin that feel like ancient symbols. "That's not what I meant by honesty."

"No?" His fangs scrape lightly over my breast through my bra, sending ripples of pleasure over my body. "Then tell me to stop."

I can't. His touch sets my skin on fire, and I'm lifting into his caress before I can stop myself. My fingers fumble with his shirt until he simply tears it off and tosses it aside. The sight of his bare chest, perfect and pale in the dim candlelight, makes my breath catch.

"Tell me you don't want me." His voice is rough

as he undresses me with vampiric speed, leaving me bare beneath him. The cool air tightens my nipples, and his eyes focus on my chest.

The feelings I've been trying to suppress since he kissed me at the gate leading to werewolf territory surge forth.

His mouth replaces the cool air on my nipple, tongue circling one peak while his fingers tease the other. The contrast between his cooler touch and my heated skin makes me gasp. He needs to feed. Blood would warm him. None of that matters right now. My hands tangle in his hair, holding him closer.

"The sounds you make," he murmurs against my skin. "They are like music to me, every sigh, every whimper, every plea." His mouth trails lower across my stomach, making my muscles jump. When he reaches the inside of my thigh, I nearly come off the bed.

"Costin, please!"

"Please, what?" His breath fans across my sensitive clit. "Tell me what you want."

"You." The word comes out breathlessly. "I want you."

He moves back up my body, and before he settles over me, his clothes have disappeared, so there is nothing between us. His weight presses me into the mattress.

"Only me," he growls. "You are mine."

I can't form words before he's thrusting inside me. The sensation is overwhelming—cold and heat, pleasure and pain, love and fury all mixed together. He takes me completely, riding me to the point of exquisite agony.

My nails dig into his shoulders as he moves. Each thrust drives me higher. I forget why I should resist him. The amulet pulses between us, but even Draakmar's warnings can't penetrate the haze of intense pleasure.

"Costin..." I beg, clutching his arms to keep him near me.

"Say it again." His rhythm increases, one hand sliding between us to touch me exactly how I desire.

"Costin. Costin. Costin..." I do, over and over, my voice rising with each perfect stroke.

I sense that his control is starting to slip. I feel it in how his frenzied movements become more urgent and less measured. When his fangs scrape my shoulder, unable to bite through the amulet's protection, the frustrated growl sends shivers through me.

Release builds like an oncoming thunderstorm, starting deep inside and spreading outward like lightning until my whole body tingles and shakes. When the sweet, fierce release finally hits, the sensations are powerful enough to make me forget, just for a moment, all the reasons we are a terrible idea.

Costin's climax follows immediately after mine. I

MICHELLE M. PILLOW

hear my name as a harsh whisper against my throat. My heart pounds and my bones feel like they're melting out of my body and into the bed. I can't move. I don't even want to try.

Costin shifts his weight off of me to lie down along my side. His hand lazily finds my stomach as he draws on my flesh. We lay tangled in his crimson sheets for a long, perfect moment. But then reality creeps back in, and I remember how I got here tonight. I trace the marks my nails left on his shoulder. The deep scratches are already healing, but the memory of how they got there burns hot in my mind. I let myself imagine what it would be like if things were simpler—if he was just a man and I was just a woman, if there weren't secrets, and prophecies, and supernatural realities between us.

Daydreaming about being normal is a useless task. Costin will never be human, and I will never be as powerful as he is.

His fingers continue to trace lazy patterns on me, and I realize they're symbols used to cast protection spells. Even now, Costin is trying to keep me safe.

"Now, will you tell me everything?" I ask, watching his fingers.

"No." His weight shifts, and he pulls his hand away from me. He doesn't move far as he settles next to me. "You first. What do you know about my sister? What did she do?"

"I know she's dangerous." I prop myself up on my elbows, trying to ignore how his naked chest looks in the candlelight. "I know she's working with the Freemonts against you."

His eyes narrow. "That's not what you meant. You said you survived her. When?"

The amulet pulses against me, almost like a warning. I ignore it. I'm tired of secrets. "In that other timeline. The one that was erased when the amulet was shattered. She and her minions tried to kill me at a gas station in Kansas."

His expression doesn't change, but I feel as if the temperature in the room drops several degrees.

"Impossible. Elizabeth was in Europe when..." He stops, something clicking behind his eyes.

"Nothing from that timeline will make sense. You were dead. I'm sure you had whatever ceremony they do for vampires. She must have come back. Now, fair is fair. It's your turn. If you want me to tell you what happened, you need to first tell me what you know about Paul's—"

"Show me," Costin demands. Before I can process what he means by that, his fangs pierce his palm. Blood wells dark and thick, too thick to be normal blood.

"I don't want to be turned."

"My blood won't turn you unless you're dying." The answer brings no comfort.

"No—" My protest is cut off as he forces his hand against my mouth. His blood drips from the wound. I sputter and gag as I thrash, trying to break free. His other arm wraps around me like steel.

The metallic taste is impossible to escape. The blood tingles on my tongue, almost painful. More than the strange taste, it's the violation that makes me want to scream. After what we just shared, how dare he do this?

The bedroom begins to fade, reality bleeding away like watercolors in the rain. A small red dot appears, focusing my unwilling gaze. A flash of light comes past my face, making me blink. Dark wood turns into large glass door coolers filled with drinks in front of a white wall as my mind is dragged forcibly back into a memory I've tried so hard not to think about.

"Show me," he whispers like a horrible mantra I try to block out. "Show me…"

ELEVEN

Salina, Kansas, Several Months Earlier...

"Take it easy, everyone. It's just a blackout. Looks like it's the whole block."

I turn to the voice. Suddenly, I'm standing in a convenience store aisle in the dark. Someone holds their phone as a flashlight. The red dot is a device running on battery backup.

This is all too familiar. I don't want to be here.

But I am here.

How? I remember this. It's a gas station in Salina, Kansas. The bus I was on stopped here in the middle of the night. But this was months ago in an erased timeline.

The cashier sounds annoyed as she continues, "I'm calling my boss. Sorry, your purchases are going to have to wait."

I try to hold on to Costin and his room. I want to remember that this isn't real. This isn't happening. It's only a memory.

The streetlights are out, but I see the running lights from the parked bus waiting for us. I'm alone in Kansas on the way to California to meet my birth mother. I left Paul and his daughter in Kansas City, where they should be safe.

"Please don't steal. The cameras have night vision," the cashier warns before muttering, "They don't pay me enough for this."

I ignore her. My eyes focus on the bus. I should never have gotten off.

"Where is she?" I hear a disembodied voice whisper. Costin? But he's dead.

Time slides and bends. The glass doors blow open. Someone screams. I try to fight against the memory—I know how this ends, I don't want to see it again—but Costin's blood forces me deeper. Dark blurs fly around the store.

Vampires. Even though I know they can't hurt me now, my body remembers the terror.

Suddenly, time jumps forward. I'm outside, pressed against an ice machine as I hide. Inside the store, metal shelves crash to the floor. I want to help the people inside, but there is nothing I can do.

My head is dizzy, and it's all I can do to remain in the moment. I hear a light tap behind me and slowly turn around to see a vampire standing in the window, smiling like a predator who just found his prey. He has a handsome face and short blond hair.

Time jumps again, and I run along the side of the building toward the back. I know it's hopeless. The monsters are giving chase, and I can't outrun them.

It happens again. Precious seconds disappear as time jumps. I'm behind the gas station. My skin feels raw from having landed on my hands and knees in the gravel. Three impressively large male vampires and a much shorter female tower over me.

The woman is vaguely familiar. Though she wears tight leather, and her straight black hair is severely angled at her chin, I picture her with longer curls and a blue gown. I've seen her in a painting in a book. Recognizing her is not a good thing. It means she's probably old and extremely powerful.

"What happens next?" Costin's voice whispers. *"Show me."*

I blink in confusion, unable to answer him. None of the others show they can hear him.

I lift my hands to defend myself. I know it's pointless, but I have to try. Blood runs down my palm from where I cut it on the gravel. I hear a collective inhale as the vampires get a whiff of my blood. I wipe it against my shirt as if it will erase the temptation.

"Please," I beg. "You're making a mistake. I didn't

hurt Costin. The fire was not my fault. This is all a misunderstanding, and I promise I will do everything I can to figure out who is responsible. I lost people too in that fire."

The woman taps her fingers against her thigh. She's unimpressed with my pleading.

"Humans," she rasps in disgust.

Usually, vampires have an air of boredom to them. Like the centuries have just added up to create a long eternity of nothingness that they're trying to fill. But right now, the way they're looking at me, they're not bored. They have a purpose, which is more terrifying than anything I can envisage. I can only imagine that what they have planned for me is not an easy ending.

"I had no reason to hurt Costin," I say. I hear more vampires landing around us, and I put my back to the gas station wall to keep them all in my sights. "We were... We were on friendly terms."

"You're braver than most blood sacks. I can see why my brother liked you," the vampire answers, flicking the back of her nails against her short hair. "Although Costin always did have questionable taste in pets."

"Costin was your brother," I state the realization out loud.

"You can call me Elizabeth," she says.

Another half dozen vampires join us behind the gas station.

"I'm a Devine." I don't know what to do. I can't fight them all.

The smirks I get in response are about what I expect.

"But are you? Really?" Elizabeth jeers.

"I didn't kill Costin," I insist. I don't have it in me to kill anyone.

I fight what's happening. Elizabeth's head bobbles, and her eyes roll like she's stuck in a loop. I need to escape this memory before it sucks me in completely and I forget this is over.

"Show me," Costin's voice whispers.

"There is no way *you* could have taken out my brother," Elizabeth continues, not hearing Costin speak. "So much for old men and their prophecies."

I don't know what she's talking about.

"We talked to Conrad," Elizabeth continues. "He made an intriguing proposition."

I sigh in relief and try to relax. My brother Conrad talked to them. All will be well.

"So, we're good? This is over?" I ask, hopefully.

"Sure, it's over," Elizabeth agrees, "as soon as we kill you."

"But..." I prepare to go down fighting. "You said Conrad made a deal."

"Oh, you don't..." Elizabeth laughs, prompting the others to do the same.

I wish somebody was coming to save me, but there's no one. I'm all alone in the world. Who would even care that this is happening?

"Sweetie." Suddenly, Elizabeth is in front of me, cupping my face. Her fingers feel like ice cubes against my skin, and the scent of ash lingers like perfume. When I stare into her eyes, I see a cold emptiness.

Rage burns through me—not only the helpless fear of that night that I can't escape, but present fury at Costin for making me face his sister again, even in memory.

"Conrad did make a deal with us," Elizabeth continues. "We kill you. We turn him. And we gain access to the great Devine empire."

I try not to cry, but I can't help it. Elizabeth lifts her fingers from my cheek to her mouth to lick my tears before lightly slapping me with her wet hand. "Brothers! Am I right?"

"I don't believe you." I don't want it to be true. Conrad is my brother. Family has to mean something.

"You do know he tried to sell you to my brother in exchange for turning him." Elizabeth is enjoying herself. "Costin refused, of course. This offer, though? Yeah, I'm going to take it."

More tears fall, and I'm shaking. I lift my hand to swat her away, but it's like slamming against a brick wall. The blow has absolutely no impact on her.

"Gah, you're so..." Elizabeth grunts in disgust. "Mortal."

"Let's eat her," one of the vampires suggests. "I'm hungry."

"Yeah, such a tasty little treat," another adds.

Time wavers and their image blurs slightly before coming back into focus. I see Elizabeth's fangs coming toward me. I try to fight, kicking and thrashing to be free.

"No, no, no..." I beg. I taste blood in my mouth.

I'm going to die. I feel only one regret. Paul. I regret that I did not have more time with him. I should have told him how much I care. We could have been in love.

Nothing makes sense. I hear my heart hammering in my head. I taste the blood in my mouth, stinging my tongue. I feel my body being held down. Vampires converge like locusts to feast upon me.

"*Stop. Go back,*" Costin's voice whispers. "*Let me see them all.*"

My attackers rewind, falling off me as I'm pushed back up. Time freezes, and I can't move. It holds me captive for several moments before I'm again on my back, thrashing to fight off my attackers. Hands claw into me to hold me down. Elizabeth's fangs scrape my neck.

I'm going to die.

Oh, fuck, I'm going to die.

Not here. Not like this. Not...

Why doesn't she bite?

A blue light flashes so fast I'd miss it if it didn't bounce off Elizabeth's ear, blocking my view. I feel a release of pressure like a pulse is sent out into the universe. The vampires fling away from me in a flurry of pitching limbs and surprised screeches.

"No!" I scream, fighting bodies that are no longer there. My fists punch at air. My legs tangle in bedding. It takes me a moment to place where I am.

Costin's bedroom.

He's withdrawing his bloody hand from my mouth, but I taste him. Still, I fight, struggling to escape.

"Easy, Tamara, easy," Costin soothes.

I blink and spit, trying to get rid of his taste.

"You're safe."

"Fuck you, Costin!" I yell, rolling away from him to land on the floor.

I lift my arms to defend myself as I look around the room. It's only the two of us, but the fear from the memory lingers. It felt so real. I was back in that moment.

Costin reaches for me as if I will just fall back into bed with him.

"You had no right to do that." I spit the words at him, still tasting his blood on my tongue. My whole body shakes with fury. "No fucking right! You just proved you're exactly like your sister. You take what you want, consequences to everyone else be damned."

"I needed to know what Elizabeth did," he says, reaching for me again. "This was too important."

I dodge his touch.

"Important? I just let you in..." My voice breaks, remembering how vulnerable I'd been moments ago in his bed. The betrayal tastes bitter in my mouth. "So I really don't matter at all. It's about beating your sister."

"It's about keeping you alive!"

"I would have told you everything. But you couldn't wait, couldn't trust me. You had to force your way into my head."

"I am not my sister," he states as if he's the one who should be offended out of the two of us. "You should take a breath and calm yourself. That time-line no longer exists—"

"But the memory does. The feelings do! I would have told you without going through that hell again." I wrap my arms around myself, hating how my body still tingles from his touch even as my mind recoils. "Your sister is an evil bitch who was trying to fill a power vacuum that is no longer there." I drop my arms. "What's your excuse?"

"You don't understand what's at stake. I needed to see which vampires sided with her." Costin moves toward me. I back away until I hit his bedroom wall. I want to run but doubt I'll make it to the elevator.

"Then explain it to me what's at stake!" I slam my palm against the wall. "Stop treating me like some chess piece you can move around the board. I am so tired of everyone telling me what's best for me. I'm not a porcelain doll that needs to be locked in the protected wing. I know you get off on controlling every—"

"You think that's what this is?" His eyes flash crimson. Good. Let him be angry. I'm pissed.

"I know it is. You can't help yourself. You're used to everyone obeying your every whim." Yelling feels good. I don't want to stop.

The crimson fades. "That is what you think of me?"

Damn him. I want to fight. Why isn't he yelling back?

"I am responsible for everything that happens in North America. If I fail, the elders will send warriors from the old countries. It'll be a bloodbath.

This is something my sister never cared about. Yes, she wants power, and your memory of her in that other timeline is not the first time she's tried grabbing for it. Joining forces with Conrad to control your family would have been too much for her to resist."

The implications hit me like a physical blow.

"That vampire you killed when I was sixteen? Robert? He said something about your sister." I try to focus on the past. It's easy since the memory feels new. "He said the North American territory is too vast for one master. He thought your control was slipping, and even your sister questioned your ability to rule."

"That was one of her many attempts at an uprising," Costin agrees. "Each time, she pushes further and tests more boundaries. The council fears what she might discover in her quest for power, what ancient laws she might break, what forbidden experiments she'll perform. I've been tasked with keeping her in line."

"If she's a traitor, why do you put up with it?" I heard what he told the vampires in the study. Any traitors would be dealt with in the same manner he dealt with Robert.

Before he even answers, I know the reason.

"She's my sister," he says. "What's happened to her is my fault."

I wait for him to say more. I need him to talk to me.

His voice drops. "Elizabeth will not stop until she finds a way to destroy what matters to me."

I feel his pain. "Who would have thought this is what we have in common?"

"My sister?"

"Siblings out to get us," I correct. I loved my adopted brother, and he betrayed me. "Conrad framed me for arson and murder and then tried to kill me. Up until the very end, I didn't want to believe the truth about him."

"It's not the same," Costin says. "Elizabeth is dangerous, yes, but she's not trying to kill me. She wants what I have. And she wants me to know she has taken it all away from me."

Something in his tone makes me ask, "And what do you have?"

"Power. Control." His eyes fixate on my amulet. "You."

I laugh, but it comes out hollow. "Me? I'm just a mere mortal who happened to get caught up in supernatural politics."

"You're far more than that." He moves closer, and I hate how my body responds to his proximity. "You tamed Draakmar. You survived the labyrinth. You've changed everything."

"And that's why you're so desperate to control

me?" The anger rises again. "Because I'm what—some kind of supernatural prize to be won?"

"Because I can't lose you." His voice drops to barely a whisper. "Not to Elizabeth, not to the were-wolves, not to Paul. I lo—"

"Don't say it's love." I cut him off. "You don't love me. You want to possess me, control me, use me in this sick game against—"

Suddenly, his mouth presses into mine, desperate and hungry. For a moment, I forget every-thing—the memory, the betrayal, all of it—and lose myself in the kiss. Then the amulet pulses, and reality comes crashing back.

I shove him away. "No. You don't get to do that anymore."

"Tamara—"

"I'm going to find Paul." I grab my clothes from the floor, dressing quickly. "And when I do, we'll figure out what this ritual really is. Without your help."

"You won't survive without me."

I pause at his door. "Maybe not. But at least I'll die making my own choices."

The amulet is warm against my skin as I leave, and for once, I think Draakmar agrees with me.

TWELVE

The penthouse lobby feels too bright after Costin's candlelit bedroom. Dawn is peeking over the city. The taste of betrayal lingers metallic on my tongue. Costin's blood. My head still spins from the forced memory he pulled out of my brain, and from the threat of blood and moonlight. His vampiric blood magic is far beyond my understanding. I didn't know vampires could extract memories like that. And I worry about how many other memories he might have taken from me.

The idea nags at the edge of my consciousness, like a shadow seen from the corner of my eye. I see tiny hints of flashing red warning lights. The battery backup on the wall at the gas station? Or something else? The smell of salt water tickles my nose, but it slips away before I can capture it, leaving only unease behind.

A doorman hurries from behind his desk when he sees me at the door.

"Miss Devine," he says, pulling it open. His uniform is too tight against his stomach. I see the buttons straining. Astrid wouldn't be pleased to see that fact.

"Hello, Simon," I answer. Astrid wouldn't appreciate me being on a first-name basis with the help, either. I don't care. Simon is a human who knows about the supernatural. For that alone, I feel a kinship with him.

"Miss Devine," he lowers his voice and leans toward me as if to reveal a secret. "A woman has been waiting all night to speak to you. She's not on the list. Lady Astrid doesn't want me to send up anyone who isn't on the list."

I see his worry.

I follow his gesture to see a figure curled in one of the lobby's leather chairs, wild curls escaping a bright scarf headband. For a moment, I'm transported back to that first meeting in California—the shock of seeing my hair on someone else's head. It was the realization that I inherited more than just mortality from her.

I knew she was in town, but I'm not prepared to see her again. My emotions are still raw from

Costin, and I'm unsure how much more I can take. I've been up all night, and I'm exhausted. I think about turning around and hiding before she sees me.

Lorelai looks up from her book, and our eyes meet. I'm struck by how we have the same hazel shade. She unfolds herself from the chair with a fluid grace that contrasts sharply with the lobby's rigid formality. Her layered dress appears handmade, adorned with the same eclectic plastic jewelry I remember. The butterfly tattoo peeks from beneath her neckline—the mark she got to keep me close after giving me up.

"Tamara." Her voice catches. She starts to reach for me but stops herself, uncertainty crossing her features. She glances at Simon, and I know she's aware of her standing as the family secret. I've only known of her existence for less than a year. "I've been trying to call..."

"I was..." How do I explain being mesmerized for a week? It's more than I have the emotional capacity to get into right now. "Unavailable."

She nods like she understands, though she can't possibly. "I hope it's all right that I came. I felt something was wrong."

I struggle to find words.

Lorelai's expression falls. "You remember me, don't you?"

"Miss Devine?" Simon hovers uncertainly. "Should I...?"

"It's fine. She can come up. You can put her on the list." I head for the elevator. Lorelai falls into step beside me. The contrast between us feels stark—her flowing bohemian layers against my rumpled clothes from Costin's floor.

We wait for the elevator doors to close before turning to each other. She wraps her arms around me in motherly affection. I'm not used to it, and my first response is to stiffen up in surprise.

"You look tired, butterfly." She uses the old nickname cautiously. "I've been so worried about you."

Suddenly, she pulls back just as I lift my arms to tentatively return the hug.

"Too soon," she says, wrongly reading my reaction. "It's okay."

She pats my shoulder. I remain silent. What do you say to the birth mother you barely know on the way to the home of the mother who raised you?

The truth is, I'm emotionally drained from my fight with Costin. I'm not sure how much more I can process at the moment.

"You remember what happened at my house?" She searches my face before looking down at the amulet I wear. "I don't know what kind of magic caused it, but I forgot about your visit for a time. Then it all came rushing back last week. I was painting in my dining room, and the protection altar started shaking. The photos were falling, and the salt was spilling. I knew I had to come."

The protection altar. All those photographs of me growing up, surrounded by salt and charms. She'd been trying to keep me safe from across the country all these years, doing what little she could for the daughter she couldn't keep.

I nod, deciding to give her the elevator-ride abridged version. "I remember. Conrad came to kill us and instead killed himself when he took my amulet. When it broke, time was reset. That is why you forgot. I fixed it a week ago."

"Does everyone...?" she starts to ask.

"No. Only you and I and..." I look up at the numbers counting up to the penthouse floor. We're almost there.

"Paul," she finishes for me.

I nod.

"It must be because we were there when it broke. That makes sense. We were closest to the magic," Lorelai says. "I'm glad you were able to restore its protection. I hate the idea of you not having it."

I think of the story she told me about goblins stealing my breath as a baby while she sat bound in a rocking chair, and of all the other monsters that forced her to give me up. I have no clue who would have sent the goblins after me or why, but it was twenty-eight years ago. It probably doesn't matter now. I wonder if they've been watching, waiting for another chance. And if not, it seems like Lorelai believes it. The trauma of those memories is etched plainly on her face. I hate to tell her, but we're about to face a different kind of monster—Astrid's cutting disapproval.

The elevator rises, and with it comes the weight of what awaits. Two mothers, two worlds, and me caught eternally between them.

"Astrid's home," I warn as the elevator comes to a stop.

"I assumed she might be." Lorelai's tone carries an edge. I don't pry. Being as I'm the result of her affair with Astrid's husband, it's already awkward.

"My father is away," I add.

Yep. Awkward.

The elevator doors open, stopping her from answering.

We step into the penthouse foyer, and I notice it no longer smells like a carnival. Hopefully, that means Astrid will be in a better mood.

Hopefully, but probably not.

I hear voices from the kitchen. This is a bad idea.

"Maybe we should go—" I start to say, but it's too late.

Astrid emerges from the kitchen, stopping when she sees us. Her gaze focuses on Lorelai, and her expression barely registers a change. Her emotionless tone, however, could freeze hell. "Lorelai."

"It's nice to see you again, Astrid," Lorelai answers politely. I wouldn't say there is gratitude in her demeanor, but there seems to be a silent acknowledgment that she knows who actually raised her daughter. "You look well."

Astrid turns to me, and I see her gaze moving over my face before dipping to the floor. I have witnessed all moods of the woman, but there is a flicker in her expression I've never seen before. Sadness? Regret? It's so hard to tell. I've never had a warm relationship with my mother, but she is still the only mother I've had most of my life. Seeing my birth mother in her home can't be pleasant.

The silence stretches like a rubber band about to snap. I stand between them, still struggling with how to reconcile these two realities—the cold, precise mother who raised me and this warm stranger who shares my curls. After decades of Astrid's calculated distance, Lorelai's open affection feels almost overwhelming. A few months isn't enough for me to know how to navigate my feelings. And this being the first time I've been in the same room with both of them... Well, I have no clue how the hell I'm supposed to deal with this.

I'm caught between these two versions of motherhood, astutely aware of their apparent differences.

Astrid in her tailored suit, every hair in place, while Lorelai's wild curls escape her scarf in artistic disarray.

Astrid is the mother who stayed. She wasn't loving or affectionate, but she was here. She gave me the skills I needed to survive as a mortal amongst supernaturals, even if I'm only starting to understand why she kept the truth from me all these years.

Then there is Lorelai, who exudes warmth, but she left because, as a mortal, she couldn't protect me. I touch the amulet at my throat, drawing comfort from its existence. Lorelai bartered with trolls to get the amulet. When my grandfather gave it to me, he never mentioned where it came from.

As different as these women are, they both tried to keep me safe in their own ways.

"I know it's early. We won't be long," I tell Astrid.

"Nonsense." Ever the proper hostess, Astrid motions toward a couch, inviting Lorelai in from the foyer. "May I offer a drink? Tea? Coffee?"

"Tea," Lorelai says. "Thank you."

Astrid's perfect posture never wavers. She nods and leaves for the kitchen.

I sink into a chair. Lorelai sits across from me, crossing her legs to twitch her foot nervously in the air. I want nothing more than to curl into a ball and close my eyes. I think of Costin in his bed. The rising sun will keep him locked in his home.

Well, in all honesty, he probably has secret tunnels all over the city where the sunlight won't touch him. I look at the windows where the sun is starting to shift the color of the sky. I can't imagine living in his land of darkness, never seeing daylight for an eternity.

"I appreciate the hospitality," Lorelai says carefully.

I turn to see Astrid rejoining us. A servant follows her, carrying a tray toward Lorelai, and offers her a porcelain tea cup on a saucer. The waif of a woman is new to the household. She walks quietly, placing her feet like a dancer. She comes to me and offers me a coffee. I take it, grateful. Finally, she brings a coffee to Astrid, who sits on the opposite end of the couch away from Lorelai.

The forced civility feels wrong, but I don't fight it. I sense the weight of unspoken history between them. It can't be easy for Astrid to face her husband's mistress and, conversely, for Lorelai to face the woman who raised her daughter.

Lorelai takes a polite sip of her tea before setting the cup and saucer on the end table beside her. "I came because I was worried about Tamara. The protection altar I built—"

"Yes, your altar of human charms." Astrid's lips thin slightly. "I remember your unconventional methods."

"They worked, didn't they?" Lorelai's hand drifts to her butterfly tattoo and directs her attention to me. "The amulet protected you."

"The amulet works because it is real magic," Astrid corrects. It's not quite a criticism, but it's close.

"Which is why I helped George find it." Lorelai's response carries a quiet strength. "We all did what we could to protect her."

How many conversations like this happened when I was a baby? How many times did these women negotiate my safety? Were those conversations this strained and civil?

The amulet pulses warmly against my skin as if acknowledging its complicated origins. Before I can speak, a wave of dizziness hits me. The room tilts slightly.

"Tamara?" Both women lean forward in concern.

"I'm fine." I press my hand to my forehead. "It's just been a long night. I'm tired."

"Constantine," Astrid says with knowing disapproval.

"The master vampire?" Lorelai demands sharply. "Has he threatened you? Does he blame you for what happened? George told me about him. Is that why the altar tried to warn me?"

Astrid stiffens at the mention of George. I

wonder if she knew he kept in touch with my birth mother over the years.

"No. Nothing like that," I lie, not wanting to explain about being mesmerized or reliving the forced memory.

"They're dating," Astrid says.

"What happened to Paul?" Lorelai looks confused. "You two seemed so good together."

Astrid sips her coffee.

"It's complicated," I say for lack of a better answer. I take a big gulp of hot liquid. It burns, but I don't care.

Lorelai gives me a pointed stare. "Uncomplicate it."

"He forgot who I was, and I tried to leave it that way. My being in his life only brought him and his daughter into danger. We're better apart." I start to take another drink.

Astrid furrows her brow and gives a slight shake of her head to stop me. She lifts her cup slowly as if to set a more ladylike example.

"But he remembers now," Lorelai insists. "I liked him for you."

"And as soon as his memories returned, knowing me put Paul's life in trouble again," I say.

"Constantine is a powerful leader," Astrid puts forth, strangely defending my choice.

"What is happening with Paul?" Lorelai asks.

I don't like the tension. I want this weird meeting to be over. "The werewolves took him."

Lorelai turns to Astrid. "There are werewolves involved now?"

"There are always werewolves involved," Astrid sighs. "Though I agree it's better when we don't have to deal with them. Feral creatures."

The elevator doors chime before I can respond. Anthony's voice carries from the foyer, "Tam? You here?"

Perfect timing.

My brother steps into the foyer with Peter in tow. Great. Now, all we need is for Costin to materialize from the shadows, and this uncomfortable day will be complete.

I glance at the window. It's too light for him to be out.

"Well, this is cozy," Anthony says, taking in the scene. His usual easy smile falters when he spots Lorelai. "Oh. I didn't realize we had a guest."

Peter hangs back, shifting his weight from foot to foot like he's unsure whether to stay or go. I wonder if he heard Astrid's jibe about werewolves. His messy brown hair falls in his eyes as he studies Lorelai with obvious curiosity. I notice Peter's nostrils flare slightly. I can practically see him cataloging her scent and wonder if he notices similarities to mine.

"You must be Anthony." Lorelai stands,

smoothing her dress. "I've seen pictures of you growing up with Tamara. I'm Lorelai."

"Funny. Can't say the same." Anthony's tone carries an edge beneath its politeness. He moves to stand protectively near my chair, just like he did when we were kids and supernatural visitors came calling.

"Hello, Peter." Astrid, ever the proper hostess, tries to break the tension. "Would you care for coffee? Raw meat?"

Well, okay, that was catty. She's *almost* always the proper hostess. I can't fault her. She's probably under a lot of stress.

"No, thank you, Lady Astrid." Peter's gaze keeps darting between me and Lorelai. I see the moment he puts it together, his eyes widening slightly.

"Peter, this is Lorelai Weber," I introduce. "Lorelai, Peter."

"We have information about your friend," Anthony says, directing his words to me. "But maybe we should discuss it when you're done here."

I straighten in my chair.

"No," Astrid commands. "Now is fine. Everyone here knows about Paul being taken."

"Everyone?" Peter asks, his usual playfulness replaced with caution. I can't blame him. Astrid was never a fan of his friendship with Anthony.

"Lorelai has certain interests in the situation," Astrid explains, her tone perfectly measured.

"Right then." Anthony claps his hands together. "Should we maybe order breakfast while we sort out this mess? I hear the candy chef is gone, but I'm starving."

Trust my brother to try lightening the mood with food. But his eyes tell me he has serious news to share about Paul. The question is, do I want to hear it in front of both my mothers?

No. I really don't.

"Whatever you know about Paul, just say it," I tell Anthony against my better judgment. "Everyone here is involved one way or another."

Anthony exchanges a look with Peter, who shakes his head in denial with a glance at Lorelai.

"She can be trusted," I say. "Please, Peter. I know you're putting yourself at risk by helping us. We won't betray you."

"I promise," Lorelai adds softly.

"You have my word," Astrid adds.

"You have our protection," Anthony says in front of his mother, so there is no mistaking his promise to his friend.

Peter sighs and then looks resigned. He gives a slight nod. "Tell them."

"The ritual the wolves are planning requires

three blood sacrifices under the full moon," Anthony says.

Blood and moonlight.

"Three?" My hand finds the amulet. Thane was so insistent on getting it off me. The stone trembles against my skin, its ancient magic stirring like a restless beast. "Paul is one. I'm the second. Who's the third?"

"That's where it gets complicated." Peter runs his fingers through his messy hair, which makes it worse. I can see he's troubled, but I also know he wants to do the right thing. Betraying his pack by talking to us is not something he'd do lightly. "The Alpha's been really secretive, even with the pack."

The amulet flares with sudden heat like a warning beacon. Draakmar's presence grows more insistent, as if he fears what Peter will say.

Peter glances nervously at the windows as if checking for watchers. Unless someone is watching from the sky, we're too high for anyone to see us.

"But from what I've gathered, they need specific types of people. Someone touched by death magic. Someone with draconic magic. Someone with forgotten magic. All three are pure mortality. They've been searching for centuries."

The stone around my neck shivers with energy, sending ripples of warmth across my skin. Draakmar stirs uneasily within the amulet. I want to tell him to calm down. His constant need for attention is becoming annoying.

"Why now?" Anthony asks. "What's changed?"

Peter shifts uncomfortably. "Like I said, the Alpha's been really secretive, but something's got him scared. Really scared. I've never seen him like this before. He's always been ruthless, but this..." He swallows hard, his voice dropping to barely a whisper. "I don't know. This is different. The other night, I overheard him talking about ancient debts coming due. I'm pretty sure he said something like even the moon herself can't hold back what's coming if they don't complete the ritual."

The amulet pulses, and I remember how Thane's hands shook slightly when he reached for it, not from desire or bloodlust but from genuine fear. Whatever is driving this ritual is bigger than werewolf politics or power grabs. Even Draakmar seems unsettled by it.

"Conrad shot Paul and killed him before the amulet erased time. His mortality was affected when the timeline reset," I say, slowly reasoning what we're facing. "He remembers both versions of events. That makes him touched by death magic."

"Draconic magic," Anthony says, staring at my amulet. "That one is pretty obvious."

"Thane offered a trade in three nights. Me for Paul." I touch my necklace, disturbing Anthony's focus on it.

"So that leaves forgotten magic," Peter says. "I don't know who that could be. No one will talk about it."

The implication hits me like a ton of falling bricks.

"Diana," I whisper. The amulet's reaction is immediate. It forcefully vibrates at her name, as if Draakmar reacts to the threat against an innocent child. "They're going after Paul's daughter."

"A child?" Lorelai stands abruptly. "They would sacrifice a child?"

"The full moon is in three nights," Anthony says. "We don't have much time."

"That's why Thane wanted you to come back. He's trying to manipulate you to get all three sacrifices together," Peter says. "You can't do it. You can't go."

"He tried to get me to take off the amulet." I grip my fist around the stone and think of Thane's words about choices and Costin's desperate attempts to keep me away. Had he known? Was he trying to protect me or control me?

"We need to get to Kansas City," I say, standing. The room spins slightly, exhaustion hitting me hard.

"We have to protect Diana. She's with her grand-parents."

"You need to rest first," Astrid states firmly. "You're no good to anyone in this state."

"I'll make arrangements," Anthony offers. "Give me a few hours to set things up safely. Peter can—"

The elevator dings, interrupting him. We all freeze, looking at each other.

"Are we expecting anyone else?" Lorelai asks.

"No," Astrid answers, her tone sharp. "We are not."

"Shit," Peter whispers, already backing toward the kitchen. "I can't be seen here."

Anthony quickly moves to shield his friend's retreat. "Go. Use the service elevator. I'll call you later."

The way Anthony protects Peter reminds me of how much my brother sacrifices to meet family expectations. Being the magical heir means living the life they want, not the one he dreams of. I wish I could make him realize it's okay to be his true self, but I know the weight of duty too well. His path is not mine to dictate. It's too bad our parents don't feel the same way.

Anthony's expression reminds me of how he looked after he broke up with Louis, that same forced smile hiding real pain. He's always been too good at pretending everything's fine. Since discovering that he had erased Louis' memories to make his human boyfriend forget their relationship, I worry my brother will never let himself be happy.

The elevator doors slide open with a soft hiss that somehow feels louder than it should. My heart pounds, and I feel Draakmar stir restlessly within the amulet. After the night I've had with Costin, after learning about the ritual, I'm not sure I can handle another supernatural crisis.

"Why don't you have a front door?" Lorelai asks, her hand drifting to the butterfly tattoo on her chest. "In California, I have three locks and protection charms on every entrance. Here, anyone can walk right in."

"We have magic," Astrid says with the kind of certainty that comes from centuries of power. Her posture somehow becomes even straighter. "The doors don't open to those who mean us immediate harm. I had the hallway removed because it was an eyesore. Besides," her lip curls slightly, "no one would dare attack the Devines in our own home."

I hear the distinct click of heels before Mabel Freemont emerges from the elevator. Her perfectly coiffed hair and designer suit look out of place this early in the morning, considering where I'd seen her hours before. But her expression of perpetual disdain is precisely as I remember it. Francis follows. His face is already red with self-importance.

"Lady Astrid." Mabel's gaze sweeps the room, lingering judgmentally on Lorelai's bohemian dress. "How quaint to find you entertaining at this hour."

I see the calculation in Mabel's eyes, the same look she had when trying to force me to marry Chester. Now that plan failed, they're trying a different approach to gain control.

Astrid rises with practiced grace. "Mabel. What an unexpected intrusion."

Francis comes in behind her and puffs up his chest, visibly dismissing the women and Anthony. "Where is your husband? I want to speak to the man of the house."

Astrid bristles. "How can I help you?"

Francis makes a show of being put out as he says, "The council has concerns about your daughter's recent activities."

At the mention of the council, my temple throbs with a sharp, unexpected pain. Something about Francis mentioning the council feels dangerous, like a half-remembered warning, but I can't place why.

My exhaustion burns away under a wave of irritation as I remember seeing Mabel conspiring with Elizabeth in Thane's court. Of course, the Freemonts would try to use this against my family. Did Mabel go straight from the werewolves to the council? She reminds me of those people who have the police on speed dial to self-righteously report every infraction of her neighbors.

"The council has no authority over my personal life," I say, fighting to keep my voice steady despite my exhaustion. The Freemonts have sought leverage since the wizard Zephronis declared my engagement to Chester impossible. "Zephronis made that clear."

"This isn't about your shameful rejection of our Chester." Mabel's lips thin as if she's tasted something rotten. "Though I must say, trading a respectable marriage for a vampire lover hardly speaks well of your judgment. Every choice has consequences, girl. You chose to spurn our family's protection, and now you'll see what it means to make powerful enemies." Her smile turns cruel. "I think Chester did well not to marry you."

Anthony moves to stand beside me. "If you're only here to insult my sister—"

"We're here," Francis interrupts, "because your mortal meddles in werewolf affairs. The Alpha himself contacted us about her interference."

Sure, he did. I feel the sarcasm radiating off me.

It's evident Mabel being at Thane's court isn't a coincidence. The Freemonts are working with both the werewolves and Elizabeth, probably hoping to use the chaos to grab more power.

Assholes.

"Really," Astrid's tone drips sarcasm. "Why would the Alpha contact you instead of coming to us directly?"

"Because we understand the delicate balance of supernatural politics," Mabel says.

Anthony snorts and doesn't try to hide his laughter.

"Something your daughter obviously has no clue about," Mabel continues. "Running around with vampires, starting fights with werewolves... The council won't stand for it."

"You're lying. There was no fighting," I grumble in annoyance. "I had an audience with the Alpha. You should know, Mabel. Or were you and Elizabeth too busy making out with werewolves?"

Anthony laughs harder, not trying to hide it.

Francis' face turns a deeper shade of angry red. "How dare—"

"How dare she what?" Astrid demands. "Tell the truth?"

"If she says she had an audience, she had an audience," Lorelai speaks up, her quiet voice carrying unexpected strength. She steps forward before Astrid can respond, and I see my adoptive mother's jaw tighten at the intervention. But for once, they're both fighting the same battle, even if they can't entirely fight it together. "You can tell your council to go to hell if they don't like it."

Mabel's perfectly shaped eyebrows lift. "Who are you to speak to me?"

"Someone who doesn't like you," Lorelai answers. I see Astrid's lip twitch in what might almost be a smile.

"This will not be tolerated. You will—" Francis starts, lifting his hand as magic forms in his palm.

Astrid cuts him off. "You have delivered your useless threats. Now get out of my home, or your lost shipment won't be the only thing the merfolk are looking for at the bottom of the ocean. And if you think I'm bluffing, I'll remind you why the Devines don't need political conniving to maintain our position."

Magic crackles in the air—not from Francis this time, but from Astrid. I've rarely seen her display power so openly. The Freemonts take a step back.

"Threaten a member of my family again, and you're fish bait," Astrid strides toward them, forcing them toward the elevator. Francis holds magic in his hand but is too hesitant to use it. Mabel frantically presses the button to open the doors. When they finally slide apart, Francis pushes her inside. As the door closes, the magic dies on his fingers, and I hear their muffled arguing coming through.

Astrid snuffs the magic in her fist and slaps her hands together as if dusting them off. "I believe we were discussing breakfast. I'll speak to the chef." She studies my face. "You look pale. Come to the kitchen. You need herbal tea, not coffee."

I follow her, too tired to argue. She pulls herbs from a cabinet and begins preparing the blend herself. The scent of chamomile fills the air, mixed with something I can't identify. It reminds me of that night with Chester and the engagement contract, how she'd made me the same tea before everything fell apart.

"Drink," she says, pressing the cup into my hands. "It will help you relax."

"Is it...?" I take the cup and stare into it. I want to ask what's in it.

"Tea?" Astrid finishes for me with a wave of her hand, urging me to drink. "Yes. It's just tea."

I probably shouldn't drink it, knowing how her special blends tend to affect me, but I'm too exhausted to resist. The truth is, I wouldn't mind a little oblivion.

"Go rest." She pats my shoulder, not looking at me as she puts her ingredients away as if nothing unusual has happened this morning.

I hold the cup and return to the living room, not sipping the hot liquid quite yet.

Anthony comes to me and whispers, "Go, Lady Astrid! Did you see Mabel's face?"

"Are you all right?" Lorelai asks me in concern.

I nod. The Freemonts don't scare me. Compared

to werewolves wanting to sacrifice me and a vampire boyfriend I'm not sure I can trust, Mabel and Francis' blustering barely registers.

"I'm exhausted," I say, wrapping my fingers on the warm mug. "But I can't sleep. We need to get to Kansas City to ensure Diana is safe."

"I'll order the family jet. You should rest," Anthony says before wrinkling his nose to tease, "and shower. You smell like wet dog and old motorcycle oil."

"Thanks, bro. You're so sweet," I drawl wryly. I catch something in his expression, a familiar melancholy I've seen more often lately. He's been throwing himself into family duties, paying more attention to me, and trying to keep busy. I know him well enough to see he's hiding from himself. But now isn't the time to push.

"I want to come with you to Kansas City," Lorelai says.

Anthony looks at me for guidance. I'm not sure that's a great idea, but I'm too tired to think of a reason to say no. If she's with us, she's not here with Astrid.

"You might not need to fly there. I'll call the lawyers." Astrid appears from the kitchen. "We have contacts everywhere. I'll have someone check on Diana and get her to safety."

I nod, trying to remember what I know about

Paul's family. "She's with her grandparents. Uh, Ben Cannon. He is a retired firefighter who has worked in construction. Skyscrapers. His wife is or was a nurse. They live in Kansas City on the Missouri side."

"We'll find them," Astrid says. "In the meantime, Anthony is right. You need to clean up and sleep."

"I should go to my hotel and do the same," Lorelai says, lightly touching her butterfly tattoo and looking at me as if she feels like she's hugging me by doing so. "I'll let you rest."

I want to ask her to stay, but the words stick in my throat. We're still strangers in so many ways, connected by blood but separated by years of absence. And yet, seeing her stand up to the Freemonts and watching her try to protect me in her own way stirs something in me I didn't expect. I glance at Astrid, not wanting to hurt her feelings.

"I'll come back tonight," Lorelai promises at my hesitation. "We can talk more then. About everything." She reaches for me, then stops herself. "I know I wasn't there before, but I'm here now. Whatever's coming, whatever this ritual is, you don't have to face it alone."

This time, when she hugs me, I don't stiffen. It's strange having a mother who hugs and can show affection so freely. It's particularly uncomfortable to know Astrid is watching us. I lift my arms to pat her back, the gesture awkward. It's brief but warm, carrying the scent of patchouli and paint that seems uniquely her. When she pulls back, I see tears that mirror the ones I won't let enter my eyes.

I glance at Astrid, who has diverted her gaze. She raised me for twenty-eight years, teaching me to be strong and never show weakness. And here's Lorelai, offering comfort like it's the most natural thing in the world. I'm unsure which approach I need more right now, but I know which one I'm more comfortable with.

"Be careful," I manage. "The Freemonts are dangerous. They don't take insults lightly."

"Oh, butterfly." She smiles, and for a moment, I see the fierce protectiveness that made her bargain with trolls for my amulet. "I've been dealing with supernatural politics longer than you've been alive. I'll be fine."

Anthony offers to escort her down, leaving me with Astrid, who watches with an unreadable expression.

When they leave, I say, "Thank you for finding Diana for me."

Astrid nods. "Children should not be used as pawns."

I wonder at her words, but she doesn't elaborate, and I'm too tired to force the conversation.

"Go," she orders. "I'll make the calls about Diana

and will come get you if I learn anything. There is nothing else you can do right now."

I turn to go, bowing my head to sniff myself. I do smell questionable. Gross.

My mind whirls. Costin. Rituals. Diana and Paul. And, above them all, three words whisper over and over through my mind.

Blood and moonlight.

THIRTEEN

I jolt awake to darkness, my heart racing before I even know why. The emergency lights pulse an angry red, each flash revealing glimpses of an institutional setting that's all wrong. This isn't Costin's intimate candlelit bedroom. My limbs feel leaden, refusing to obey as I fight through a druggy haze. The phantom smell of salt water and metal hits me like a physical blow, and my stomach lurches as forgotten memories claw their way to the surface. Time is running out. I can feel it in my bones.

Dammit. Did Costin mesmerize me again? The thought sends anger coursing through me.

I push myself up, fists clenched for a fight, only to recognize my bedroom at the penthouse. The familiar space feels wrong, tainted by whatever's trying to surface in my mind. I must have slept through the entire day.

Fuck! Precious hours wasted while Paul and Diana...

My head begins to clear, but the urgency doesn't fade. I'm alone and can't blame Costin for this murkiness. Something darker is at work.

I try to piece together what happened. Astrid had insisted I rest while she made calls about Diana's safety. I came back to the bedroom and took a shower. The last thing I remember is Astrid's tea. It is the same blend she used the night they had tried to make me sign the engagement contract with Chester. I should have known better than to drink it, but after dealing with the Freemonts and werewolves, I was too exhausted to resist. I wanted a little forgetting.

I did this to myself.

Diana.

The name hits me like a punch to the gut.

My fingers fumble for my phone, nearly knocking over the sandwich and soda someone left on my nightstand. The screen glows accusingly, showing dozens of notifications. My stomach growls like a waking monster, but the hunger feels distant compared to the dread building in my chest. I force myself to take mechanical bites of the sandwich while scrolling through messages with trembling fingers.

Multiple missed calls from Anthony and texts from unknown numbers flood my screen. One message makes my blood run cold. *"The grandparents aren't home. No sign of the girl. Trackers are out now. Hold for more details."*

My heart stops. The half-chewed sandwich tastes like dirt in my mouth. We're too late.

How the hell could I sleep with this going on? The guilt crashes over me. Each wave is stronger than the last. Every wasted second could mean Diana and Paul's suffering. It could have brought us closer to whatever horror the wolves have planned.

The amulet pulses against my chest, matching my racing heartbeat. Draakmar stirs restlessly within, and I swear the dragon's agitation feels different when I think of the child. There's something he's trying to tell me, something I'm missing.

"Any news? When do we leave? I need to be there." I text Anthony back, taking multiple bites to finish the sandwich. My head clears, and I get up to use the bathroom.

Blood and moonlight.

The words echo in my head like a death knell. Two nights until the full moon. The werewolves already have Paul and now Diana is missing.

My phone dings as I return to the room. Anthony

has written back, *"Just landed in Kansas City. If she's here, I'll find her. I got this."*

I start to type back, but it dings again.

Anthony writes, *"I took Lorelai with me. Nice lady. She wanted to help. Our mother thought it best if she was not in the city right now. Sorry if that's weird."*

"It's weird," I answer, before adding, *"Thanks for doing this."*

A shadow moves across my wall—too solid to be cast by the city lights below and too deliberate to be natural. My pulse quickens as the temperature seems to drop. I know who it is before I turn around. I can feel his presence like a physical weight.

"Did you know, Costin?" I demand, anger burning through the last of my grogginess.

My hands shake with barely contained frustration, but beneath the anger is that familiar spark of awareness that invariably ignites when he's near. His presence fills the room like a physical force.

I'm starting to hate him for it.

At least, I'm telling my lying self that.

"Did you know they'd go after Paul's daughter?" I continue. The amulet burns hotter against my skin. Draakmar feeds off my fury. "A *child*, Costin. They're after a child."

"I warned you to stay out of this," Costin says. His voice carries that ancient weight that reminds me he's been a witness to centuries. What is one human life compared to a creature who has seen so many? "Werewolves are feral, dangerous creatures. I was trying to keep you safe."

But I don't feel safe. Nothing does. Not when an innocent child's life hangs in the balance. Not when time is running out.

"Safe? I'm not yours to keep safe, Costin." I laugh in disbelief, the sound harsh and bitter in my throat. The predator in him is close to the surface, and despite everything, I'm aroused by it. I only partially believe what I'm saying. "I can take care of myself."

He moves closer, moonlight catching the fresh blood on his hand. I'm not scared for myself, but from the idea that he's been feeding. The sight of blood on his skin should repulse me. I tell myself it does. I'm too much of a coward to ask him how he ate. Or who. I am too afraid to acknowledge how the predator in him calls to something wild in me.

"What is it about this man?" Costin demands. Before I can retreat, his fingers catch my neck. They're warm and are further proof that he's been feeding. His eyes swirl with possessive power. I feel the jealousy radiating off of him. There is a desperation I've never seen before, a crack in his perfect control that makes him even more irresistible. His thumb traces over my pulse, and I hate how my body aches for his touch even as my mind screams to pull away.

I'm so used to thinking of him as strong and powerful. Now, to see the vulnerability takes me aback. The great Constantine, master of vampires, actually looks afraid.

"What is it about Paul that makes him so special?" he asks, this time more like a plea as he tries to understand.

"He saved my life. He helped me when he didn't have to. I've told you all this, Costin. He should not be punished because he was kind to a stranger. His parents are hurt, his daughter's been taken, and it's all my fault. They're on the supernatural's radar because of me. They fit the requirements for this ritual because of me. If they'd never met me..." My voice breaks. "Diana would be safe at home, not being used for some werewolf ritual."

There's more to what I feel for Paul than gratitude. I know we both know it. I can't help but wish he'll leave it at that.

I am not so lucky.

"Why do you love him?" Costin's voice drops to a dangerous whisper. He stands unnaturally still, a predator poised to strike. The blood on his hand gleams in the moonlight, a reminder of what he truly is. I wish I could read the thoughts behind those ancient eyes and translate the micro-expressions that centuries have taught him to hide. I wish, just once, I had the same power over him that he holds over me.

I want to tell him I don't love Paul, but the lie sticks in my throat. There's a part of me that desperately wants what Paul represents. I want normalcy, equality, and a life where I'm not constantly reminded of my mortality or treated less than because of it. In the supernatural world, being human is seen as a flaw, a weakness to be protected or exploited. But Paul... Paul never saw me that way.

I want to belong. I want to be able to hold my own without having to depend on others to take care of me. Paul saw me as an equal, not something to be controlled or sheltered. I miss that feeling.

The memory of it makes my chest ache, even as Draakmar's restless presence reminds me I can never return to being just human. Not now. Not with an ancient dragon's power protecting me and a child's life hanging in the balance.

"Tell me." Costin stares at me expectantly.

My voice chokes in my throat. The amulet burns against my skin. Draakmar senses my turmoil. Why has everything become so complicated? A few days ago, my biggest worry was avoiding Chester Freemont. Now I'm caught between a master vampire and a ritual sacrifice, with an innocent child's life in the balance.

His fingers tighten on my neck, not enough to

hurt, but enough to remind me of his inhuman strength. "Will you ever love me like you do him?"

The question carries an edge of desperation.

I don't know what to say. I don't allow myself to think about love with Costin. It's too dangerous and complicated. He's lived for centuries and will live for centuries more. I'm just a mortal, a tiny blip on his timeline that will fade in the blink of his immortal eye. The depth of my feelings for him terrifies me because I know I'll never mean as much to him as he does to me.

I need to refocus my thoughts and resist the temptation of his eyes. With time running out for Diana, how can I think about love at all?

"If you won't tell me. Show me," Costin whispers, his voice dropping to that dangerous velvet tone that makes my knees weak. Crimson bleeds into his eyes like spilled wine, hypnotic and terrifying. "Show me why he matters so much to you."

His grip tightens on my neck. Before I can react, his fangs tear into his palm. The scent of ancient vampire blood hits me. It's powerful and intoxicating.

"No!" I try to scramble away, but supernatural speed makes resistance futile. His arm bands around my back like steel, crushing me against his chest as his bleeding palm presses against my mouth.

Draakmar's protective presence feels distant as Costin's blood magic takes hold.

The thick, metallic taste floods my tongue. I thrash against him, but it's like fighting a marble statue.

"I need to understand." His voice carries a desperate edge that scares me more than his strength. This isn't the controlled master vampire I know. This is raw and dangerous. "Show me everything."

The world blurs and shifts, reality bleeding away like watercolors in the rain. I try to fight his blood magic, but a riptide is pulling me under.

"No, we don't have time for this!" I try to fight, but his blood chokes the protest back.

It's too late. The room spins violently, and I feel myself being torn backward through time. Fragments of memory flash past like broken glass as my mind finds the right one. I see Diana's terrified face, Paul's gentle smile, and the vampires appearing from the shadows. I don't want Costin to see any of this. I don't want to relive these moments. I don't want to feel.

The memory he's searching for crystalizes with brutal clarity. It hits me like a physical blow, and I feel Costin's presence watching and judging. His blood magic makes everything sharper, more vivid than I want it to be, and I'm helpless to stop it as the present dissolves...

Hotel, Downtown Kansas City, Several Months Earlier...

If places carry emotions, then this hotel room radiates desperation and despair. Paul and I are tangled in sheets, the aftermath of passion still humming through my body. There's an undercurrent of fear we can't ignore, but for this brief moment, it doesn't matter. My fingers trace symbols on his skin, patterns I learned from my supernatural family but never thought I'd use. His hand catches mine, pressing my palm down to stop the movement.

Through the blood magic, I can feel Costin's jealousy spike at this intimate moment.

"I hate that I brought you here." Paul's voice carries the weight of a man who's seen too much. He stares at the stained ceiling tiles. A pencil stuck in one of the panels catches my attention, and I stare at it until my vision blurs with unshed tears.

"I hate that I brought chaos into your life," I answer.

Part of me knows I am reliving a moment that happened, though it feels real. I sense Costin on the edge of my mind like an unwanted voyeur, his presence growing more intense as he searches for something specific in this memory. And yet, it's hard to resist the feelings just as it was the first time. They again pull me into the scene.

Paul's brow furrows, and he turns onto his side to study me. "I have to ask you something I've been wondering about."

My stomach tenses. "Ask."

He cups my cheek. "What particular thing were you supposed to find in the enchanted forest game?"

A tiny laugh escapes me. He's referring to a game called Hunter and Hunted. I told him about, when I was younger, Anthony and his friends invited Conrad and me to play with them in the woods. Everyone drew a card and searched for that object. The woods were enchanted, and we couldn't leave until we found it. I got separated from the others. Branches kept scraping my skin because the forest was so dense. I had been terrified.

"A fairy ring," I answer, thinking of my object. I had no clue at the time what that was. "I thought it was jewelry. Turns out it's a ring of mushrooms."

"How did you get out if you didn't know what you were looking for?" he persists.

"My grandfather ended the game when I didn't come home. He came to get me." I briefly touch my amulet. "I think he would have liked you."

Through the blood magic, I feel Costin's grief at

the mention of my grandfather. Their friendship had spanned decades, and a promise to George forced Costin to watch over me. Even now, years after his death, Costin is keeping that promise... though perhaps not in the way either of them had imagined.

"Show me everything," Costin whispers in the back of my mind, and I feel him drinking from my past.

The memory shifts like smoke caught in a sudden wind. Costin's blood magic pulls us forward, hungry for understanding. Paul and I are sitting up now, tension thick between us as his expression grows serious. I want to stop reliving this.

"Who would want your family dead?" Paul demands.

The question hits me like a physical blow, then and now. This was our first time together, and instead of afterglow, we got this. I try to resist showing more, but Costin's blood magic won't let me hide.

I don't have an answer. In this erased reality, my mother, father, Anthony, and Costin were all dead. Killed in the birthday fire. My chest aches with phantom grief for deaths that never happened, lives the amulet restored when it broke. The memory feels too real. Through Costin's magic, I can feel both timelines overlapping.

My family is alive now, but the memory of their

deaths still haunts me. I mourned at their graves. That kind of pain changes a person. Even now, that grief settles over me like a thick, smothering blanket, and I can't breathe.

"Show me everything," Costin's voice demands, each word driving his blood magic deeper. The pressure builds behind my eyes until I think my skull might crack.

My temple is pounding, and the more I fight against the memory, the worse the pain becomes. I already have these answers. This only leads deeper into Conrad's betrayal, Paul's death in that timeline, and Diana's innocence being shattered. Why is Costin forcing me to relive this? What is he really looking for?

The blood magic won't let me hide. Finally, I'm forced to answer just as I did that day. "They were some of the most extraordinary magics in the world, but feared and loved are not the same thing. They probably have enemies I don't even know about."

Through Costin's power, I feel the bitter irony of those words. I had no idea then that the real enemy was sitting at our family dinner table.

As I follow the memory, the pain in my head lessens.

Costin's presence grows heavier. He's watching intently now, seeing through my eyes as Paul pieces together what I couldn't.

"Who would want you dead?" Paul's eyes tell me he already suspects an answer. Even now, through the blood magic, I can see the moment he figured it out before I did.

"No one. I'm nobody." The words taste like ash in my mouth. Even as I say them, I know they're not true. In this erased timeline, the birthday fire had killed most of my family, including Costin. Then came the second explosion at Conrad's birth mother's apartment. And the third that almost took out Conrad's old foster family. It's a pattern I had been too blind to see, too hurt to acknowledge.

"Who had the addresses for all three fires?" Paul demands.

Paul's words come faster now, each one hitting like a physical blow. Through the memory, I feel Costin's grip tighten on my real body, his presence a cold shadow as he watches this intimate moment between Paul and me. There's something possessive about how he holds me as if he's trying to anchor me to the present even as we dive deeper into the past.

"Conrad's family. Conrad's remaining sister. Conrad's birth mother. Conrad's foster family..." Paul says, laying out the evidence of my brother's betrayal.

I try to fight against reliving this moment, but the vampire's blood magic won't let me escape. The conversation continues exactly as it happened. I try to scream at Costin to stop, but I can't overwrite the past. I feel tears on my cheek.

"And if you're out of the way, who gets all that Devine power and money?" Paul's tone softens at my tears. "Who is there now making all the decisions regarding the estate? Who is dealing with the lawyers? I know you don't want to see it because you've lost so much, but I say this because I care. Often, the simplest answer is the right answer."

Hot tears slide down my cheeks as the truth I didn't want to see becomes clear. Even now, with Conrad dead and the timeline reset, this moment cuts deep. I want Costin to stop this. I don't want to feel it. I don't want to remember how much I trusted my brother, how blind I was to his darkness.

The memory of what happened later—of Conrad's death when he stole my amulet—tries to surface, but the blood magic keeps me locked in this moment. Costin wants to understand, to see how Paul broke through my defenses when no one else could.

"Tamara, I'm sorry," Paul continues. His voice sounds distant through the haze of that past and present, "but I think Conrad is trying to kill you."

No, no, no, no, no...

The memory shatters like glass fragments. They cut deep as Costin yanks his bloody hand away. Reality crashes back with a brutal force. His grip is almost painful, and I can feel him trembling. We stand in the bedroom as if no time has passed.

"Did you get what you wanted?" I whisper, my emotions raw. The taste of his blood lingers on my tongue. "Paul figured it out before anyone else. He saw the truth about Conrad when I was blind. He protected me. He risked everything to help me. And now he and his daughter's in danger because of it."

"He loved you." Costin's words come out like an accusation.

"Yes." I don't deny it. The amulet hums against my chest. Draakmar's presence is returning now that Costin's blood magic has released me.

"And you love him." It's not a question.

"Costin, don't..." I whisper, pressing my palm against the amulet to steady myself. "There is no point in talking about that past. It's all been erased. None of this changes that the werewolves took him. They need him because he died and came back when the timeline reset. His mortality is touched by death magic."

"It's not erased for you and him." Costin's voice is laced with bitter understanding. "He remembers. You remember."

I nod. There is no point in denying it. Draakmar stirs, sensing the growing tension.

Costin releases me so suddenly that I nearly fall. "Get out."

"What? Why? This is my room." The taste of his blood remains as a reminder of the intimacy he forced between us.

"Get. Out." His eyes blaze crimson, and I see the monster he tries so hard to contain. "Before I do something we'll both regret."

FOURTEEN

Asshole!

I make it halfway to the door before Costin says, "Wait."

The word pisses me off more. What the ever-living hell is wrong with this guy?

Get out. Wait. Get out...

Fuck him and his supernatural authority. I don't care if he's a master vampire king or ruler of every paranormal creature on the planet. He's being a jerk. I may be just a lowly human but I'm not a child, and I'm not going to obey like one. Every second we stand here arguing is time wasted. Paul and Diana need me.

I reach for the doorknob, my hand shaking with anger and the leftover effects of his blood magic. I know he has the physical power to stop me from leaving, and I half expect him to do so.

"If you leave now, you'll do something rash."

"For fuck's sake, I'm not an idiot!" I cry.

"Tell me you don't plan to confront Thane."

I hate it when he sounds all calm and reasonable, like I'm the irrational one for yelling.

"You'll most likely start a war with the werewolves," he insists. The amulet pulses as if Draakmar agrees with the vampire's warning.

"Shut up, or I'll throw you in a lake," I try to tell the dragon. I don't think Draakmar hears my thoughts the same way I hear his.

"You're the one who told me to get out." I don't turn around as I attempt to sound calm. My hand rests on the doorknob, gripping it tightly, but I can't quite make myself leave.

"I should not have lost my temper with you." His tone is measured.

"You think?"

"The idea of him touching you..." He stops himself. I don't have to see him to know he's struggling for his precious control. When he speaks again, his voice is tight. "You make me forget myself, and I can't afford to be distracted."

I snort in disbelief and roll my eyes. "So now it's my fault you're an asshole?"

"Did you just call me an asshole?" he asks in surprise.

"What? Too modern for you? What did they say at the dawn of time? Arsehole?" I might be brave enough to yell at him, but I'm not brave enough to let go of the door in case I push my luck too far. I wonder if Astrid will rescue me if I scream loud enough.

"Would you be reasonable and listen? There is too much at stake for us to be arguing like this. Elizabeth is plotting, the wolves are circling, and you foolishly insist on running headfirst into danger every time I turn around. If I didn't mesmerize you, I wouldn't get anything else done. We need to keep cool heads."

"Did you just call *me* foolish?" I shake with unspent anger. Where's a sharp wooden stake when you need one? Not that I could actually kill him, but I'd like to bash him over the head with it a few times. I stare at the door so hard I don't see it. "Cool heads? Seriously? Are you kidding me right now? You are so tightly wound I'm beginning to think you'll implode at any moment."

Part of me has always tiptoed around supernaturals, trying not to make them mad for fear they'd eat me or worse. A lifetime of hearing you're less than will do that to a person. But that ends now. Two innocent lives are worth more than supernatural politics.

I finally turn to face him, letting my rage show on my face. I don't think I could hide it if I wanted to. My tone is condescending, but I don't care, as I explain, "I don't need you to manage me. I need you to help me find Paul and Diana. I need you to actually do something instead of playing these power games. No more riddles. No more cryptic comments and half-truths. Just say what you mean for once."

He's across the room in a blur, hands braced against the door on either side of my head. I fall back against the hard wood. Apparently, he's not going to hide his anger either.

My heart hammers violently. Oh, fuck. Maybe I should try screaming for help now.

"You want me to help you save him? Risk your life for his? Support you going to reunite with the mortal who holds your heart?" His voice cracks slightly on the last word, revealing a rare vulnerability. "Is that what you're asking of me?"

"Costin—"

"You want truth? I've lived centuries, Tamara. I've seen supernatural and human empires rise and fall. I've watched you your entire life. And here I am, jealous of a human who had you for mere days." His eyes shift from anger to sorrow. "I can't get the image of you two out of my head."

"I never meant to..." I don't know how to answer him. I can't bring myself to worry about his immortal turmoil. Diana and Paul's situation is much more urgent.

I take a deep breath.

"This isn't about your jealousy, or about us," I say. "Werewolves are torturing Paul, and his five-year-old daughter is missing."

I shouldn't have to keep explaining this. Why won't he hear me?

"Stay here. Stay safe." His forehead drops to mine. I feel him tremble with the effort it takes to restrain himself. "Let the wolves have their mortal. Please. I can't watch you die for him. Let me keep you safe and I'll find Diana. I'll bring her to you. I promise."

The casual way he dismisses Paul's life makes my blood boil.

"The mortal has a name." My voice comes out harsh. "Paul has a life. I don't want Diana to grow up without a dad. She already lost her mom."

His expression becomes unreadable.

"You're not surprised by any of this, are you?" The realization hits hard. Costin wasn't there when Peter explained everything to us, yet he already seems to know. My stomach twists in knots. I hate feeling like this. "If you value what we have at all, tell me the truth, Costin. Did you know about all of it when they took Paul? Do you know about what they want to do at the ritual?"

"What are you talking about?" His confusion seems genuine. "All of what?"

"Peter came by the house this morning."

"And?" He gestures as if it's useless information.

"Did you know there need to be three sacrifices?" My voice trembles with uncertainty.

He frowns and doesn't answer.

"Peter said the Alpha needs the blood of three mortals for his ritual to work." I watch carefully for any change in his expression.

"And?" he repeats.

I sigh. "It needs the blood of three mortals, each tied to magic but not magic themselves. Draconic, death, and forgotten."

His face doesn't give anything away.

"Me, because of my connection to Draakmar. Paul, because of..." I hesitate. Paul is such a sensitive subject with us, and I don't want to relive the past again. "Because of what happened when he died before. He's death magic. And Diana because of something she doesn't even know she has."

I see the war in his eyes—the master vampire who demands obedience versus a man with feelings. I know which of the two is the dominant personality, and to be honest, it breaks my heart. The vampire will win every time.

I touch my amulet. "How much did you know?"

His fingers tighten on my throat, just for a second, before he exhales sharply and lets go.

"Admit it. You let the werewolves take Paul. You knew they were coming, and you let them have him." I try to push at his chest, but he doesn't move away. "I don't want to believe it, but that's what I do, isn't it? I don't believe in what is right in front of me because I don't want to face it. That's what happened with Conrad, and he tried to kill all of us. I made excuse after excuse for my brother. And that's what's happening with you now. I've been making excuses for your misogynist behavior. You're a vampire. You're old as dirt. You come from a different time. You mean well. You don't know better."

His eyes flash crimson. I ignore the threat.

"What the fuck is wrong with me? Why do I keep...?" I shake my head and steadily meet his gaze. "No more, Costin. We're not in the Middle Ages, and you are not feudal lord of the manor. You need to evolve. This time, you've gone too far. Diana is just an innocent child. I'm not going to abandon her. Paul is a kind man who doesn't deserve this. There is nothing you can do that will change my mind."

"Enough," he commands hoarsely. The color of blood overtakes the whites of his eyes.

The threat hangs between us like a static charge

building before the storm breaks. We both know he can overpower me if he wants. He could drop me off the side of the penthouse before I even knew I was moving. He can mesmerize me into oblivion. He can force me into compliance.

The fear should be overtaking me. It's not. This time, when Draakmar stirs, I don't feel afraid. I feel powerful.

"No," I say softly. "Paul and Diana need my help. I'm not turning my back on them. And I can't be with someone who would stand by while a child is killed."

"You have responsibilities to your family, a duty not to let the wolves win." His fingers brush my cheek with surprising gentleness before curling into a fist against the door. "If they need all three powers, then the werewolves can't complete their ritual without you. Stay away, and this all ends."

"Ends how?" I refuse to back down. "I won't hide while others suffer. That's not ending anything. That's running away, and you know it. I'm not a coward."

"No, never that." He leans closer like he's going to kiss me. His hand slides gently over my throat, thumb tracing my pulse. "I can't let you sacrifice yourself. The Alpha won't just hand them over to you because you ask nicely. There is no way his plan ends without bloodshed."

Draakmar agrees with him. The dragon thrashes wildly for attention.

Suddenly, Costin pulls back, studying me. "What's happening to you?"

"I don't know." At least it's honest.

He puts the back of his hand on my forehead. "You're warmer than usual."

I grab his wrist and pull his hand away. "Don't change the subject."

Though I get what he's saying, I feel like I'm standing on top of a furnace. Only I'm not sweating.

Costin steps back, and the crimson fades from his eyes. "You should know me better than this by now. Do you really think that I would let them hurt a child?"

"How would I know that? You're a closed book. You drop enigmatic half sentences and then look at me all moody like a... like a..." I'm so frustrated the words struggle to come out. "...a moody goth teenage boy."

"I did not know they wanted the child," Costin states. "There was no reason to suspect it. Wolves don't turn children if they can help it."

"Keep talking," I demand, wanting more from him.

"But I knew something bad would come of all this. That is why I didn't want to arrange the audience with the Alpha. Werewolves are not to be trusted. They are rash, treacherous creatures who live on emotion and impulse, bound to the moon and as changing as the tides."

"But you knew they were after Paul?" I keep my gaze steady on him.

"Yes."

"Why would you let them take him?"

"The Alpha had threatened to take you but had heard rumors we were together. He tried to barter for you. I said no." His guard slips, and his voice carries real emotion. "They wanted someone touched by magic. Namely, you, because of the amulet. When they suggested taking Paul instead..." He looks away. "I let them. I didn't know about the full ritual at the time, and I never knew they were after a child. At worst, I thought they'd turn him into a howler."

He doesn't need to spell it out, but I can connect the dots. If Paul were a werewolf, then Costin thinks that would change my opinion toward him. Instead of competing against a human, he'd be competing against a werewolf. To a vampire, he would be the clear winner in that rivalry.

Did Costin's decision to let them take Paul really come down to pure old fashioned male jealousy? Was that his secret?

"Werewolves are impulsive creatures who act on emotion rather than reason," he continues, like he's trying to justify his thinking. "I assumed they initially wanted leverage against the vampires through you because of our connection. You're so defiant and keep running away from me. I can't protect you during the daylight hours without mesmerizing you into safety. Then, when you demanded that audience, I knew Thane would make a play to lure you in. That is why I couldn't let you have a meeting without me there. Whatever promises he made to you are lies."

"Damn it, Costin, why didn't you tell me this from the beginning? This is what I'm talking about. Why the hell do you keep doing this? Keeping secrets, and making me guess?"

"Why would I tell you everything? So you can look at me like you are now? Why would I give you that choice? I knew you'd sacrifice yourself to save him." His voice is rough with emotion. "You're mine to protect, Tamara. Yes, I promised your grandfather that I would watch out for you. But even if I hadn't, you would still be my responsibility. Mine to..."

He cuts himself off, jaw clenched. He gives a small shake of his head, biting back his words.

"Yours to what?" I whisper, wanting him to finish the sentence. "You have to talk to me. I can't read your mind."

Instead of answering, his mouth crashes into mine. His kiss is desperate, almost bruising. It reeks of panic like he's afraid I'll disappear if he lets go. I'm not sure what it means or how I know it. Is it fear of losing me, fear of feeling too much, fear of this power he can't control?

A fang nicks my bottom lip, and I taste a hint of blood from the tiny wound. I should push him away. I should leave. Instead, I grip his shirt to keep him close as heat floods me. The amulet grows hotter, radiating flames, but neither of us pulls back.

Costin deepens the kiss, and I feel the moment the predator gives way to something more vulnerable, more human. I realize that for all his strength, for all his power, I've become more than just his weakness. I'm his tie to humanity.

"Don't..." he whispers, choking on the word. I sense the need in his trembling hands as they frame my face. "Don't leave me."

The admission does not come easily for him. I feel it in the way his body tenses and how his fingers curl possessively into my hair. Vampires don't admit weakness. Their whole survival depends on being the emotionless predator. I often doubt they can feel things like the rest of us. And for someone like Costin? A master vampire meant to lead them all? Admitting to his feelings would be seen as the ultimate failure.

I want to trust him, but I've been burned by my own willful ignorance too many times.

"I can't lose you," he says against my mouth. "Not to the wolves, not to Paul, not to death." His fingers trace my pulse. "If it comes to it, there are ways and things I can do to save you. There are ways we can make sure you can't be used for the ritual. If you're not mortal, they can't..."

He stops himself, but I see the calculation in his eyes. He's already planning how to save me, no matter the cost.

"No. Promise me you won't do that." I don't want to hurt his feelings, but no part of me wants to be made into a vampire. The idea of drinking human blood makes me gag. And to never see daylight?

"You don't have to be scared."

Sure, the idea of eternity in the abstract sounds romantic, but I have seen the toll that reality takes upon people. I think of my parents, disillusioned in a practical marriage. I think of what it would be like to deal with the supernatural bullshit until the end of time. I just want to be normal. It's all I've ever wanted. And if I can't be normal, then at least I know who I am. I don't want to be a monster. Of course, I'd never call him one to his face. He can't help he's a vampire.

"I don't want that." I need to be clear. "Don't turn me."

His fingers twitch against my skin, then pull away. He's hurt I rejected his offer. His jaw tightens.

For a moment, I think he might argue, might try to convince me of immortality's benefits. Instead, he nods once, the gesture carrying the weight of a vow. But something in his eyes makes me wonder if he could keep that promise if truly tested.

He leans into me. I should stop this. I'm too emotionally vulnerable to make good decisions. I can't think straight when he touches me. But when his fangs graze my throat, I pull him closer. My body presses into him with a mind of its own. The amulet heats between us, and for once, it feels like permission rather than a warning.

I should stop.

Fuck, I need to stop.

I need to think. I need to reason.

"Let me in," he pleads as if feeling my internal struggle. "Trust me enough to let me protect you."

Damn, he's sexy. I can't help myself.

"Trust me enough to let me make my own choices," I counter, even as my fingers work at the buttons of his shirt.

He laughs softly against my neck, but he doesn't sound pleased. "Choices? What choice is there when every path leads to your death?"

I pull back enough to meet his gaze. "Then help me find another path."

This time, when he kisses me, it's different. It's slower, deeper, like he's memorizing every sensation. His cool hands slide under my shirt, and I shiver at the contrast between his touch and my fevered skin.

I can't resist. I'm being drawn to him as if he can't turn off the magnetic pull of his power.

"You're really burning up," he murmurs, touching my forehead. The contact sends shivers over me. "This isn't normal. Are you unwell?"

"I'm fine. It's Draakmar," I answer. "His connection has gotten stronger. It's like he is attempting to tell me something, but half the time, it's like listening to a language I don't understand."

I can't focus on the dragon's warnings when Costin's proximity makes my skin tingle.

"It's fine." I wave the concern away and pull his lips back to my greedy mouth. His tongue presses past the seam of my lips, tenderly dipping inside. Passion shoots through me at the taste of him. I moan in pleasure, imploring him to give me more.

We crash into each other, frantic, as we stumble toward my bed. Our clothes crumple under our eager hands as I fight to be free of them. I hear material rip before he throws it to the floor.

He lays me down, and I sink into the bedding. Costin moves with inhuman speed, caging me under his body. I breathe in, feeling as if I'm pulling his breath into my lungs. The torturous need becomes unbearable.

I ache with mounting passion. Every point we touch feels like raw electricity. Yet, his weight keeps me grounded as desire courses through my veins. His body presses into mine, so close my breasts yield to the hard muscles of his chest. He groans, a purely animalistic sound.

I'm struck by how right it feels to be with him, despite everything. We're so dissimilar. He's immortal strength and I'm frail mortality. By all rights, we don't make sense.

He pulls up just enough to gaze down at me. I see the red hunger filling his eyes, begging me. I can imagine all the things he's not saying. Stay alive. Stay safe. Stay mine.

The vulnerability in him makes my chest ache. For all his power, I hold him captive. And somehow, he has become my undoing as well. I'm not equipped to resist him. The thought frightens me but also makes me burn hotter. This isn't just about the primal need of our bodies.

I pull him closer, working my legs along his hips. I see the predator in his gaze. I feel the brush of his fangs as if he wants nothing more than to bite my flesh. He can't as long as I wear the amulet.

The pleasure of his touch vibrates to my core. His mouth again claims mine, teasing me with his fangs but not cutting into me. His possessive kisses try to mark me as his. The kiss deepens until my lungs burn for air and I have to push him back. I pant heavily, as he waits for me to pull him back to my mouth.

I can't resist this. Each nerve is electrified as it reaches toward him. The sound of my rushing blood fills my ears. I've spent my entire life struggling against supernatural control, but there's something incredibly intoxicating about surrender.

I shiver as a sensitive trail follows his hand over my ribcage. I writhe beneath him and push up my hips, trying to get him to end the ache between my thighs. Instead, a palm finds my breast, massaging it deeply. I don't want him to stop. I never want this to stop. I try to be strong but can't control myself with him. I need him to touch me and end the torment.

My head swirls with thoughts and warnings, but I don't listen. Costin has been there my entire life, standing in my shadow, watching, waiting, protecting me when I didn't even know I needed protection.

And then the truth hits me as his hips settle between mine, and his grip tightens on my breast, keeping my nipple at full attention. I've fallen in love with him. I'm terrified, and I'm in love.

The realization takes me aback, and I hesitate.

"I need to taste you," he murmurs against my throat. Those damn fangs tease the skin over my pulse. The amulet prevents him from breaking through, but the pleading in his voice makes me quiver.

This is madness.

My hands tremble as I reach for the chain around my neck. The amulet is my shield against supernatural danger. Without it, I'm vulnerable.

My sex pulses with denied pleasure. I want him. Not just the careful, controlled version of himself he shows the world, but all of him, both the vampire and the man, the darkness and the light. I need him to give me what my body craves.

I finger the necklace before slowly pulling the chain over my head. I feel exposed without my talisman, and my heart beats faster at the dangerous thrill.

"Are you sure?" Need radiates off him, and yet he holds himself perfectly still.

I nod and offer my neck.

The predator inside him emerges. Costin groans and buries his face against my shoulder. Fear should be clawing at me. But instead I feel anticipation of the bite. His power wraps around me like a physical caress. My body arches into him, wanting more.

I tense and wait for him to drink, only to be disappointed when he doesn't.

My nerves tingle. Costin's mouth travels along my unprotected body. Soft light dances along his perfect muscles. He's so beautiful it makes me ache.

He kisses a winding path to one breast, then the other, and back again. With each press of his lips, I stiffen and wait for that sharp, painful stab into my flesh. When it doesn't happen, I release a small gasp of disappointment, only to tense when his mouth returns. Each contact is calculated to amplify my need.

His hips rock, hinting at the rhythm to come. I cry out in frustration, my fingers tangling in his hair to force him closer. I open my legs, wrapping them around him to pull him in. He's too strong for me to force down. His tongue traces patterns on my sensitive flesh, over my nipples, and down the valley of my breasts. I squirm beneath him, pushing and pulling, trying to end the building ache inside me. I forget where we are. The room fades into the fog of oblivion. Nothing matters but this moment.

I need him.

I want him.

I love him.

He knows exactly how to touch me, how to drive me to the edge and keep me there. His supernatural strength holds me effortlessly in place when I try to move. Control is just an illusion. I never had it. I will always be at his mercy.

My vampire.

The desperation courses through my blood like a fire needing to be extinguished. I hear myself begging, but the sounds feel far away, and I don't know if I'm thinking it or saying the words aloud. "Please, Costin, oh, please..."

When his fangs graze my inner thigh, I inhale sharply and try to force him toward my sex. I need to feel him against me, releasing the growing tension in my body. All the stress, fear, frustration, and doubts whirl around in my head. I am helpless against them.

"Mine," he growls against my skin. The possessive tone should anger me, but instead, it sends the fiery heat pooling low in my belly.

Then, finally, he bites down on the tender flesh of my inner thigh. All my frantic thoughts instantly stop under a sharp sting of white heat and then the warmth flooding through me. Pleasure-pain drowns out every thought but him.

His hands grip my hips, holding me still as he intimately drinks. I feel the pull of his mouth as he sucks against my skin. I don't know if it's the erotic sensation or the blood loss that's making me lightheaded. All I know is I don't want him to stop.

The more he drinks, the warmer he becomes. I have no concept of time. When his mouth finally pulls away, he leans his head back and makes a strange noise of pleasure. I watch as his jaw bites at the air as if he is forcing himself to stop before he kills me. I feel the tickle of blood dripping down my thigh to the crack of my ass.

And still, I'm not scared of him, at least not of this part of him.

"Please," I beg, not even sure what I'm asking for.

Costin leans over me and licks the wound with a loud moan before flicking his tongue along my sex. I can't control myself as I convulse in response.

He rises over me like a dark angel, all dominance and barely contained violence. I see my blood swirling in his eyes and staining his lips. I feel the tremor in his body as if he's trying to rein in his power. But his touch remains gentle as he brushes the hair from my face. "Tell me you're mine."

It's a command I can't deny. I nod and manage on a breath. "I'm yours."

His mouth crashes against mine, desperate, demanding. Like he's trying to brand me with his kiss. I taste my blood, and his continual growls of pleasure vibrate through me.

There is a fierce tenderness to the way he draws his body to mine. When we finally join, it is pure ecstasy. I feel connected to him. My nails dig into his shoulders as he drives deep and hard, claiming me completely. The sensations are overwhelming. His supernatural strength lets him set a pace that would break a mortal man. Each thrust feels like he's trying to mark me from the inside out.

His mouth crosses over my throat, and his hot breath makes me shiver in anticipation. I turn my head, offering myself again to him. His fangs pierce my skin at the height of our passion, and the dual sensation sends me spiraling over the cliff. I've never felt anything like it. The sting of his bite only intensifies my climax. I cry out as release comes over me in waves.

I feel him drinking, taking my essence into himself, and somehow, it makes everything more intense. His grip tightens as my blood fills him. When he finally breaks away from my throat, his mouth finds mine again. I taste a coppery sweetness as his kiss deepens.

For one perfect moment, there are no threats, no rituals, or complicated choices. There's just us, connected in the most primal way possible. I feel his power surrounding me, filling me, claiming me in ways that go beyond the physical.

"Stay with me," he begs against my mouth. "Choose me."

I want to. The feel of him still courses through me, and his body presses to mine. I want to promise him everything. But dawn will come to shed its hateful light, and with it, all our complications will return.

He settles on the bed next to me. Seeing my

penthouse bedroom draws me back into reality, a place I don't want to be.

His hand moves over my neck as if tracing his bite. He leans to nuzzle my neck, licking me.

Costin pulls back, studying me. "Did I hurt you?"

The concern in his voice makes my heart ache. "No."

"You've always been strong." His whisper tickles my ear. "Stubborn. Defiant. Beautiful."

Something has shifted inside him. It's in his expression and in the way he holds me. There is a vulnerability I've never seen before.

"I meant what I said," he murmurs, fingers caressing my skin. "I can't lose you."

I search for the amulet in the bedding, finding its familiar weight. I lift my head and slip it back around my neck. The stone pulses warmly, but it feels different now, less like a barrier between Costin and me and more like a bridge. Perhaps this is what I've been fighting all along, the inevitable truth that my place is here, balanced between his darkness and my light.

"Then help me," I say softly, reaching to caress his jaw. "Help me save them. Not because you care about Paul or Diana, but because I do. Because letting innocent people die isn't who either of us wants to be."

I let my touch linger on his face, and he leans into it like a creature starved for gentleness.

He's quiet for a long moment, and I feel the tension return to his body. Finally, he presses a kiss on my temple. "You should sleep."

It's not a no. From Costin, that's practically a yes. I curl into him, knowing that dawn ticks closer and he'll have to go underground soon.

That moment comes faster than I anticipate. He pushes up from the bed and is dressed before I have time to question it. "I have some important vampire matters I need to attend to before dawn."

I don't like the vagueness of that statement. "What matters?"

"Nothing you should be concerned about. There is a message from the European council that needs answered. They do not like to be kept waiting. We'll talk more tomorrow night. Get some rest."

I want to tell him I slept all day and I'm not tired, but he drank a lot of blood. Between that and Draak-mar's feverish surges of power, I feel the lethargy seeping into my limbs.

There are still secrets between us and choices to be made, but something fundamental has changed. I'm no longer just his to protect. He's mine to protect, too.

FIFTEEN

This time, when I wake up disoriented, it is to daylight and the lingering sensation of Costin's touch. My neck and thigh itch where he fed, and my body aches as a reminder of all that passed between us during the night. I feel closer to him than I ever have. There was a vulnerability in him I've never seen.

That has to be real, right? I didn't imagine it.

I want to trust Costin, but it comes hard.

The amulet radiates warmth against my chest, its magic trying to heal the marks Costin left behind. The wound might fade, but the mark will not.

I realize I've been in this room way too long. I'm hiding. That's not good.

I look at the nightstand, hoping to see food.

MICHELLE M. PILLOW

There is none. Trust Astrid not to enable laziness for too long.

I go to the bathroom to stare at the horror show looking back at me in the mirror. Dark circles mar under my eyes, and my hair is a wild mess of untamed curls. My skin is pale from blood loss, which makes the dried crimson streaks more pronounced. The puncture wounds are healed over. Two pink dots remain as evidence of his feeding.

"In two nights, the werewolves will try to sacrifice Paul and Diana," I whisper to my reflection as if saying the words out loud will make the idea manageable. It doesn't. I don't know what to do. There is a sick anticipation building in my stomach. I want it to be over, and yet I don't want the night to arrive. The two conflicting feelings battle inside me.

Do I go into hiding? If the wolves don't have me, they don't have a complete ritual.

Although, I can't imagine the Alpha shrugging his shoulders and just letting the two humans go free in response.

A sharp pain shoots behind my eye, and I press my fingers into my temple, closing my eyes tight. It only lasts a few seconds. I blink several times to clear my vision. It's weird but hardly concerning.

I have to figure this out.

Do I try to amass an army? Use my position as Lord Constantine's girlfriend to...? To what? Start a

252

war between vampires and werewolves? That would only lead to supernatural chaos and so many more deaths. Besides, that's too big of an ask. No one will want to go to war over three mortals and a ritual. The supernatural community probably would laugh if I even suggested it.

Then what?

I touch my amulet. "What do you think, Draakmar?"

I feel the creature stir like a sleepy child turning in a warm bed, refusing to wake up.

"Thanks," I drawl sarcastically. "That's a lot of help."

It might be helpful if I knew what this ritual was for. I mean, the fact they're going through all this trouble and calling it a ritual signifies that it's not a good thing. What the hell is wrong with supernaturals? Are they so bored they have to invent new ways to fuck things up? Why can't a ritual be like... I don't know. Is world peace too dull?

I stare at the mirror.

"Too bad zombies don't get respect from the supernaturals," I mutter, pushing my hair back from my face. "I might actually have a chance."

My brain goes onto autopilot as I start making myself look presentable. I pull my hair back and put on some makeup, making sure to cover up the healing bite wounds. After I dress to the lowest of

Astrid's standards, I leave the room searching for breakfast.

Astrid's voice drifts from somewhere in the penthouse, pulling me toward it. From the one-sided conversation, it sounds like she's talking on the phone. "The Freemonts are involved. They've been seen with the Alpha..."

The mention of the Freemonts triggers something. Another sharp pain lances through my temple, and I stumble. I press my palm over my eye. This is worse than the first time.

The hallway feels like it tilts sideways, and I grab the wall to steady myself. The scent of salt water and diesel fuel fills my nose, so intense and sudden it makes me woozy. Images flash through my mind like a strobe light, each one hitting harder than the last. I see Chester's face illuminated by red light, feel the press of uneven metal against my back, and hear the distant sound of chains clanking.

None of it makes sense.

The pain becomes more intense. I suck in a deep breath and hold it. Astrid's voice fades as if she's being pulled away from me. The penthouse disappears, and I feel as if I'm flashing through time.

Flash. I'm sixteen, peeping through the spyhole in the Devine library, watching as Mabel and the vampire Robert plot to overthrow Costin. Sweat trickles down my spine.

Flash. Chester's hands are glowing with magic. He reaches for my throat, and I feel the power stinging my skin. His voice whispers, "What are you even doing here?"

Flash. Cool fingers caress my face. Costin's eyes swirl with red. "Sleep now. Forget..."

My lungs force out my breath with a rough pant, and I realize I'm on the floor of the penthouse hallway, propped against the wall. The walls stretch like a bad acid trip. My stomach tenses. My headache throbs in time with my quick pulse, and each beat releases waves of pain throughout my skull.

I try to decipher the images flashing through my thoughts, but the memories feel like shards of broken glass, cutting deeper each time I try to grasp them.

"Mom," I cry, desperate for help. I never call her that, but it's all the sound I can eke out.

"Tamara?" Astrid's voice pierces through the fog, closer now. She appears in the doorway to the library, her phone clutched in a white-knuckled grip. Her heels click against the marble floor with rushed precision. "What's happening?"

I try to answer, but my thick tongue feels clumsy. I taste blood. The metallic flavor floods my mouth as another fragment surfaces. I can't lift my arms to reach for her as she leans over me.

Flash. Chester's face is bathed in blinking red

lights, his eyes gleaming with smug satisfaction. The image vanishes as fast as it comes, leaving a lingering echo of clanking chains and the phantom sensation of magic burning against my throat.

When my sight returns to the present, Astrid kneels beside me on the floor. "You're bleeding. Tilt your head back."

The amulet pulses against my chest like a second heartbeat, its heat matching the fever in my blood. Deep within me, Draakmar thrashes as if the dragon is writhing to shake the memories free.

Astrid grabs my hair and forces my head back. For once, I feel like her perfect composure cracks. She pulls me against her chest to prop my head against her shoulder to keep my face pointed at the ceiling. I feel her pinching the bridge of my nose. Tiny pulses of magic come from her fingers.

"There we go," she soothes. "It's just a little nosebleed."

The words are unconvincing, and I wonder which of us she's trying to persuade.

"I can't..." I try to explain. My body convulses. Draakmar keeps trying to pry open the locked door.

Another memory hits like a physical blow. I taste burned meat and the sound of magic crackles through the air. Something presses against my throat, and I hear the distant howl. It's too painful, and I try to fight it. The fragment shatters, leaving me gasping.

The pain lessens, and my vision clears. Astrid holds me tight, her fingers pulsing magic into my nose. I still taste blood and reach for my face to wipe my mouth.

As my mind clears, the feeling of being held by her becomes awkward. She releases my nose, and I push up to sit against the wall. She drops her hand and adjusts her tangled legs to a more ladylike position before moving to stand.

"What did you see?" Astrid asks, reaching to pull me to my feet.

My legs feel disconnected from my body. "How do you know I saw something?"

She arches a brow and hooks my arm to lead me toward the living room.

I shake my head. "I don't know. Chester? Red lights?" I close my eyes, scared to pry too deep for fear it might start again. "The shipping office?"

"The shipping office," Astrid repeats, frowning. We continue walking slowly together. My feet shuffle on the floor.

I open my eyes. "I know it doesn't make sense. Chester was never at the shipping office, but it feels like I lived... Costin."

"Costin?"

I sigh. "I think he must have erased a memory."

Another memory.

"Of the Freemonts and the shipping yard?" she clarifies, bringing me to the couch to sit down.

I see dots of blood on her blouse. My blood.

I touch my nose. It's stopped bleeding. "Chester, at least."

"Has that vampire done this to you before?" Astrid puts her hands on her hips, not sitting next to me. Her expression frosts over, and I know that I cannot refuse to answer truthfully.

I nod again, feeling very much like the little kid caught doing something wrong.

"Tell me exactly what you remember," she orders.

I sink back into the couch, pressing my fingers against my temples as if I can physically pull the memory into place. "Just Chester and our shipping yard. Red warning lights. The sound of those enchanted security chains. You know, the ones that used to be there. I think they took them out because they kept attacking gnomes or something—I can't..." The images spiral away like leaves in a whirlwind, leaving only the residue of terror behind. "Maybe I dreamed it?"

"Perhaps you should rest. You look pale." Astrid's tone carries a hard edge beneath the concern. "The tea—"

"No." The word comes out sharper than

intended. "No more tea. No more forced sleep. I need to focus. Diana is missing, Paul is captured, and the Freemonts..." I struggle as the kaleidoscope of fractured memories threatens to return. "They're working with the werewolves. They have been for years. I don't know how I know that, but it feels true in my bones. The Freemonts, Costin's sister, and the wolves... this all has something to do with them. And blood and moonlight."

Astrid sets her phone on the coffee table with deliberate care. "Slow down. You're mumbling your words."

"It's like..." I rub my temples and search for words to describe the sensation. "Like trying to catch reflections in a broken mirror. Every time I think I see the whole picture, it shatters into something else. There are too many pieces."

How many times? How many memories did Costin take from me?

I want so badly to trust him, but the evidence keeps coming back to all these secrets that feel like lies.

"There are spells, but they are painful and complicated," Astrid says carefully. "The easiest route is for him to tell us what he erased."

"I can handle pain," I answer, needing to know the truth. I hope it's true. "Do what you need to."

Astrid shakes her head. "No. Even if you were to

survive the magic needed, you wouldn't come out the other end the same."

"So we'll confront him tonight." I lean my head back on the couch. "Have you heard from Anthony about Diana? Is he still in Kansas City?"

"Diana is not there. The grandparents are in the hospital. They were severely attacked, and the police are working under the assumption that they're dealing with a kidnapping home invasion scenario." Astrid doesn't sugarcoat it. "They had also reported their son missing when he did not call to check on his daughter, which initiated a wellness check. I told Anthony to manage the situation in Kansas City for us before coming home. We do not need the humans meddling in our affairs. Our fixers are handling the police locally. The investigation into Paul will be closed."

I don't know what to say.

"Are the Cannons...?" I think of the nice man I met in that other timeline. Paul's father was a kind and loving soul.

"We're taking care of it," she says.

"What does that mean?"

She looks at me like I should know the answer already. I half expect her not to say.

"We won't hurt them," she assures me, "if that's what you're asking. It means that their medical bills will be taken care of, and we'll see to it they have the best doctors. Memories might have to be erased. The police reports will be handled depending on the outcome of this whole situation. If we don't stop their plans, all of this preparation might be for nothing. But they matter to you, so they matter to this family."

That last sentence might be the nicest thing she's ever said to me.

I can't feel pleasure in it, though.

"The wolves won't..." It's a stupid question, and I stop myself before I finish it. Of course, the werewolves will hurt Diana. That's the whole reason they took her.

"I should tell you that I sent Lorelai with him. She wanted to help, and I thought it best to get her out of the city." Astrid's voice carries that familiar dismissiveness toward humans. It's how she's always handled complications by removing them from the equation. "There is nothing she can do here but get in the way. This battle is not for mere mortals. We can't be distracted by... well."

I don't tell her that Anthony already told me.

"I understand," I answer, recognizing the pattern. Astrid is managing every detail, just like she managed the truth about my birth for twenty-eight years. Some things never change. However, I noticed she at least told me about sending Lorelai away this time. Maybe that's progress. At least Lorelai will be safe.

"Go put on your shoes," Astrid orders. "I'll have the chef make you a breakfast sandwich to go."

"Go where?" I frown.

"Constantine's," she says, her eyes dipping to my amulet. "He can't come to us, so we're going to him. We are Devines. And Devine ladies do not wait for men to grace us with their presence. If we left the world to men, we would have lost it long ago."

The change in her toward me is starting to make sense. I wield Draakmar's power through the amulet. I may be mortal, but I now have access to powerful magic. This makes me closer to an equal in her eyes.

It's not quite what a daughter wants from a mother, but then I don't live in a world of perfect families and happy endings. I live in the real world. This world. The supernatural world.

SIXTEEN

It feels strange standing next to Astrid as the elevator descends into Costin's underground sanctuary. Everything about my mother is stately. She's changed into black slacks and a dark red blouse. A black scarf covers her head so only her sunglasses show. There is no trace of my blood on her as if the nosebleed never happened. She takes her scarf down and unwraps it from her face to let it drape over her shoulders.

I see my warped reflection next to her in the elevator doors. I wish I could say the same for myself. I wear jeans, sneakers, and a long-sleeved T-shirt under a cardigan. It's too late to do anything about it, but I'm not elegant. Not like her.

The metal box carries us deep beneath the city. Astrid stands perfectly still, her chin lifted as if she's posed for her entrance. "I spoke to your father earlier. He won't be returning from Europe to help with this situation." Her tone carries no surprise or disappointment. "He sends his regards."

Of course, he does. I wonder if he's with another woman, creating another family drama. It wouldn't surprise me if he returned with a new sibling or twelve in tow. The thought of his benign neglect doesn't hurt like it used to. Maybe because I now know the truth. Davis Devine might be the smiling face of our family's power, but Astrid has always been its spine.

I want to ask her why she stays married to my father, but I won't. Those fleeting glimpses of affection between them hardly seem more than an old habit. Once, when I tried to broach the subject, she told me, *"Life is not meant to be easy. It is meant to be lived."*

The doors open to reveal Costin's gothic home. The air feels weighted with anticipation. It's tomb-quiet, with soft lighting casting long shadows across the cold mausoleum-esque stone. A servant appears as if he's been waiting in the shadows for just such a moment, bowing deeply—to Astrid, not to me, despite my being Costin's... whatever I am. There is something familiar about him. I'd seen him being fed upon through a cracked door. His clothes are perfectly pressed, and I notice all the usual feeding marks are covered. The vampires knew we were coming.

"Lady Astrid." The man's voice carries genuine reverence. "Lord Constantine awaits in the library."

"I know the way." Astrid doesn't break stride as she leads us through corridors I didn't know existed. Of course, she knows his home's layout. She probably knew him before I was born, back when the supernatural world was even more of a boys' club than it is now. Though, to be fair, I've spent most of my time in his bedroom.

We pass under arched doorways and between towering bookcases that disappear into the darkness above. The timeworn volumes look like they would hold many secrets, bound in materials I don't want to identify. Firelight flickers from ornate sconces, making the shadows dance across the stone. Everything in Costin's home is carefully curated to remind visitors of his age and power, from the medieval weapons mounted on walls to centuries-old tapestries.

I'd be lying if I said I wasn't more than a little intimidated by all of it.

We pass by several servants who all stop to hold still as Astrid passes. She keeps her head up high. I think of all the meetings where men like Francis Freemont and my father dominate conversations while their wives sit silent and decorative.

Yet here's Astrid, commanding respect without raising her voice, solving problems while her husband chases his latest distraction. The supernatural world might pretend to honor tradition, but the real power waits quietly and knows when to strike.

"Remember, you are a Devine," Astrid says as if reminding me to be strong.

Doors are pulled open at our approach, releasing a rush of cool air to greet us as we enter. The library stretches two stories high, its walls lined with books. A massive fireplace dominates one wall, its carved mantle depicting a hellish battle. I see a pile of bodies carved in great detail as if they have been dropped from the mantel above.

The firelight outlines a leather wingback chair positioned near the hearth. Movement catches my eye as Costin rises from it. I find it odd that his clothing choice matches Astrid's. He's dressed impeccably in black slacks and a blood-red shirt. The firelight casts over his features, making him look more like a statue than a man.

"Lady Astrid, welcome. To what do I owe the pleasure?" he asks, though his eyes fix on me. His expression is neutral, but I see tension in his shoulders.

"Lord Constantine." Astrid moves to sit in a chair next to his without waiting for an invitation. The firelight plays across her stern features. I know that look. I've been the recipient of that look.

I look around before slowly going to a smaller chair placed against the wall. I reach for it to carry it over when Costin suddenly takes it from me. He places it next to his chair before resuming his seat.

"It's time to return what you took from my daughter," Astrid states.

The word daughter sounds intimately weird coming from her.

Costin grins. "I've taken nothing that wasn't freely given."

His gaze drops to my neck, where his marks are hidden beneath makeup. I automatically lift my hand to cover my neck. Draakmar's connection stirs within the amulet. The dragon feels restless.

"She means the memories you took from me," I explain before Astrid can respond. I move closer to the fire, letting its warmth chase away the chill of the underground, and slowly sit down next to him. "The ones you erased. I want them back. All of them."

"No." His expression doesn't change, but something swirls within his gaze.

No? Just no? I'm not sure what to say to that. There's no denial or reasoning. Just... no.

Astrid looks at me expectantly, like this is a learning opportunity.

MICHELLE M. PILLOW

"That's not your choice to make," I say.

"Some memories are better left buried," he counters. His fingers trace the arm of his chair as if examining the leather.

I open my mouth to counter, but Astrid cuts me off.

"That is not for you to decide," Astrid says, her tone holding just enough chill to be a threat. She crosses her ankles and adjusts her position to face him more directly. The firelight catches the diamond on her wedding ring, sending rainbow prisms dancing across the wall. They're out of place in the darker room. "This is a Devine matter and a Devine decision. It is only out of respect for my late father-in-law and his affection for you that I am giving you a chance to mend this affront. The Freemonts are making moves against us. Whatever you buried about them, we need to know. You need to tell me."

"I—" I try to interject. This is a strange argument. Neither side is yelling, and yet I feel like they should be.

"With all due respect, Lady Astrid," Costin's eyes catch a glint of fire, and his voice sharpens with a dangerous edge, "you don't understand what's at stake. This is not a Devine problem, not exclusively." His fingers stop their tracing and curl into a fist. "You have no right to come into my home and make demands of me."

"I—" I try to say again.

"You have no right to steal from my family," Astrid counters. "Those memories belong to us."

"I think—"

"You will return them," Astrid continues.

Every time I open my mouth, it feels like they talk over me. Ugh, what am I? Five? I'm tired of feeling like a little kid waiting for the adults' attention. They aren't even pretending to include me in the conversation. I hate when they act like I'm not in the same room.

Costin's expression is controlled like a predator waiting to pounce if forced. I see the tension rippling through him. I also know that look on my mother's face. They might not be screaming and flailing their arms, but a fight is brewing.

"I made a choice to protect—" Costin begins.

"To protect me?" I interrupt loudly, carrying over their quiet tones as I force them to listen.

They both look at me in surprise.

The amulet feels warm against my skin, a constant reminder of its presence. I lean toward them and direct my attention to Costin. "Like you protected me when you let the wolves take Paul in my place?"

His jaw tightens, and a muscle ticks beneath his skin. "I didn't know they would come for you regardless."

I can see he doesn't like the miscalculation being pointed out to him, especially not in front of Astrid. But I'm tired of tiptoeing around supernatural egos. Paul and Diana do not have much time left. We need to figure out what the wolves are planning. I need to understand what blood and moonlight means.

Astrid removes her scarf and drapes it over her chair's arm with deliberate precision. The unhurried movements show confidence but also contemplation like she's buying time to gather her thoughts.

"You've been watching over her since she was a child." Astrid's gaze drifts to the battle scene carved on the mantle, and she sighs. "I am not here to fight you. You've been a family friend for a long time. We have not forgotten that."

I stand and move so they are forced to look up at me. My hands shake, and my voice is rough as I say, "Stop treating me like a mere mortal. I tamed a dragon and stopped the apocalypse. I survived the labyrinth. I have proven myself capable of handling far more than any of you ever expected."

"This is different," Costin answers. "You are not ready for this war."

"I'm already in it," I snap.

"None of us are ready for this war," he continues, ignoring my anger.

"War?" Astrid's eyebrow arches at Costin. She smooths invisible wrinkles from her slacks.

There are few things more annoying than being pissed off and having the targets of your irritation staring at you like they're calm and rational. I want to scream in their faces and shake them into listening.

"I've been trying to stop it," Costin answers. "The fewer people looking, the better my chance of discovering what's happening. I wasn't sure who I could trust."

"Stop it! Stop it! Stop it!" I cry, waving my hands like a lunatic. The amulet heats. Draakmar is all for unleashing my anger. "I'm right here. Tell me!"

Costin's hands grip the arms of his chair, his knuckles turning white as if he might rip them from the seat. Firelight makes his skin look almost translucent as veins rise along his temples and snake down his cheeks.

"I need to protect you," he whispers, looking up at me. I see desperation dancing with rage. "It was the only way."

"The Freemonts threatened her?" Astrid clarifies.

Costin hesitates before slowly nodding once.

"Whatever happened at the shipping yard is clearly about more than the Freemonts," she concludes. "It's much bigger. Who else do you suspect is involved?"

Costin doesn't move as he stares at me. I see he's torn and trying to control himself. Then, blinking slowly, he looks at the floor next to my feet.

"Elizabeth has been plotting against me for as long as I can remember, since before we were turned. She's rash and has no power with the vampire council. They've condemned her methods. I worry what they would do if they discovered the lines she's willing to cross." His expression darkens with something that looks like guilt. "Even if she managed to kill me, they would never let her have my throne." His eyes dart to me, and then Astrid with a wry smile. "She's a woman, after all, and they are ancient men."

Fucking misogyny. I don't have the energy to rant against the supernatural patriarchy right now. But it's freaking annoying.

"It seems she's found another way to unseat not only me but the council of elders. The Freemonts provided her with the resources and connections. The werewolves were her means." His chair scrapes against the floor, the sound harsh in the library's quiet as he stands. He turns his back to me and tilts his head to stare at the ceiling. "None of them expected Tamara to be at the shipping yards in the middle of the night."

"I worked the night shift," I say. "My parents thought it would be safer with less supernatural traffic in the offices."

I see the ghost of a smile threaten his mouth, but he doesn't look happy. "So you told me."

I don't remember telling him that.

"If you had remembered what you saw..." He presses his lips together and finally returns his gaze to mine.

"Your sister would have killed her," Astrid finishes. She doesn't sound surprised.

"Not just Elizabeth." His eyes flash crimson. I'm beginning to recognize the subtle changes in his moods. Before, I thought his monstrous characteristics were simply to incite fear, but they're just micro expressions revealing so much more when one knows how to read them. "The Freemonts, the wolves, their allies. I made her forget to keep her alive."

"I don't need protection." I quiet my tone and move toward him. Pleading, I add, "I need truth, Costin. I need to trust you."

I see real emotion crack through his careful control. He reaches for me but stops short of touching my face. "Everything I've done has been to protect you."

I ignore the fact Astrid is watching us. "You say you want me to choose you, but how can I when you won't let me make my own choices? When you hide parts of my life from me?"

His expression softens slightly. He touches my face. "Tamara..."

"Tell me," I whisper, mimicking his touch. I stroke his cool cheek. "Let me fight beside you."

"I can't tell you what I don't know. There was no time for me to see everything before I suppressed them. I don't know everything that happened that night."

"Then give me back the memories you have stolen."

"It will hurt," he warns.

"Then let them hurt. Let me choose what risks to take." I keep my hand against him. "Let me decide what I can handle."

"The girl has dragon fire in her veins now." Astrid's voice cuts through our private moment like a blade. She hasn't moved from her chair, but her presence fills the room. "Whatever you're protecting her from, she's faced worse. Show her."

"Constantine, please." I touch the amulet. "I'm protected now. They can't kill me."

"Death comes in many forms, and the stone can't stop them all," he whispers, and I see the war in his eyes. The need to protect me battles with his desire to trust. His gaze lingers on the amulet before trailing up to my face. Finally, he nods. "If I do this, there's no going back. It won't be like the last memory with Robert in the Devine library. That memory I carried. This one I suppressed. Do you understand the difference? I can't stop the pain once it starts. What you'll remember will change things."

I catch his wrist as he tries to pull away, stopping him. I sense him trembling slightly. "Everything's already changing."

"You have to take off the amulet," he warns. "Draakmar can't protect you from this part. His magic will interfere."

The amulet flares hot against my chest, warning me not to do it.

I hesitate before nodding. "I need to know."

I lift the necklace over my head and push it into my jeans pocket.

Costin's thumb traces my lower lip, and I feel the familiar pull of his power. The firelight dims, causing shadows to gather around us. Books rattle on the shelves, the pages noisily trying to escape as if desperate to be read. I glance up at them. They must be reacting to the pull of his magic.

"As you wish." He leans to kiss me softly. Blood trickles out of my nose. Shadows rush over me, bringing with them an intense agony.

Pain shoots through me from his mouth, exploding inside my head like someone is beating the back of my skull with a hammer. The taste of copper floods my mouth, mixing with his kiss. I try to cry out for him to stop, but the sound catches in my throat. I can't run from it or fight back. The magic holds me trapped between memory and reality. The blood spills faster from my nose, hot against my lips.

I hear Astrid's voice as if from the bottom of a well. "Be careful. If you kill her by bringing this memory back, Constantine, there won't be anywhere in this world you can hide from me."

My ears pop like balloons bursting underwater, taking with it all external noise. Blood runs from my ears down my neck, soaking into my cardigan. The library blurs and fragments. Books appear to be falling like stone walls crumbling into darkness. I feel my legs give out, the muscles turning to jelly. Costin's hands keep me propped up even as my arms fall limp at my sides.

And then, all I register is the shipping yard's smell of salt water and diesel fuel. The darkness and pain pull me into the memory of that forgotten night.

SEVENTEEN

Devine Shipping Offices, Nine Years Ago...

The night air carries the scent of salt and diesel as I walk along the edge of Red Hook, Brooklyn. The supernatural port is a far cry from Manhattan, where my family keeps a penthouse, though I've heard worry of gentrification cleaning up the neighborhood. My parents never let Conrad and I come here as kids. They said it was too dangerous for mortals. I think they still believe that, as it took a lot of convincing to give me this job at my father's shipping company.

To human eyes, this stretch of waterfront is a study in urban decay where abandoned warehouses loom against the dark sky, their broken windows like empty eye sockets warning people to stay away. Chain link fences topped with razor wire warn trespassers to keep out of the crumbling docks. That doesn't stop the occasional vagrant from trying to sneak in. They never make it far. I've been told there are rumors amongst the homeless populations that a serial killer takes victims here or that there are monsters or ghosts. One of those I know to be true. I suspect two.

Hell, maybe all three. I mean, it's possible we have a haunting.

I rub my arms and glance around to make sure I'm not being followed.

Even the police don't look too closely when patrolling. Their eyes slide right past, part courtesy of old magic worked into the very foundations of this place, part my family's generous contributions to their various funds. Bribes is too dirty of a word for fine society, but that's what they are. They're bribes. Money can hide a lot of secrets.

I press my palm against the scanner hidden in a graffiti-covered wall. It's a combination of biometrics and magic. The glamour ripples to let me pass. I step inside to reveal the true face of Devine Shipping's supernatural port. Merfolk security guards patrol the underwater perimeter, their powerful tails leaving phosphorescent trails in the dark water. Enchanted chains hang between reinforced pylons, clinking soft warning songs when anything unauthorized approaches. If that doesn't work, they attack like vines, entwining and strangling anything that tries to pass.

We don't talk about the dead gnome worker found hanging one morning. I didn't see much, but his little hand was still clutching a beer bottle when they took him away.

Above me, gargoyles perch on the warehouse corners. I never see them move. I'm told they're not just decorative stones but rather living guardians with claws and eyes that track movement. I'm not worried about them. I'm used to being around enchanted and dangerous things.

The above-water dock stretches into the harbor, its wooden planks inscribed with runic symbols that glow a faint blue under my feet. I know the ones to step over as they send an uncomfortable tingle up my leg when I press against them.

Massive cargo ships float at their berths, though at least half are glamours hiding supernatural vessels beneath. Supposedly, some of the older artifacts fare better inside Viking longships and pirate sloops rather than a metal haul. The way I understand it, this has something to do with natural wood instead of high-tensile steel and the imprint of past events giving them power. I suppose any ship that survived since the Medieval period and still floats has to have some kind of ancient power infused into it. Then there are those creatures that must be contained with iron hulls, like the 19th-century warships. I once saw the manifest for the iron warship was a single fairy.

I had to learn all this when I took the job. Shipping manifests for the containers cannot be altered, and their vessels are not interchangeable, no matter how much logistical sense it makes.

"We're not a human shipping company," my father reiterated repeatedly.

To my right, an underwater loading bay opens in the pier. The sound of flowing water erases all else for a brief moment. I watch as the current settles. A mermaid surfaces, her webbed hands clutching manifests in waterproof cases as she crawls on the dock. Merfolk look nothing like they're portrayed on television... well, okay, that's not true. Some horror movies come close. She nods as she passes, her gills flickering in the security lights.

I scan my badge at three more checkpoints before finally reaching the office building. Each floor serves a different supernatural shipping need. There are pixie-sized mail rooms for internal communications, reinforced receiving areas for beastly cargo, temperature-controlled storage for sensitive, magical items, holding tanks beneath the water, and a deep shaft under armed guard that drops into the earth. I don't ask what goes down into the pit.

My tiny office is on the third floor, overlooking

the water. It's nothing special. There is a desk, computer, filing cabinets, and a coffee maker that's seen better days. But it's mine, and I'm kind of proud of the fact.

The fluorescent lights flicker to life as I enter, casting harsh shadows. I hang my coat on the rack, settling into the night shift routine. Out of habit, I look out through the wire-reinforced windows to the water. The view helps pass the long nights. I watch the play of moonlight on the water and the graceful arcs of merfolk diving between ships. The sound of waves mingles with distant foghorns and the occasional splash of merfolk surfacing to check sensors. A strange glow emanates from some containers, but I've learned not to look too closely at those. It's the boxes that don't have visual warnings that scare me the most.

I start a pot of coffee and get ready to settle in. The shipping office feels different at night. I like the late shift. It's calmer, quiet.

Yes, my father owns everything around me, and he gave me this job—an entry-level position, the bottom of the corporate ladder, supernatural nepotism at its finest. But, hey, it's a start. For once in my life, I'm not just the mortal Devine daughter who needs protecting. I'm employee number 38655, a shipping clerk on the night shift. Knowing about the supernatural world makes me qualified to be here, or at least that's what I tell myself. There are days I'm way over my head.

I need this to work. I need to prove I can take care of myself.

During the day, this place bustles with supernatural energy. There are merfolk negotiating passage through their territories, pixies delivering internal mail between departments, and even the occasional dragon representative discussing Norwegian air space regulations. But at night, when I'm alone entering manifests into the system, I can pretend it's just a regular office. Just me, a computer, and endless shipping records that need to be digitized.

I boot up the ancient machine and pull up the current manifests while my coffee brews. The irony is not lost that for all my family's magic and money, I'm staring at a green screen, first generation, older than me piece-of-shit computer. The shipping world loves its paperwork, supernatural or not, and every item needs documentation. I have filing cabinets full of special permits for dragon-flame forged metals, environmental impact studies for merfolk cargo routes, quarantine certificates for magical creatures, and wizard council approval forms. My security clearance is nonexistent, which means I can only read the manifests of the more mundane cargo—art, antiquities, and specialty items that need to cross between human and supernatural territories.

A massive shadow glides past my window. One of the guards is doing the rounds. Its wings scrape softly against the building's edge. I've started leaving snacks out, though I'm not supposed to. They're security, not pets, but I swear the harpies check on me more often since I started sharing my candy stash.

My coffee mug, proudly declaring "Devine International Shipping," sits on a coaster beside my keyboard. A small protection charm hangs from my lamp. It was a gift from the office pixies after I helped them reorganize their mail room. My filing cabinet is plastered with notes in multiple languages, including Atlantish, which looks like water spots. It's not much, but it's mine.

Wait, why is my coffee mug on my desk? I always put it away before I leave. I reach to pick it up and notice a chip on the rim. My arm brushes the computer, and it feels warm.

Someone was in my office.

I take stock of my surroundings and find that the stack of finished manifests in the basket is misaligned. I frown, grab the stack, and begin flipping through it. I have my own system to remember where I left off the night before. This isn't it.

Pulling out a form that's not where it should be, I frown and take it to the computer to check it. This manifest doesn't make sense. Container FMNT-666 lists art supplies, paintings, designer clothing, cigar crates, and the usual Freemont family imports. But the weight is wrong. Way wrong. And someone altered the order from a regular cargo ship to piggy-backing on an ironclad.

The cargo hasn't been cleared from the ship yet. There is no way the form belongs in the done bin. I pull the original documents from my filing cabinet to compare against what's in the system. According to the record, FMNT-666 is still two days out in the middle of the Atlantic, even though the ironclad just docked.

My stomach drops.

That absolutely cannot happen.

Shit. I'm screwed. This is a big fuck up.

Three months into my attempt at independence and I've stumbled onto what looks like fraud. If I report it, I'll probably be fired. If I don't report it, I'll definitely be fired when someone finds out. So much for proving I can make it on my own.

And why did it have to be the Freemonts? They're family frenemies. No part of me thinks they'll be understanding.

Shit. Shit. Shit.

"Think, Tamara, think," I whisper, my hands shaking. Who could bypass the shipping yard security? No one will believe I didn't have something to do with this.

A splash outside draws my attention. One of the merfolk guards is gesturing urgently at the water. Others surface, their webbed hands making quick signals I'm not trained to understand. The dock runes flare a bright yellow.

This is worse than I thought. There is no time to think.

The harpies react first, launching from their lookouts with screeching sounds that set my teeth on edge. They circle the water where the merfolk are gathered, their wings casting massive shadows in the security lights. One hovers near the windowsill, studying me before darting along the building.

Warning chains begin to clank. Their ungodly sound rises in pitch until my ears pop. On my computer screen, a warning message scrolls past in green, *"Unauthorized magic detected in shipping lane four. Multiple containment breaches detected. Security protocols engaging. Lockdown."*

I should do something. There's a procedure for everything here, but for the life of me, in my panic, I can't remember what it is, and I hesitate.

I stare at the manifest. Who could do this? The Freemonts are powerful enough to alter shipping records. What if they smuggled in something and set me up to be the fall guy? Or does someone else want this to look like my mistake? My heart is beating so fast that I feel like I might puke. I glue myself to the window, watching for a sign of what hell is being unleashed.

The merfolk disappear beneath the surface in perfect synchronization, leaving only ripples in their wake. The security lights along the dock flash red, reflecting off the water like blood. A large shadow swims under the ships and the dock runes spark like fireworks.

The lights in my office flicker and dim.

"That looks worrisome out there." Chester's sudden appearance makes me jump. He stands in the doorway, clearly overdressed for the shipping yard. This is the first time he's shown up here. None of the Freemonts come to pick up their containers.

This feels wrong in so many ways. His being here can't be a coincidence.

He comes inside, making the tiny office feel suddenly so much smaller.

The overhead lights go off, taking the computer screen with them as the power goes out. The security lights flash through the window, making Chester's shadow dance across my office wall.

His eyes glance down at the paperwork on my desk, and he sighs. "What's all this?"

"Your shipment is not due for a few days," I manage. I push the original manifest toward him, though I'm not sure why. Maybe because it's his family's shipment. Perhaps because I'm an idiot. All I can do is hope he knows nothing about the switch, and I can buy some time to figure out what to do.

He taps against his thigh like he's playing a piano. Blue magic twines his fingers before fading. It feels like a threat, but I may be overreacting.

Please let me be overreacting.

"Did someone call you to pick something up?" I step back from him and bump up against the filing cabinet. "Because it's not here."

He tilts his head, watching me. I see a kind of perverse pleasure in his eyes. Finally, he reaches for the manifest on my desk and picks it up. He then reaches for the altered manifest that was in my done bin.

"That's not what this says." He holds up the forged paper.

"The weight doesn't match the original," I say. "Someone changed a shipping order. I'm sure there is a reasonable explanation for—"

Magic flows from his fingers into the paper. Symbols emerge on the manifest in glowing script, and I make out the words *Sanguis et Lūnāria*.

I have no idea what it means.

The air presses down on me, and I find it hard to breathe. This room is too small, and the way he looks at me makes my skin crawl. If I scream, maybe a harpy will pluck me out of the window and get me out of here.

I doubt it.

I dare a glance at the window. The creature in the water moves closer to the dock. "What is happening out there?"

Chester moves too fast. The papers flutter to the floor as he darts at me. I scream in fright at the sudden attack. The harpies don't come to save me.

Chester's hand wraps around my throat, and I feel magic tingling against my skin like a heating stove. I struggle to get away but it's useless. The pain is getting worse by the second. If I don't push him off soon, I will surely sizzle into a pile of ash.

"What are you even doing here?" he asks. "It's the middle of the night."

"I work the night shift," I whisper, terrified by the way he's glaring at me. "Fewer supernaturals, and there's security. It's supposed to be safer."

Chester tilts back his head and laughs. "That is the stupidest thing I've ever heard."

My throat burns where he touches me. I'm going to be sick.

"Please, I don't know anything," I beg, hoping he'll determine I'm a waste of his time.

"I was hurt when you canceled our last date," he says, studying my face.

I know it's a lie. The date was an obligation arranged by our parents. "I'm... sorry?"

"You know they have big plans for us, don't

you?" he continues, his tone soft like he's not holding my neck. His smile reminds me of his father. It's the same entitled smirk Francis gets when bragging about his latest mistress at supernatural gatherings.

I try to look out the window at the water but can't turn my head. "Who?"

"Our parents." Chester grins. "The wedding is practically planned."

"Why?" I find the idea of marrying Chester utterly repulsive.

"Family alliances. Power. The usual reasons." He acts like I should be grateful to receive this information. In reality, I just want to push him out the window. I wonder if we're high enough to do any damage.

"I don't believe you. I'm just a human. Why would you want to marry me?" The pain of his touch makes it hard to sound brave.

"To secure my family's future." He tilts his head, and his smug look fades into confusion. The flashing red lights illuminate his expression. "They really didn't tell you?"

"I don't believe you," I repeat. My parents are a lot of things, but I don't think they'd engage me to someone without telling me.

Or is that just naïve?

I already know the answer. Duty comes before

love.

I've seen how Chester looks at me, just like he's doing now. It's why I've avoided him. To be completely cliched, I'd be nothing but another notch in his bedpost, and that thing has already been whittled down to toothpicks.

"Let's end this. Marry me tonight," he says, giving what he probably thinks is a charming smile. "Let's join our families."

He has to be joking. It's not funny. The idea of having a life like Mabel and Astrid, turning a blind eye while my husband screws other women... no thank you. I'd rather dive face-first into those murky waters out there than marry this tool.

The thought of danger in the water brings me back to reality.

"I can't play this game now," I try to push him back, and my eyes go to the phone on my desk. I have to call someone for help. "The shipping yard is under attack. I have to—"

"I figured that might be your answer." Chester cuts me off. There is no love lost in his expression. He appears more annoyed than anything.

"The security systems—" I try to explain rationally before he cuts me off again.

"Are doing exactly what they're supposed to." His hands glow brighter.

"Ches—"

"You shouldn't have come to work tonight." His grip tightens on my throat. "If the council finds out about tonight, they'll execute anyone who knows about this cargo. Even you, despite your family name."

"Ches..." I gurgle for breath as I claw at his choking hands, struggling to be free.

"The wolves aren't the only ones who can harness old magic. When the power shifts..." He gives a small laugh. "You know, never mind. I don't have time for the whole Bond villain speech. Sorry, Tamara, you should have said yes to me while you had the chance. Too late now."

The blue glow of his magic wars with the red security lights on his face. As his power intensifies, so does the burning on my neck. He presses closer. I feel his body brushing against mine. My position doesn't allow much leverage, but I still fight. I slap his arms and try to knee him in the groin. My blows only seem to fuel his attack. His gaze narrows as he focuses on his deadly task, but his eyes spark with pleasure. He likes it.

My eyes roll in my head, and my vision blurs. A shadow appears to detach from the wall behind him. The temperature in my office drops so fast Chester's breath fogs against my face. Costin materializes behind him, and my initial relief quickly turns to fear. What's he doing here?

"Release her," Costin commands. He's one who is used to being obeyed.

When Chester doesn't comply, Costin grabs his arm and jerks him back. Chester flies through the air and hits the wall.

My lungs feel as if they're on fire. I drag in a ragged, loud breath, holding my bruised throat with protective hands. I feel the hot amulet dislodge from my skin, where the pendant pressed into my flesh. So much for my grandfather's claim of its protection. A minute more and I would have been dead at Chester's hand.

"This doesn't concern you, vampire." Chester's voice shakes.

I turn from them, still gasping as I try to make my way along the window to a corner. There aren't many places to escape to in the tiny office. Below, I see the water has gone completely black as if something's swallowing all of the light. The merfolk are gone. Most of the runes on the dock have burned out. Suddenly, the water churns in the red light, and something massive rises to the surface. I can't quite make them out, but the container appears covered in large symbols that match the writing on the manifest.

"What are you trying to smuggle in?" Costin demands, his attention fully on his prey.

"What are you doing here?" Chester demands. "This doesn't concern you."

I pass the window and manage to huddle in the corner of the room, hoping they forget about me.

"What is in that container? What are the were-wolves planning?" Costin growls, the demon in his voice. His eyes churn with crimson, and his face distorts into that of a monster. Bared fangs threaten Chester, who throws a barrage of fireballs at the vampire. Costin dodges most of them but catches a couple on the forearm. He hisses in pain.

"You can't do this," Chester warns. "You know what will happen if you kill me. The council—"

Costin moves faster than my gaze. Before I realize where he is, he has Chester by the throat. "Will never find your body."

"Kill me, and they'll give Elizabeth your power," Chester says, squirming in fear. "The Freemonts are too powerful. Even for you, bloodsucker."

I'm surprised when that threat seems to work. He tosses Chester at the door. The man stumbles, backing away as he keeps his eyes on his enemy.

"That shipment is going to be lost at sea. I'll take care of the rest." Costin's fangs catch the red light, and I can't stop staring at them. The creature terri-fies me. In return, I barely seem to register with him. "And you're going to let it happen."

"She's seen too much. The Alpha will never let

her live," Chester warns. He raises his hands, magic gathering. "Let me take care of her. No one has to know we were here."

Suddenly, the lights flicker back on. Chester's relief is almost palpable, and he grins. "You're too late. We have it." His gaze flickers to me, and he winks. "Kill her, or the others will."

I clutch my neck. Not only is it bruised and sore, but now I have a full-blown vampire alone with me in the room, and he looks mean enough to feed.

Chester flees. I hear his feet running down the hall toward the elevators. I should be grateful, but all I can think about is how this will probably cost me my life.

"Please," I mouth, shaking my head as I hold my neck to hide my arteries. I know it's useless. If he wants me, he'll get me. "No, no, please, no."

Costin seems torn between following Chester and looking at me. Finally, he comes toward me, and I lift my hands, cowering. Everything inside me shakes.

Pale fingers come at me. I flinch as they wrap my arm. I have no choice as he lifts me to stand before him.

His eyes take in my expression, and slowly, the worst part of the monster fades. "What was in the container?"

"Art supplies? Cigars?" I manage.

Costin's brow furrows in displeasure. His eyes swirl, and I feel myself being compelled to answer.

"I don't know," I whisper. "I swear. The weight doesn't match the original manifest. The paperwork's been forged. I didn't do—"

"Do you know anything useful?" He has that same patronizing tone I get from my family. I hate it. "Tell me."

"Chester's a creep who follows his father's example with women. I'm not about to become another Mabel Freemont, pretending I don't know about my husband's mistresses." I don't mean to say it, but it's the truth. The words feel forced out of me. "I don't want to marry Chester Freemont. I'd rather you eat me."

His lip twitches up at the corner. Light reflects in his eyes, making him look human... well, almost. "Don't tempt me."

I should be scared, but there is something a little sexual in the way he says it. This is not a side of the vampire I remember seeing as a child.

The crimson swims harder, and his gaze pulls me into his will. "Do you have any idea what you've stumbled into?"

I shake my head, unable to look away from him. In the distance, I hear a werewolf howl. Costin tenses as if torn on what he should do next.

"Did you see anything about the shipment that

can be of use to me?" he demands, more specific in his questioning this time.

"Magical words. Um," I try to remember what showed when Chester's magic infused the documents. "Something like...?" I shake my head. "I can't remember."

I feel like claws are reaching into my brain and forcing memories out. I try to pull away but can't.

"What was it?" he asks as if trying desperately to unbury the thought.

"I don't know. I don't speak the old languages." I'm too scared and sore to focus. "There were so many strange symbols."

I see confusion passing his gaze. "Try to remember. It's important."

"I don't know," I repeat, sounding lethargic, even to my own ears. "What does all this mean?"

"It means the Freemonts are working with the Alpha to traffic in magic that could reshape the supernatural world. This magic is powerful enough and scary enough that it could get everyone involved killed just for knowing about it. And I have no clue what it is or how to stop it."

"Are you going to eat me now?" I can't take my eyes off him. Frankly, if he says yes, I'll probably lean my head to the side and let him. I have no willpower left to resist.

"Is that an invitation?" He grins.

How can he smile at a time like this?

Before I can answer, he adds, "Sorry, castoff, not tonight. Your grandfather asked me to watch over you. I'm going to keep that promise."

Costin cups my face, and his touch feels different than usual. The way his fingers caress my cheek is less protector and more... My mind starts to drift. ... more something that makes my pulse quicken despite my fear.

"I should call my father. We need to report—"

"Sorry, castoff, but you can't remember this night. Some secrets are better left buried in the ocean."

"No, wait—"

But his eyes are already swirling with power. "Sleep now. Forget..."

The moment starts to blur and fade. His expression is neither triumphant nor controlling but sad. His face begins to disappear into the darkness as my consciousness slips away.

"Sleep now," his voice whispers. "Sleep."

CHAPTER
EIGHTEEN

Consciousness returns like steady waves lapping against a shore, each one bringing more sensations than the last. I want them to stop. I don't want to leave oblivion. My body aches from being thrown against the filing cabinet and choked. I feel the bruises forming along my back and ribs. The taste of blood lingers in my mouth. It hurts to breathe. Not only because I suspect my ribs might be broken, but my throat is strangled and raw. My head throbs with every heartbeat, a racking pain so deep I dread the next pulse.

"...couldn't stop Elizabeth then, and now she's allied with the wolves." Costin's voice drifts through the fog. He sounds exhausted.

What's he doing here?

He continues, "The shipping manifest showed—"

"You should have come to us immediately." Astrid's tone is hard despite its quietness. "Instead, you erased her memory and let my family continue working with the Freemonts."

I'm lying on something softer than the floor. A couch, maybe? The leather feels stiff against my fevered skin and I'm sticking to it. My muscles protest as I try to move, so I don't.

"I made a choice," Costin says. "If she remembered what she saw that night, Elizabeth and the Freemonts would have killed her and made sure the body was never found. I cut a deal with Chester. With her memory gone, there was no threat. We made it look like the shipment was lost at sea. I did what I had to do to save her life."

"You should have told us," Astrid answers.

"I told George. He agreed with me. Tamara needed protection. She was already in danger with the amulet's prophecy."

"And you both should have told *me*." Astrid's irritation is growing.

"Because you and I are so close?" Costin almost sounds mocking. "You're a magic. As are the Freemonts. Your families are friends. They came to your country estate as much as I did. Why would I trust you with this if George didn't?"

"We are hardly friends," Astrid denies. "It's easier to keep an eye on them if they're close. Besides, Mabel leveraged that damned lost shipping container for those invitations. The woman is insufferable. I wish I had lost her at the bottom of the ocean."

"I'm trusting you now."

"What's changed?" Astrid asks.

"Everything." His voice drops. "I can't keep lying to her. Draakmar's influence is pushing the memory fragments to the surface. There are parts from that night that I don't even know, like what happened before I arrived and what she discovered in those records. I didn't have time to watch what I was suppressing when I buried the memory. The wolves had the container and were already leaving the shipping yard. I tried to go after them, but I was too late. I spent months trying to figure out where they took it. Whatever was in that shipping container disappeared. We need Tamara's full account."

Hearing my name, I manage to blink open my eyes. The ceiling ripples above me. We're no longer in the library but in what looks like an office and sitting room. A large metal shield hangs on the wall behind a desk. It's not as dark here, but the candlelight still makes the shadows dance. When I try to peel myself off the leather, the room spins dangerously.

"Careful." Costin appears beside me, his hand steadying my shoulder. "You're all right. I'm here."

I try to answer, but I croak.

"I'm here too," Astrid appears behind him. She tries to push him aside to touch me. Costin doesn't relinquish his place.

I want to tell them this isn't a competition as I witness the stubborn set to both of their jaws.

"The transition back can be disorienting," Costin says.

That's an understatement.

I try to speak again and only grunt. I reach for my neck. The amulet is there. My skin feels tight under my ears and down my throat. I feel dried blood.

My throat is raw, like I really did just face Chester at the shipping yard instead of nine years ago. I again attempt to sit up, and Costin automatically helps me. He sits next to me, almost too close to my sore body.

"How long?" My voice comes out rough. I look down. My cardigan is stiff with dried blood. I hold my neck. "My throat..."

"A few hours." Astrid stands over me, her posture rigid. "You've been screaming."

"Do you know who we are?" Costin asks.

I realize they are watching to see if the experience has altered me. Both of them stay very still, waiting for my answer.

I can't resist. I furrow my brow and look confused. "Castoffs?"

Astrid's eyes widen, and she gives a soft gasp. I see magic flare against her fingers.

Costin arches a brow. "Very amusing."

"Tamara!" Astrid scolds as she catches on a second later. The magic dissipates. "That is not funny, young lady."

I start to laugh, but it hurts. I groan instead. "Oh, ow."

Astrid lifts a goblet toward me. "Drink this."

"I'm not tired." I refuse to take it.

"It's not that. It'll help with the pain," Astrid insists.

My ribs hurt when I breathe too deep, and the promise of relief is too much to pass up. I take the goblet.

"Drink," my mother orders, gesturing her hand as if to tip the goblet toward me.

My hand lifts it to my lips. The bitter liquid burns as I swallow, but it instantly lessens the pain.

"What did you see?" she asks when I lower the goblet. "Tell us everything. In detail."

When I speak, my voice is better. I tell them everything, every detail. It's as clear as if it just happened.

"That bastard," Astrid mutters under her breath when I mention Chester's attack. Then, to Costin, she said, "You should have lost him at the bottom of the ocean."

"I still might," Costin adds.

"When I woke up at my desk the next morning, I didn't remember any of it. I didn't even remember coming in to work the night before." I think back to that following morning. Everyone had been so disappointed in me, and the shame of it had followed me for years. My father never gave me another chance. "I thought I fell asleep on the job. Mabel was there yelling about a lost shipment. Since I was the shipping clerk, everyone assumed I mis-keyed the entry and sent the shipment to the bottom of the Atlantic."

At the time, I knew nothing about the container belonging to the Freemonts, and the event was significant enough to get me instantly fired. I remember feeling lucky they didn't think I lost it on purpose. The exact contents of the shipment had been unknown, and Mabel never hinted at what was so important, but I assumed it was likely something highly valuable or magical.

"When I think of how many years and how much money has been put into paying the merfolk and other sea creatures to search the ocean floor for it..." Astrid purses her lips together and shakes her head.

"I'll reimburse you," Costin dismisses.

"It's the principle, not the money," Astrid quips.

"The container," I interrupt as I try to focus through the lingering pain and bring them back to what's important. "It wasn't on the right ship. They changed the manifest to put it on an ironclad. It arrived earlier."

Costin's hands curl into fists.

"The magic must be old and powerful if they needed an ironclad to contain its power for the journey," Astrid reasons.

"Did anyone ever figure out what was really in it?" I ask.

Costin and Astrid exchange a look that makes my stomach clench.

"Wait." I sit up straighter despite my protesting muscles. I feel like the answer is right in front of us. "I think I might know what they were smuggling."

My hands start to shake at the realization. They both stare at me, eagerly waiting for me to explain.

"Well?" Astrid demands.

"In Thane's sanctuary, I saw an altar with words carved into it. Blood and moonlight. I told you that, Costin. Remember?"

Costin frowns in disappointment. "That means nothing. In vampire and werewolf traditions, blood represents sustenance and familial bonds. It's how we are born into our new life. While the moon governs our existence as our powers are tied to the lunar cycles."

"No, it has to mean something," I insist. I feel so sure about this. "You weren't there. Thane acted like it was important."

"I'm sure he did. Thane's beliefs tend to lean toward mysticism," Astrid almost seems dismissive. I half expect her to pat me on the head and call me a cute, simple human girl. "The altar is probably some sex prop he uses to seduce women."

The potion she gave me is making my stomach tingle, like the magic is attacking the pain in my ribs. I take a deeper breath. It's distracting me from what I'm trying to say.

"Blood has long been tied to both birth and death, while the moon waxes and wanes, symbolizing renewal and decay," Costin says. "Both could be said to represent duality—life and death, light and dark, creation and destruction."

"Right, a sacred covenant," Astrid inserts. "For those who rule the shadows.

"Alchemists saw the moon as a mediator between worlds," Costin adds, "and blood as the vital essence connecting the mortal to the divine. People put faith in many things. None of that helps us."

"Just wait..." I struggle to find the words to politely tell them to stop talking while I try to think.

"I'm sorry, Tamara. He's right," Astrid agrees. "Vampires and wolves saying 'blood and moonlight' is as generic as humans saying 'heart and soul.' They're bound to the blood and moon like humans are bound to the physical—*their hearts*—and the metaphysical—*their souls*."

"Would you just listen?" I order, pressing my hand to my temple. I gently rub to ease the headache behind my eye. They keep talking over me. It's annoying. "Both of you. Just give me a minute."

They stop talking and stare at me.

"I know it means something. Those same words appeared on Chester's manifest that night," I explain.

"Chester's manifest said blood and moonlight?" Costin looks to Astrid, who shrugs in return.

"Yes, but it wasn't English. It was another language, just like the altar." I attempt to say the ancient words. "*Sang... sang-something*?"

"*Sanguis et Lūnāria*?" Costin fills in.

"Yes," I nod. "Thane said it means blood and moonlight.

Costin goes completely still. "Are you sure?"

Even Astrid's perfect posture stiffens.

"Yes." My voice is weak as I feel waves of power.

"You saw the altar with those words?" Costin's voice carries a dangerous edge.

"Yes. When we had that audience with the Alpha, and Thane took me aside." I watch his expression darken. "We didn't exactly go into detail about... Well, I mean, you weren't exactly in a sharing mood yourself. Then Elizabeth and Mabel showed up. We left, and you were aggravating me. And then that memory came back from when I was sixteen, and you ripped out Robert's heart in our library."

"You killed Robert in our library?" Astrid demands in surprise. "Mabel's vampire lover? That's what happened to him?"

Costin scratches the back of his head. "I cleaned it up."

"We'll discuss that later," Astrid promises in annoyance as she takes a deep breath. "Tamara, describe this altar."

"It's twisted metal and stone." The idea of that room makes me shiver. "Thane has it in a circular chamber beneath a glass ceiling."

Costin stands. "I'll be right back."

I stand to protest, but he disappears in a blur.

Astrid moves to take his seat and pulls me back down. "Have another drink."

I obey, lifting the goblet to my mouth. When I swallow, I shake my head. "I can't believe they've been planning this for nine years. The ritual, the sacrifices..." My head spins as I try to connect it all. "Did they know what would happen to me? About Paul and Diana? That seems like so many pieces to fall into place. Chester wanted to kill me that night."

"I would assume they didn't expect you to become what you are." Astrid's gestures at my amulet. "They probably thought you were just a mortal who saw too much. They couldn't have known you'd be the dragon's chosen one."

"But I am just a *mortal*." The word tastes bitter. "Draakmar, the prophecy, all of it is borrowed power. The amulet's power."

"No." Costin suddenly reappears, holding a thick tome of a book. His hand finds mine. "You were never *just* anything, Tamara. Never to me."

He starts to pull me close, and my arm brushes up against the book. At the contact, Draakmar's consciousness slams into me, and the amulet flares with a warning. I jerk away from Costin. The dragon's frenzy floods my senses, and I can't understand why the creature is agitated. My vision blurs and turns red. Pain shoots through my skull, worse than the memory recovery. Blood trickles from my nose again.

"Tamara?" Costin reaches for me as the door bursts open.

"My lord!" A servant rushes in, terror plain on his face. "Werewolves in the foyer. They're trying to access the elevator."

Costin stiffens and turns his head sharply toward the door. "My sister is nearby. I feel her. Tell the men to seal the tunnel and then hide."

The servant runs to do as he's ordered.

Astrid's already moving, magic crackling around her hands as she snatches the book from Costin. "I'll protect this, and I'll handle the wolves. They won't expect magic." She sweeps toward the door, her heels clicking against the stone. "Keep Tamara safe."

I try to protest, but another wave of dragon worry rips through me. Through distorted vision, I watch Astrid disappear with the book, leaving Costin and me alone.

"The pain should pass," Costin says, reaching to steady me. "Just breathe—"

I hear stone scraping against stone. Movement flickers near the fireplace. A blurry figure materializes from the shadows, emerging from what must be one of the underground tunnels. Elizabeth steps into the flickering firelight, her biker leather-clad form a contrast to her brother's elegance. I blink rapidly, forcing my vision to clear. I can't see how she entered the room.

"What are you doing here?" Costin hardly sounds welcoming. He puts himself in front of me as if to shield me from her.

"Ah, brother dear, that hurts me," Elizabeth purrs. Her smile is razor sharp. "Aren't you happy to see me?"

Costin's body fills with tension.

Elizabeth holds up a finger and tilts her head to

the side as if listening to something in the distance. She gives a short laugh. "Oops, sounds like they sealed the tunnels to the underground city a little too late."

"You're not welcome here." He stays in front of me.

"Is that any way to greet family?" She moves further into the room, each step deliberate. Her gaze sweeps over the space, lingering on the blood-stained couch where I'd been lying. "Are we having snacks?"

"What do you want?" Costin's voice carries deadly calm.

Elizabeth leans to the side, and her attention fixates on me. She wiggles her fingers to wave. Her fangs extend as she takes a step closer. "Well, hello there, my little amuse-bouche."

I lean closer to Costin.

"Oh," Elizabeth wrinkles her nose. "What did you do to the poor thing? She looks like roadkill. Didn't our mother tell you not to play with your food? I honestly can't remember. It was so long ago."

"What. Do. You. Want?" Costin reiterates.

"You're especially testy today." Her predatory smile never falters, but it never reaches her cold eyes. "I'd have thought centuries would have mellowed you. If you don't want to share your treat, all you have to do is say so. Rude," she lifts her brows in mock affront, "but fine."

I grip Costin's arm as another wave of pain threatens. The amulet feels heavy against my chest, and I feel Draakmar begging to be unleashed.

"Actually," Elizabeth studies the back of her hand, "I came to deliver a message from Thane. Time's up. He wants to know if your toy has an answer to his offer. Her for Paul."

Elizabeth shows her fangs, the gesture practiced to instill fear. She's enjoying her sick game. Her eyes swirl with blood and power. I can tell she would like nothing more than to rip out my throat.

Elizabeth directs her gaze to me. "Though, maybe we should find you a bath first. All the dried blood might give the wolves ideas."

NINETEEN

"The answer is no," Costin says, grabbing my arm like he's going to lead me from the room.

"Do you always let him speak for you?" Elizabeth jibes. "I guess the rumors of your strength are just that... *rumors*."

"You heard him," I say. "No."

"If you knew my brother, I don't think you'd be so eager to be under his..." She gives me a once over, and it feels a little sexual in nature. It makes me uncomfortable. "...thumb if you knew how he really treats women."

"He treats me fine." Okay, so it's debatable, but a united front feels like the right call.

Her eyes move deliberately over me, and she laughs. "Yeah, so I see."

I self-consciously touch the blood under my ear.

"We're leaving. Try not to destroy anything before you go." Costin makes a move for the door.

Elizabeth's form blurs and shifts, her body dissolving into that of a bat. She darts with supernatural speed. One second, she's by the fireplace. The next, she's blocking the doorway to prevent us from leaving. Her wings beat as she hovers before us, and she lets loose a high-pitched screech.

Costin shoves me behind him toward the corner. "Stay back."

He launches himself at his sister, his own form shifting mid-leap into a larger, darker bat. They collide in the air, wings striking, bodies tumbling in violent circles as they tear at each other. The sounds they make are deafening—leather wings beating against stone walls, inhuman shrieks echoing over the room.

I watch them closely, sidestepping to stay out of the way when they somersault too close. I bump into the couch, but I don't care. I can't look away.

I scream as Elizabeth's bat form darts toward me before turning at the last second, leading Costin on an aerial chase around the room. I know she wants to hurt me, but the amulet's magic stops her. Costin pushes her toward the ground, smashing her into an end table so that the legs splinter into thick pieces. They fly so fast they're barely more than dark trails, crashing into the walls and ceiling with bone-crushing force.

They shift back into human form in mid-air. Elizabeth's heel catches Costin's jaw with a spinning kick that sends him crashing through his desk. She follows through with impossible speed, grabbing a broken table leg and driving it toward his chest. He catches it inches from his heart, using her momentum to flip her over his head so that she lands upside down against the wall above his desk.

"Stop this, Elizabeth," Costin growls, rage filling his tone with gravel. "Enough!"

Elizabeth falls to the floor, hands first, catching her weight before twisting to her feet to stand as if it's no great achievement. Decorations from the wall clatter around her. Rage pours out of her. "Enough? Remember when you arranged my marriage, brother? That is what I used to beg of Marcus. Enough. Enough. *Enough!* But it never was."

"I didn't know—" he tries to answer.

She picks up the metal shield and hurls it at him like a frisbee. When he deflects it, she's already moving, her supernatural speed blurring her figure as she continues her attack.

Costin blocks several strikes, but her last hit catches him in the ribs with a sickening crack. They grapple out of the open office door. I run to follow them, keeping them in my sight. They smash through a stone column, toppling it. Dust whirls from the ceiling.

"Liar!" She shifts into bat form, darting behind him before materializing to drive her knee into his spine. "I told you exactly what kind of monster he was. I wrote to you, telling you what he was doing to me."

Costin spins, transforming as he leaps into flight. His larger bat form catches her in its claws, dragging her up toward the ceiling. Elizabeth shifts back to human mid-flight, using the momentum to flip them both. They crash through another column, more stone crumbling around them.

I want to yell at them to stop, but this is a feud I have no authority over.

"He killed me," Elizabeth snarls, grabbing a chair and smashing it across Costin's back. "And you let him."

"And you killed me." Costin's voice carries genuine pain as he transforms again, swooping low across the room.

Elizabeth follows. Her smaller bat form is more agile as she chases him through the debris. They play a lethal game of cat and mouse, shifting between forms to attack and dodge. The ceiling cracks from their impacts. Blood rains down from both of them, staining the floor beneath their aerial battle.

What if Elizabeth kills him?

That very idea petrifies me.

I can't lose him.

I press myself against the wall as they tear past me back into the office. The hallway looks like a war zone—columns cracked, suits of armor scattered, decorations and blood everywhere. My head still throbs from the recovered memory, making it hard to think past my fear. I poke my head around the doorframe to watch without going back inside.

Elizabeth has materialized directly in front of Costin, and he shifts back to his human form. Her hand finds his throat, pinning him against the wall. A broken chair leg presses against his chest like a wooden stake, ready to end him.

"Elizabeth, don't," I beg. I rush into the room, looking for a weapon. I grab the heavy shield and use all my strength to strike her in the side and knock her away. It bounces off her, barely making a dent.

She snarls and leans harder into her brother. "I want to do to your pet what Marcus did to me. And I want you to watch."

I jump at her, intent on wrapping my arms around her neck to distract her enough to give Costin time to free himself. She swings her free arm, launching me across the room. It's only by the amulet's power that I don't break my bones against the stone wall. I drop to the floor, panting and sore.

"But I can't go against our mighty master, can I? It doesn't matter that I'm your sire and the eldest by vampire right. Only one of us was given actual power," she continues, still poised with her stake as if I'm not a concern. She tightens her grip, and her knuckles turn white as she drives the wood forward. "The council would never let a woman rule. Especially not a murdered wife who dared to kill her vampire husband."

Costin doesn't look at me. He could shift to escape, but something in his eyes tells me he won't. There's too much guilt there, too much history.

I need to do something, but my body is still weak. The amulet pulses, but I am no defense against vampiric strength even with it.

Elizabeth's head snaps toward me, her eyes blazing crimson. "Don't worry, dear. Once I finish with my brother, you'll get your turn. Unless..." Her smile turns cruel. "You'd like to make that trade with Thane now? Costin for you."

I can't answer. Why isn't Costin finishing her? Surely he can put up more of a fight.

"Or would you prefer to save Paul?" Elizabeth laughs.

I can't answer. The choice is impossible. Costin or Paul? It's like asking to choose between love and an ideal. Or would it be love and guilt? My feelings for Paul are confused. I had been so sure of them at one point and of the mortal, normal life he represents. But that old mantra circles around in my head. Knowing me might cost him everything—his parents, his daughter, his life.

Diana's face flashes in my mind, and I remember her trusting smile when she showed me her stuffed dog, Mr. Plop. How can I sentence a child to grow up without her father? She's everything I never had a chance to be—innocent, perfect. I fantasized about being her mother, a real mother, not like the two I have.

"Do you see how she hesitates?" Elizabeth mocks her brother, laughing. "That is how deep her love flows for you. She can't even choose saving you."

It's not true. I open my mouth to say the words but can't force them out. I can't do that to Paul and Diana.

The thought of losing Costin makes my chest ache in ways I can't explain. The amulet pulses against my skin as if Draakmar senses my turmoil and wants to help. The dragon has no answers, only that underlying fury ready to surge.

The truth is, I doubt Elizabeth will keep her word either way. She's toying with us. This is all a game to her.

Both vampires suddenly tilt their heads in unison, listening to something I can't hear. A smile curves Elizabeth's lips, but it's different than before. The change in her expression is subtle, almost intimate like she's sharing a private joke with someone far away.

"Well, that's my cue." She presses the stake harder against Costin's chest, drawing blood before stepping back. She drops the makeshift weapon on the floor. "This has been fun. We should play again sometime."

"Elizabeth," Costin warns. He lets her pull away and doesn't try to stop her.

"Alpha Thane sends his regards." The way she says his name carries weight like she's savoring the taste of it. "Now there is a man who knows how to protect what's his."

Costin's eyes narrow, and I detect the moment he recognizes something in his sister's tone. There's a familiarity there that seems to surprise even him.

"You and," his voice drops into disgust, "a *wolf?* No, Elizabeth, that's too low, even for you. Thane is—"

"He's what?" Elizabeth's bitter laugh cuts him off. "At least he understands what it's like to be looked down upon by other supernaturals, to be underestimated and ignored, to have everything taken away because of what you are."

Costin's lip curls in disgust. "The treaties exist for a reason. The last time wolves and vampires tried to align, they nearly exposed us all to the mortal world. Or have you forgotten the Blood Riots? There's a reason we keep to our territories."

"Oh yes, brother. The precious treaties." Elizabeth's voice drips acid. "Tell me, how many of those territory lines did you draw yourself? How many packs did you force into these urban wastelands while you claimed the prime hunting grounds? At least Thane doesn't pretend to be civilized while he takes what he wants."

"This can't just be about power," Costin denies. "As my sister, you have—"

"Nothing that is my due. The council, the vampires, the magics... They all believe they're so superior with their rules and hierarchies." Her eyes flash as she paces, each movement precise and deadly. "They have all these arbitrary rules about what magic can mix, about what creatures should remain separate. The treaties were written by old aristocratic males playing at civilization, brother. You may be content to play lord of your underground kingdom while bowing and scraping and licking the boots of those fossils who declare themselves your betters. Then there are the magics, like the Devines, who perch in their gilded sanctuaries, declaring themselves too pure to mix with lesser beings. But Thane sees through their pretense. These boundaries they've drawn, these rules they've made are nothing but chains forged by cowards afraid of true power."

The way she says it makes my skin crawl.

"That's about to change," she promises. "I will not bow to lesser men who think they are more."

I watch them like a play, not knowing how I can make the situation better. Costin doesn't try to fight her anymore. Even when she comes towards him, he doesn't lift his arms in defense. She runs her finger through the blood on his chest before lifting it to her lips.

"Thane knows what it means to be treated as lesser. The wolves may be as ancient as our bloodlines, but they're seen as animals, dogs, barely civilized. Just like women are seen as decorative toys to be traded and married off with no other value." Her gaze fixes on me. "Ask your vampire about that. Ask him how many times he's moved those he considers to be lesser around like pieces on a chess board to cement his power."

"Elizabeth—" Costin warns, but she cuts him off.

"You have until tomorrow night, little dragon tamer." She goes toward the door, her movements confident. "Come to us willingly, or we'll start cutting Paul into manageable pieces. Diana, too." Her smile is cruel. "I wonder if the child's screams sound different than her father's. Thane's quite curious to find out."

"If you touch that child—" Costin starts forward.

"Oh, *now* you care about children. Please!" she snorts.

"Elizabeth, I'm warning you," he orders.

"Or you'll what? Kill me? We both know you lack the balls. You need me alive to validate your eternity." She glances between us. "I wonder if your pet will be as understanding when she learns the truth about what kind of man you are." Her attention fixes on me. "Ask him about what he did to me."

With that, she transforms into bat form and disappears down the hall, leaving us with the wreckage of their fight and the weight of her threats. The sound of her wings fades, replaced by my own ragged breath.

"Are you hurt?" I see guilt etched on Costin's features.

I shake my head in denial. "What did she mean?"

He doesn't answer.

"Costin, talk to me. This doesn't work if we keep secrets." How many times do I have to remind him of that fact? "You arranged her marriage, and the man killed her. What else?"

"It was a different time," he says as if I wouldn't understand. He lifts his finger to his chest, lightly rubbing the blood on his shirt as if he wishes to erase it.

"The medieval period. I know." This isn't news. I know he's ancient. I take small steps toward him.

"Marriages were about political alliances. We were at war. A noble match was made to cement allies. I was her guardian, and it was my duty to find her a husband and make sure that she was taken care of."

I think of how my uncle, Mortimer, tried to force me to marry Chester for the sake of political alliances. I think of my parents' arranged marriage. I could argue that times are not so different.

"And he turned out to be a vampire?" I prompt.

I see his guilt. It's almost palpable. When the siblings were fighting, there was a moment when it almost looked like he wanted her to kill him.

"I didn't know what he was. When I met him, Marcus seemed like any other nobleman. Elizabeth was young. I thought my sister was being dramatic and fanciful, as was her nature. I knew she was not pleased with the marriage. Marcus' castle was isolated and far away from the amusements of the royal court. She did not want to live in the mountains. When she made claims of Marcus eating people and draining their blood in his dungeon torture chambers, I didn't believe her. She begged me to let her come home. She spoke of unholy acts, and even the priests did not give credence to the ramblings of a silly girl. We thought all she needed was a stronger hand and time to learn her place. I did not know until later that my sister became pregnant. Vampires cannot conceive children. At least not naturally. Dhampirs are rare and require spells. Marcus killed her after he made her watch as he impaled her lover."

As horrific as this is, I can see there's more to the story that he's not saying. I see the shame in him. I see how it's eating away at him, piece by piece, the centuries of guilt compounding upon itself.

"How young?" I asked softly, pausing on my way to him.

A ripple works over him, and he presses his lips tightly together. "She had just turned fourteen when they married. And she was nineteen when she died."

I read once that girls as young as twelve often married. Life expectancies were different back then. But, still, as a modern woman, I can't help but feel repulsed by the idea.

"And she turned you?" I clarify, remembering what Elizabeth had said during their argument.

"Sired," he corrects. "Yes, she is my sire."

"But you're male, so you were given the power," I conclude. As much as I hate Elizabeth and think she's an evil bitch, I can get where that would make her angry.

"I will not deny that it had something to do with it, at least in the beginning. But my sister does not have the temperament to lead others. She is selfish and cruel and will stop at nothing to grab power for herself." His eyes meet mine, and I see the sadness. "But she is my sister, my blood both human and vampiric, and I cannot end her."

I resume walking towards him, but something in his expression tells me to stay back, that he would not welcome my comfort at that moment.

"I should make sure that the werewolves are expelled from the foyer and Astrid has made it to safety." When he speaks, his tone is cold and in control. It is the old Costin, the one I cannot read, the perfect master vampire. "Stay here. I will have somebody bring you to the dining hall. I do not know what human food they have in the kitchen, but you must eat something and get back your strength. It has been a long morning."

With that, he leaves in a blur of movement.

I stand amongst the destroyed office and stare after him, trying to process everything I have learned —my recovered memories of the shipyard, the sins of his past, the grievances of his sister. Exhaustion fills me, but I know I cannot give in to it. There is a battle ahead, and I'm going to be forced to fight it whether I want to or not. Too much is at stake.

Costin's dining hall feels more like a medieval great room than any place meant for eating. Or an abandoned movie set. It reminds me that I'm in the home of someone born when even dining was a show of power, when lords held court over feasts that lasted days. Astrid's weekend parties have nothing on those guys.

If I close my eyes, I can imagine knights filling the room, their drunken, boisterous laughter ringing out as serving wenches walk between them refilling goblets. In reality, it sounds like a tomb. The only noises are the ones I make.

Today, those goblets wouldn't hold wine, and the feast would be of a live variety.

I can't forget I'm dating a vampire. I can't

romanticize what he is because of lust. I have to remember his darkness, not just the glimmers of light I want to see. As much as I hate it, Elizabeth's words stick in my head. There is so much I don't know about him.

I might not wish for his vampiric fate, but I empathize with him. I can't imagine being forced to survive only on blood and moonlight.

Blood and moonlight. Everything keeps coming back to that.

The thick stone walls rise to a vaulted ceiling where wrought iron chandeliers cast flickering light from gas candles made to look real. A massive fire-place dominates one wall, its mantle carved with scenes of hunts—though I notice the prey looks suspiciously human. The hearth is large enough to roast an entire deer, as they would have in Costin's human days when feasts meant survival through winter.

Tapestries depicting ancient battles hang between tall windows that must be rigged to show false daylight, as we're underground, and sunlight would kill the vampire guests. The fabric has faded over centuries, but I can still make out knights on horseback, their banners carrying sigils I don't recognize. I wonder if any show Costin's family crest from when he was human nobility. The thought is surreal—this man once lived in actual castles, commanded actual servants, and arranged actual medieval marriages. While I grew up watching cartoon versions of his world, he lived it.

The table could seat fifty, lifted above the others on a platform and stretching longer than my apartment when I tried living on my own. Dark wood gleams with age and polish and is scored with marks that might be older than America. I sit alone at one end, pushing food around my bowl and running my finger over the wood's scars. I wonder who sat here before me and stabbed the surface to forever mark it like a name carved into a school desk. A few feet away, I see what appears to be claw marks, evenly spaced fingers from when someone must have been pulled across the surface.

I rub my clean face. Thankfully, the dried blood is gone. However, the aches still linger.

I take a bite of the stew, but I don't taste it. Everything feels like dirt in my mouth. My body needs sustenance after the memory recovery and Elizabeth's visit, but my mind can't focus on eating. The silver settings and crystal glasses feel like artifacts from a museum, making me intensely aware of how out of place I am in this world. Out of everything, I doubt the silver is real. If it is, it would be reserved for trusted human guests. Vampires don't like touching the metal.

The amulet hums against my chest, stronger than before Draakmar woke. Since confronting him head-on in the underground city, his presence feels palpable. Like he's inside my thoughts, trying to tell me something just beyond my understanding. The stone's protection seems to have changed too. It's less a passive barrier and more an active conduit to give me the dragon's messages.

Too bad I don't speak cranky dragon. The ancient's messages are hard to decipher.

Draakmar is older than this room, older than Costin's human memories of nobility and power, heck, older than humanity. His agitation has been growing since Elizabeth left as if the dragon is trying to warn me to be careful. I touch the stone, hoping for clarity, but all I get is that familiar sense of ancient power and growing urgency.

I try to message back with my mind, *"Use your words, Draakmar. Your human words."*

I don't think the creature hears me.

"You need to eat." Costin appears in the doorway. His clothes have changed, but his face still carries the weight of his sister's visit. He moves to stand behind my chair, his cool fingers brushing my shoulder. His formal posture and perfect manners don't seem contrived in this setting. They're muscle memories bred into him during his human era.

"Are the werewolves gone?" I ask.

He nods and turns his attention to my food. "Eat. Your body needs strength."

"I need answers more." I set down my spoon, the metal ringing against the dish. His skin doesn't look as translucent as before, and his wounds are already healed. I wonder if he stopped to feed. "Talk to me. What is going on with you?"

He's quiet for so long I think he'll refuse. Finally, he takes the chair beside me, turning it to face mine. In the candlelight, his eternal youth seems more like a curse than a blessing. It's like I forget sometimes how long he's lived. I know the truth, but it gets buried in my short timeline with him. There is so much I don't know, might never know, might never understand.

But is it mine to judge?

I think of my worst sins, the ones that keep me up at night, the ones that fill me with shame. Would I want to be judged for those moments over all the rest?

I think of Paul and Diana, where they are now, all because they showed kindness to me, a stranger. That is my biggest shame and my eternal guilt. If they die, that is what I will carry inside me. Tears enter my eyes at the thought.

We stare at each other, unable to speak. There's an exhaustion between us that settles like a thick, smothering blanket. So much has happened to me in a short time. It's hard to believe I'm not who I was six months ago.

Is this my life now? Threats and apocalyptic adventure? It's so far from the normal, *mortal* life I dreamed of.

"Costin—?"

A servant appears, making me jump. "Lady Astrid has returned with the book. She awaits you in the library."

Costin is instantly on his feet. I think he must feel relief not to have to talk about his feelings.

I stand, and my legs are still shaky from every-thing that's happened. The amulet's heat intensifies, and I swear I can feel Draakmar's consciousness pressing harder against mine. The dragon's whispers have become almost like a white noise. Whatever's in that book, the dragon already knows it's not good news.

We step past the destruction from Elizabeth's attack, and I see a servant already cleaning up the mess in the office. Costin doesn't seem bothered by the splintered furniture and crumbling stone columns as he leads me to his library. It's lighter than we'd left it, and I can see the details previously hidden by shadows. It's funny how light can change the feel of things. Where before it was gothic and unwelcoming, it now feels regally romantic. Well, except for the whole researching the ritual that wants to kill me thing.

Unlike the battle-scarred corridor, this space feels like a sanctuary. There is a musk, subtle in the air, of decaying parchment. Shelves extend from the floor to the high ceiling, filled with leather-bound volumes. I would say there are too many to read in a lifetime, but then Costin is immortal, so that's not true.

Astrid waits for us at a wide oak table, perched on a chair, reading the tome open before her. If she battled werewolves while keeping the book safe, there are no signs of it. Magic weaves around her fingers as she turns a delicate page without actually touching it.

"So many pieces..." she muses, not looking up. "They must have been planning this for decades."

Her voice is so calm. If I didn't know her, I wouldn't know if she was angry or impressed.

I come closer to see for myself. It's not surprising that I can't read the ancient text. That's one of many regrets I have from my childhood. I wish they would have taught me more about magic and the old languages. Being mortal, my education was focused more on protecting myself, not wielding or under-standing true power.

Astrid's finger hovers over lines and I follow even

though I can't read. "They would've been waiting for the right combination of sacrifices."

My eyes find words I do recognize, "*Sanguis et Lūnāria.*"

Costin appears as silent as a shadow beside me. "I remember reading this centuries ago when the book first came into my possession, but I don't recall the details."

"The sheer complication of putting this together... It's a wonder it could even come to pass," Astrid says.

"The more complicated, the more dangerous. One thing I've learned is with time, any combination of things can happen," Costin answers.

"What does it say?" I prompt so one of them will translate it for me.

"All right, let's dig in. As we know from Peter, this ritual requires three specific types of power." She turns a page so we can see the intricate drawings of an altar. It is the same one Thane showed me in his sanctuary. The words "*Sanguis et Lūnāria*" are drawn across the illustration.

The amulet burns against my chest. Draakmar's consciousness presses harder. He doesn't like this.

"Death magic to anchor it, draconic magic to amplify it, and forgotten magic to channel it," she continues. "Paul's death in the erased timeline marked him with death magic that acted as the anchor so this could start. You have Draakmar's power amplified through the amulet. Dragon magic is ancient, some of the most ancient, born before time was time."

"We already guessed this much," I say slowly. "Why Diana? Surely, there is someone else who forgot magic. Think of all the people walking around with erased memories. Not to be callous, but they're a dime a dozen. Why hurt Diana? She's just a kid."

Astrid waves her hand over the book to turn another page. This time, there is an illustration of a child surrounded by pure light.

"Children possess magic in its purest form," Costin answers. "They're innocent, untouched by time. They still carry the magic of coming into creation before rules, and society corrupts them."

Astrid nods. "It's why they can see things adults can't, why they believe in magic so easily—Santa Claus, the Easter Bunny, imaginary friends, monsters under the bed. Most lose this power as they grow up, but some..." She looks up at me. "Some children retain traces. The book calls it forgotten magic because it's what everyone has a touch of before they forget how to use it."

My throat tightens, and terror shivers its way over me.

Costin touches my shoulder and adds, "It's deeper than that. Diana underwent a magical ordeal, and then the amulet took those memories away from her. She retains that childlike ability to believe in magic without questioning it. She's touched by draconic magic and a descendant of death magic. She has been touched by all three."

"She's perfect for the ritual," Astrid agrees. "Young enough to channel pure power, but old enough to survive the initial surge."

"Fine," I feel my frustration rising, fueled by Draakmar's restlessness. I hate feeling helpless. I throw my arms to the side, raising my voice so that it echoes around us. "But why? Why even do this ritual? What's it for? What's it going to do? End the world? Why is everybody always trying to end the freaking world? Don't they understand that it's going to end them too!"

Costin and Astrid remain calm. I find it annoying. I want them as worked up as I am. I feel the dragon's growing rage, and it amplifies my own. I want to give in to it. It feels good, tempting.

"Why go to centuries of trouble?" I demand. Nothing can be worth all of this sacrifice. "Why do all three of us have to be sacrificed?"

I don't want to die. I don't want them to die.

"It's a power redistribution." Astrid leans over the book as if reading before answering, "When the moon is full tomorrow night, they'll use her forgotten magic as a conduit to strip power from all supernatural beings."

The amulet flares are so hot I gasp and lean forward to drape it away from my skin. Draakmar's fury floods through me. That's why he's been restless and angry, why he tried to surface when he did. When they steal all supernatural powers, they'll try to take his as well. But it's not just the ritual that gets him agitated—it's Diana's role.

"Draakmar." I press my hands flat against the table to steady myself. I take several deep breaths. "He's saying something to me about Diana."

"Tell him we know. They're going to sacrifice an innocent child to reshape the supernatural world," Costin says in disgust.

"It's not just that." I shake my head and grab the amulet. It burns my palm, but I close my eyes and try to listen. Draakmar's insistent presence feels different. "He knows something about Diana's magic that we don't."

"The ancients are notoriously vague. Let us know if he says something useful, but we don't have time to decipher his riddles." Astrid takes a deep breath as if centering herself. "They have orchestrated their plan perfectly. They have one shot to get it right. Tomorrow's full moon is the first total lunar eclipse since the amulet shattered and the timeline reset. Paul's death magic is still fresh, your connection to Draakmar is at its peak, and Diana..." She presses her lips together. "They won't get another chance like this one. The moment the Earth passes directly between the sun and moon, it will create the blood moon."

"Blood and moonlight," I whisper.

Astrid nods. "Blood and moonlight."

"*Sanguis et Lūnāria,*" Costin adds.

We stand in silence, feeling the weight of the revelation. Astrid was right. There are so many little pieces fitting together. It feels like impossible odds. My mind spins with the magnitude of it all. "If they strip all supernatural powers, what happens? To vampires, to magics, to—"

"To everything," Astrid puts forth. She glances at my amulet like she wishes she would have smashed it long ago.

"They'll redistribute it the way they want. Thane and Elizabeth want the same thing—dominance over the vampires and anyone else who opposes them. It's a match made in hell. It will never last. Once the thrill wears off, they'll destroy each other with their greed for more," Costin says.

Astrid smirks. "The Freemonts are vain enough to think they can control where the power goes and use that chaos to establish a new order. They don't understand what Elizabeth is capable of or what she's willing to do to get what she wants. Even the other vampires fear her particular brand of ambition. Mabel has always been jealous of us Devines because deep down, she knows she's nothing but a two-bit hack who married poorly."

They're talking more to each other than to me.

Astrid's perfect posture somehow becomes even more rigid. "And now they ally themselves with wolves. As if Thane's feral pack of backwoods bikers could ever maintain the delicate balance we've built. The treaties may seem restrictive, but they've kept the peace for centuries. Without them, we'd be back to territorial wars in the streets, wolves hunting in broad daylight, vampires draining whole neighborhoods dry. The humans would notice, and then where would we be?" She smooths an invisible wrinkle from her silk blouse. "The wolves forget there's a reason they were restricted to industrial zones. Their kind can't control their baser instincts. In the 1950s we tried giving them a small town. After two weeks it looked worse than those nuclear test sites."

"Elizabeth should know better," Costin adds.

"How do we stop them?" Everything in me is filled with panic. I don't want this battle. I want to curl up into the fetal position and never move. I think of Draakmar and the sleeping ancients like him. Power that old and raw could tear the world apart.

"Elizabeth knows vampire weaknesses and how to neutralize our defenses," Costin says. "I can't know everyone she's turned against me during the years, but I can guess. She's always resented the old order, just like the wolves resent their territories. But there's a difference between resentment and revolution."

"The dogs won't go against their master. Thane is a dictator. Peter is terrified of him. We can't expect him to do more. They'll have the ritual site fortified." She stands and leaves the book on the table. Waving her hand, she magically forces it to close. "I'm going to make sure Peter is safe. If Anthony were here, that's what he'd want us to do."

I'm glad Lorelai and Anthony are safe in Kansas City. As much as I'd like my brother at my side, I can't ask that of him. Plus, I suspect Astrid won't call him to come back. She'll want to protect her son and the Devine magical heir.

They don't say more. They don't have to. I think of Diana, so young and innocent, being used as a conduit for this ancient magic. Of Paul, marked by death, forced to anchor it. Of all the carefully laid plans leading to this moment. And I know that it's my fault. If I had just walked away from them the first time we met, not accepted their help, not dragged them into the supernatural world to save myself. If I had done the right thing, none of this would be happening.

Guilt eats at me, consuming my insides as it burrows in deep.

Draakmar's fury shows no hint at lessening. It makes it hard to hear past the anger. The dragon's knowledge stays just out of reach like I'm trying to remember the details of a dream. Whatever the creature is trying to tell me about Diana, I pray I figure it out before it's too late.

TWENTY-ONE

Astrid leaves as the threat of tomorrow's blood moon hangs over us. It's still hours away, but I feel it pressing in. The library feels more ominous than before as I walk past the collection of secrets. I can't help but worry each book holds a different key to destroying everything I care about. All these rituals, prophecies, and curses. I think of the wizards who must have divined them in the first place. Why bother? What is the point in giving someone the recipe for destruction?

Costin strides to the fireplace, tension radiating off him. I move toward the table to stare at the leather book until the texture blurs. There is no reason to open it, but I hate that it exists.

"Do you think your sister can be reasoned with?"

I ask. "If we talk to her and explain how bad all of this..."

Talk to her? I hear how useless my suggestion sounds. What's my next great idea? Vampire family therapy session? Hug it out? Apologize?

When I look up, he's staring into the flames.

"I should have protected her." He's so quiet I almost miss the words. I'm drawn to the raw pain in his voice and move closer to better hear. "She wasn't always like this. She was so young, so full of life. Before Marcus..."

I reach for him and hesitate. My hand hovers over his back, not making contact. I want to comfort him, but I'm afraid he'll pull back inside himself and stop talking.

"Tell me," I urge.

"We were nobility by birth." He doesn't turn from the fire, but his hand lifts, like he wants to reach for something he sees in the flames. "Our father wagered away everything we had. Lands, money, jewels, alliances. When he died, the vultures descended. All he left me was a crumbling castle and a tarnished title."

"That must have been tough," I say.

"I was barely a man myself when they sent me home from the battlefront. Then Marcus came to collect a debt. He saw my sister. You wouldn't know it now, but she was sweet, a little shy, and so pretty despite the fact food had been scarce. As her guardian..." He stretches his hand deeper into the fireplace, too deep. "I thought I was doing the right thing."

"Costin, don't!" The smell of burning flesh propels me into action. I move around him and tug at his arm. He allows me to remove his charred fingers from the flames. It has to hurt, but he doesn't let it show.

His eternal youth fades into a hollow gaze, revealing the burden of his immortality. "We struck a deal. Marcus paid a handsome bridewealth for Elizabeth's hand. Anyone else would have wanted a dowry, something I couldn't afford. He had money and could take care of her. By any standard it was a powerful alliance with wealth, position, and protection for Elizabeth. Though if I'm honest, I was happy to send my responsibility away and to have my money problems solved. I was able to pay off my father's debts and restore my family name."

I hold his wrist and watch as his charred fingers slowly heal. "Costin, you have to forgive yourself. It was a different time. You're a different person. I know that is not the man you are today. Look how you've protected me my entire life. You've changed. You're a good person. I see that."

"Time does not change facts." His laugh holds no humor. "I didn't listen when she wrote to me. I told myself she was being dramatic and that she needed time to adjust. Even when her letters spoke of blood and screams in the night, of servants disappearing, of Marcus' inhuman appetite..." His voice breaks. "I failed her."

I keep holding his wrist. Suddenly his burned fingers turn, wrapping around my forearm to hold me, tightening desperately like I'm keeping him in the present. They dig into my flesh.

"It never occurred to me that I never saw Marcus outside during the day. Maybe I didn't want to notice it. I didn't know what he was. Not until Elizabeth came home and slaughtered everyone in the castle. Everyone but me."

I watch his hand on my arm.

"No, me she tortured so I could experience what I'd sentenced her to. She made me feel every moment of what she'd endured. Then she brought me back, made me like her. She thought being my sire would change our dynamic and give her control." His free hand cups my cheek, stroking my face with his thumb. "I've spent centuries trying to protect her from herself, trying to atone. But I couldn't stop her from becoming everything she hated."

I lean into his touch. "You were young, trying to do what was expected—"

"Don't make excuses for me. I am long past

denying my truth. I was wrong." His crimson gaze holds mine, and I see past the master vampire to the man beneath. "The things we do to protect those we love are sometimes worse than what we're protecting them from."

The double meaning isn't lost on me. I think of his attempts to protect me—erasing memories, making choices for me, trying to keep me safe.

"When I saw you as a child, you reminded me of her. Sweet, a little shy but also wild and rebellious." He closes his eyes. "And then that night at the shipping yard, I saw you as a woman, the same age my sister was when she was turned. I wanted nothing more than to protect you from this supernatural world, to take the pain of it away."

I remember thinking of him as the vampire always lurking in our shadows when we were growing up. I never knew why. He said it was because he promised my grandfather, but I see now it was more than that. His loneliness, and the guilt over Elizabeth, drove him to protect me.

"I'm not your sister," I whisper.

"No." A faint smile curls the side of his lip. "What I feel for you is not how a brother feels about his sister."

I wrinkle my nose. "I'm going to pretend that's romantic and say I'm very glad to hear it."

He traces my lower lip. The gentle touch sends

shivers through me. "I can't lose you too." The words come out rough, almost broken. "Not to Elizabeth, not to the ritual, not to my own mistakes."

"Then trust me," I whisper against his fingers. "Let me make my own choices."

"Can you forgive me someday?" His other hand slides into my hair, cradling my head. The firelight plays across his features, softening them. All calculation and painstaking control fades into raw need and vulnerability.

"I already have." I find I mean it. With what we're facing, being angry about the past hardly seems worth it.

When he kisses me, it's different than before. I feel the soft intensity vibrating through me. His lips move slowly like he's attempting to extinguish centuries of loneliness. I want to give him comfort and take care of him.

I lean closer, my hands untucking his shirt until I discover bare skin. I let my fingers travel around his waist. He feels warm against my palms, and his deepening kiss makes me forget everything for an exquisite moment. Desire floods me, weakening my knees. He holds me against him.

Why can't we exist only in this moment?

"Tamara." My name sounds like a plea. His hands journey down my sides, sparking trails of pleasure in their wake. I want to be closer to him, feel his skin against me. He's so still compared to my heavy breathing. It gives the illusion of calm, but I feel the hard beat of his racing heart.

Reality fights its way back into my brain. Draakmar is restless and wants to force his will to the surface. I ignore the dragon. Instead, I pull Costin closer, my fingers digging into his flesh. My vampire needs me. I feel the hole in him crammed with eternal guilt and damnation.

We're surrounded by the sanctuary of the library's candlelight. The world can't touch us, or at least it feels that way. Tomorrow brings the blood moon. It ticks closer with each second. I can't do anything about that right now. But in these few precious minutes before that raging storm, I need to forget everything but basking in the safety of Costin's arms.

Costin needs to know I trust him after what he shared, and I want to show him. I take the amulet off and set it on the table. Crimson hunger floods his gaze at the offer. His mouth claims mine again before trailing down my neck. His lips discover my racing pulse. I'm completely exposed. Without the barrier between us, every sensation is heightened. His fangs scrape lightly over my feverish skin, and I tense in anticipation of the white heat of his bite. His lips explore, promising and teasing, as his tongue licks long trails. He doesn't bite, but the thrill of knowing he might at any moment sets my nerves on edge. I shudder in response.

His strong hands glide under my shirt, long fingers splaying across my back. There's an excitement in knowing how powerful he is and how easily he can overtake me.

"I don't want boundaries between us," he whispers against my throat, the tickle of his breath brushes against me like a feather making me shiver.

I lift my arms. He takes the invitation and pulls my shirt off me in one fluid motion. The air caresses my skin. Electricity hums through me in the form of desire. I love the supernatural grace in which he moves, the flex of his perfect muscles beneath tight skin. I feel like we're dancing to a song only we can hear.

His hands slide down my arms to cup my breasts through my bra. Thumbs brush over the sensitive peaks until I can't suppress the moan of approval. The lace disappears as quickly as my shirt, only to be instantly replaced by his mouth. He pulls my nipple into a deep kiss, taking his time as if he's trying to savor my taste.

The air feels cool against my heated skin, raising goosebumps for his hands to chase away. He takes his time and caresses me slowly as if memorizing my form, learning every curve and hollow of my body.

All those moments doubting how I feel seem

foolish now in light of what might be the end. My clock is finally running out. I survived my childhood, Conrad, the labyrinth, and an apocalyptic prophecy featuring an ancient and powerful dragon. By all rights, any of those should have killed me. How much luck can one mortal woman have? I'm afraid I'm fresh out of second chances.

The need is too great. I want him to end my torment. I try to unfasten his shirt buttons, but my hands shake. The anxious thoughts racing in my head might be suppressed, but they won't go away completely. I focus on my body's growing needs, trying to stay in this moment and push out everything else. The ache in my stomach unfurls, radiating from my sex like tentacles to overtake every tingling nerve ending.

Costin helps me undress him, shrugging out of the expensive fabric to reveal perfect skin. His fingers are completely healed from the fire. Golden light caresses him in ways I want to. His body jolts beneath my touch. I take my time exploring him as he did me. I trace the muscles of his chest, following the definition down to his waistband. A low growl escapes him when I brush past his arousal, the sound more monster than human.

As if by an unspoken understanding, we take our time. I feel the barely contained vampire beneath his skin, full of need and hunger. His fangs are fully extended. And yet he doesn't attack. I see him struggling for control.

"Are you sure?" His voice is rough with need, and his eyes fill with blood as he stares at my neck. I know what he wants. He's always trying to protect me, even from himself.

Instead of answering with words, I pull him into another kiss. This time when his fangs graze my lip, I press forward purposefully letting him taste my blood. It flavors our kiss. Some of his control breaks. He moans deeply as his body shudders against mine, and I feel him licking the wound.

The unmistakable lift of his arousal through the smooth material presses hard against my hip. I need more. I need to end the torment raging inside me. I fumble with his pants until his hands join mine to help. An eternity passes before I'm able to take his length in my palm. The air between us is thick with anticipation. I find it hard to catch my breath.

"Tamara." My name almost sounds like a curse in his gravelly voice. His hands free me of my jeans and I kick off my shoes so I can step out of them. He finds my hips, fingers digging into my ass as he lifts me easily off the floor. My legs wrap around his waist, feeling his muscles straining beautifully against my inner thighs.

`I feel connected to him. There is an invisible thread sewn between us that can never be severed.

He places me on the surface of the oak table. I instantly lean back to give him access to my body. My arm slides into something and I hear the ancient book fall to the floor with a heavy thump. I jump at the sudden sound, but he doesn't seem worried about the book.

"Leave it," he says when I turn my head to check.

He continues exploring my length, using the new angle to run his hands down my legs. He massages and caresses a sure path. The amulet bumps against my hand, but I don't want to wear it. I like the danger of being at his mercy.

The wood is unforgiving against my bare skin, but I barely notice. All I can focus on is the way he is looking at me.

He kisses me everywhere. The contrast between his pliable tongue and sharp fangs sends a shiver over my heated skin. There seem to be two realities —the one we're in and the one I feel when I'm with him like this. One of his hands pins my hip, holding me in place as he lavishes attention on first one breast, then the other. I squirm to feel him between my legs.

"Please," I manage, though I'm not sure what I'm begging for. My fingers tangle in his hair, trying to draw him closer, torn between pulling him to my mouth and pushing him between my thighs.

He lifts his head, eyes blazing with crimson promise. "Tell me what you want."

The sound of the monster is thick in his voice. One hand trails down my stomach, fingers playing along the edge of my sex, teasing my need. "Tell me."

"You," I breathe. "Just you."

His mouth follows his hands. He keeps my hips in place with one hand as the other works magic between my legs. They thrust into me as his mouth clamps down on my clit. I writhe for more.

Just as I'm about to find release, he stops. I cry out in protest and try to sit up.

He keeps me on the table like a feast he's about to devour. When his mouth finds my neck, I turn my head in invitation. I wrap his waist with my thighs and force my body to slide to the edge. His fangs scrape my pulse point, and the tiny sting only heightens every sensation.

He growls incoherently against my throat and enters me with agonizing slowness, like he's still trying to maintain some control. I use all my strength to pull him closer to impale myself on his thick cock. We've fucked before, but it's never felt like this.

"Do it," I command, not caring who hears my cries. I force a violent rhythm against him, bucking for release.

Only this moment matters. His fangs pierce my

skin as his cock penetrates my body. The dual sensations are overwhelming—pleasure and pain mixing until I can't tell them apart. It's too much. My stomach tightens, and I become lightheaded. Costin's hungry mouth pulls hard against my neck. My arm drapes over his back. He's taking too much blood. I slap his shoulder in warning, but his body is moving over mine. That deep need for sweet release wars with self-preservation.

My vision dims, and I worry I might pass out from the intensity.

When he finally pulls back from my throat, his lips are stained red. The sight frightens me a little. I have no time to react as the pleasure takes over. His hips pound into mine with heated abandon, driving me hard against the tabletop. My head tilts back, and I shut my eyes.

"Mine," he growls, gripping my thighs to keep me next to him.

He stops moving until I open my eyes. He holds my gaze, not resuming the frenzied pace. The slow, measured strokes are too much. Our bodies strain together, pushing and pulling, until the primal need takes over.

My heartbeat hammers in my ears, and I can barely hear anything else. My nails dig into his shoulders. The bittersweet pleasure builds between us. A cry is ripped from me. Climax hits me so hard I freeze into a trembling mass. He follows immediately after, my name a broken cry against my injured throat. For a long moment, we remain perfectly still, connected in every way possible. But as the tremors subside, his forehead drops to mine.

"You are like fire and daylight," he whispers in awe, "like you could burn away the darkness inside me and make me human again. I wish I could be that for you."

I catch his face between my hands, making him look at me. I see the marks healing on his shoulders from where I gripped him. "I don't want to burn away your darkness. I want all of you—light and shadow both. I know you're a vampire, and there is no coming back from that. Just as I am human, and you accept me for my mortality."

What I don't say is that I don't want to be a vampire. I don't want to drink others to live.

Something breaks in his expression. His mouth finds my neck again, fangs scraping but not breaking skin as he licks the wound as if to help it heal. Next, he pulls me to sitting and kisses me gently, still tasting of blood and passion.

When he releases me, it's to pick up the amulet. He hands it to me. "You should put this back on."

I do, watching him lift that horrible old tome from the floor and place it down next to me. I hate that book and everything in it. The firelight casts long shadows across the library walls, and the weight of history and prophecy feels like it's closing in once more. I want to throw the book into the flames and watch it burn. If only it were that easy to stop the ritual.

The amulet heats as if the dragon is angry at being ignored, and with it comes the strange sensation of memories trying to surface. Not mine this time, but older. Ancient.

"Stay with me," he whispers against my lips, drawing me away from Draakmar's needy demand for attention. "Whatever comes tomorrow…"

I kiss him to shut him up, not wanting to think about blood moon rituals or choices yet to come. I need time to stop. Right now, in this moment, I just want to feel loved.

TWENTY-TWO

"Stay with me."

Costin's voice echoes in my mind, mingling with Draakmar's insistent white noise. I try to put them both aside, but it's difficult.

I didn't want to leave him, but when I got Astrid's text telling me I needed to come home, I had to. I used to think that, as a vampire, Costin had one weakness—the sun. I now know he has at least two more. Elizabeth and I are the others. I worry about him in this battle to come. I can't ask him to harm his sister, but she's a rabid animal that needs to be put down.

Dawn creeps over the city, and my mind keeps drifting back to Costin's bedroom, where I left him in that half-dead state that vampires experience. Astrid and I had interrupted his sleep the day before, and he stayed awake through the following night. The blood I gave him during our lovemaking, combined with the new sunrise, had finally pulled him under. Part of me aches to still be there, safe in that moment, hiding in his underground sanctuary. But Paul and Diana don't have the luxury of time.

The penthouse feels empty when I slip inside. There is a melancholy that comes over every movement. I wash up and grab clothes from my room, trying not to think about how this might be the last time I see it, the last time I brush my hair, wash my face, and look in the mirror.

When I emerge dressed, Astrid is waiting for me. She stands outside my door, leaning against the hallway wall. Her expression is carefully neutral, but I see worry in the set of her shoulders. She nods for me to follow, and we walk, not speaking, toward the living room.

"You're sure about this?" Peter asks before I actually see him sitting in a chair.

He's slouched over like a kid trying to hide from monsters, knees drawn into his chest. I expect Astrid to lecture him about putting shoes on her furniture, but they share a look instead. It's clearly an unlikely alliance born of desperation.

"Tell her what we discussed," Astrid says.

Peter releases his legs and places his feet on the floor. He angles his body toward us without standing. "I can show you the tunnels that will take you close to where they're holding Paul, but Diana..."

He glances at Astrid.

"Go on," Astrid says. "We have a deal. You are protected."

"They're keeping the girl somewhere else," Peter continues. "The death magic shouldn't mix with forgotten magic until the ritual. They want to keep it separate so that they're stronger."

The amulet pulses steadily against my chest, like a second heartbeat, counting down the hours until moonrise. Draakmar's presence feels different after last night—less agitated and more focused. It is as if the dragon knows what I'm about to do and approves of me taking action.

"I couldn't find where they are holding her," Peter says. "I'm sorry, Tamara. I tried."

I nod. I'm disappointed, but at least it's something.

"If you want to go, it should be during the day. We're stronger during the full moon," he says.

"Then we should leave now," I answer.

He stands, and we follow Peter to the elevator. Astrid waves her hand over the button panel, and it swings open. I've never seen it do that before. She reaches inside and flips a seemingly random sequence of switches. The elevator begins to move, and she waves her hand to close the panel.

At my stare, she says, "Private entrance to the supernatural city. You never know when you're going to need to disappear."

We ride the elevator down, past the lobby, into a sub-sub-basement I never knew existed. When the doors open, it looks like we're stepping into an old maintenance tunnel.

Astrid's heels click behind us as we descend a concrete walkway. The sound echoes off stone walls, making me think of prison corridors.

"The pack doesn't know I'm helping you," Peter explains as he leads us past a series of iron doors. I can't see inside, but my idea of a prison might not be far off. "If they find out..."

His hands shake slightly as he pulls out an ancient-looking key. It has a werewolf head on the head. He turns it in his hands.

"They won't." Astrid's words carry absolute certainty. She touches Peter's shoulder, and I see him relax slightly. Sometimes, I forget how long she's known him, how she's watched him grow up along-side Anthony. "Not from us."

"What are all these doors?" I ask, glancing back.

"Holding cells," Astrid answers. "Don't worry, they're empty. Mostly. You don't need to worry about them."

"But we have a tunnel to the wolves?" The idea does not bring me comfort.

"We have a magical portal that will open to various locations depending on the key used. Peter has the wolf key." Astrid motions Peter to go on. She reaches along a ledge next to the ceiling and pulls out a flashlight to give to me.

Peter slides his key into what looks like an electrical panel, but when he turns it, the whole wall shifts. The grinding of concrete rubbing against concrete makes me wince. Dust fills the air. Behind the false wall, darkness opens wide like a hungry mouth ready to swallow us whole. No part of me wants to go in there.

"The marks will guide you," Peter explains, pointing to symbols that glow faintly along the walls. "Follow the wolf tracks to find Paul. But be careful—some of these tunnels are older than the city. There are things down here that even werewolves avoid. You don't want to get lost."

I click on my flashlight. The beam catches dust carried by currents of stale air. The passage ahead feels ominous, heavy with threats of ancient magic.

I hesitate to step inside. I see something flicker in Peter's expression as he looks at me—that old boyhood crush. He knows about Costin and Paul, but there still seems to be a lingering hope that maybe someday...

There will never be a someday for us. I think logically he knows that.

"Maybe I should go with you," Peter says, his voice trembling.

"No." Astrid's tone allows no argument. "If they catch you helping her, Thane will kill you. Anthony would never forgive me." She touches his arm. "You've done enough showing us the way. A car will be here shortly to take you to the country estate. You will be safe there until this is over."

"Just... be careful, Tam. These tunnels change people. And Paul..." He hesitates. "They haven't been kind to him."

The way he says it makes my stomach clench. "You've seen him?"

"Thane made the pack watch his demonstrations. He wanted to ensure us that Paul was really touched by death magic." His voice carries genuine fear. "Thane likes to remind us of what he's capable of."

I place my hand on his trembling shoulder. He's terrified.

"Thank you for helping us, Peter," I say with a small squeeze. "Astrid's right. You should go to the estate until this is over."

He nods, then turns away quickly.

"I'll make sure he's safe. Be careful," Astrid looks at my amulet. "Don't take that off."

"You'll find Diana?" I ask. "You'll tell Costin I'm sorry I didn't wait for him?"

"I'm doing everything I can," Astrid says.

I pretend not to see the shine in Peter's eyes as Astrid leads him back the way we came.

I step inside the tunnels. They remind me of the labyrinth, and I tell myself that if I survived the supernatural challenges of those trials, then I can survive a walk through werewolf territory. I hold my fist around the amulet.

I can't be killed. I can't be killed. I can't be killed...

I follow the faint green glow of wolf paws. The tunnels grow older and less even as I continue alone. Centuries of supernatural traffic have worn down the stone path. The air feels thick with magic and smells of decay. Water drips somewhere in the darkness, each drop sounding in lonely echoes. My flashlight beam catches on claw marks scored deep into the walls. I don't want to know what caused them.

I can't be killed. I can't be killed.

The wolf tracks lead me deeper, past abandoned chambers that smell of old slaughterhouses. I don't want to think about what unimaginable torments they have seen. Finally, I reach a section that feels like it's been maintained a little better than the tunnels. Iron doors line the passage, each marked with various spells against supernatural strength. The locks are simple enough, meant to keep creatures in, not humans out.

I peek into the small windows. The first appears

empty but has a horrible smell. The next has a troll having an invisible tea party with himself and a rock. His eyes meet mine, and he turns his back as if I'm interrupting. I find Paul in the third cell.

The space is barely larger than a closet, with walls of rough stone that weep moisture. The drip-drip sound from within would be torturous after a few minutes of listening to it. A single lamp burns with enchanted fire, casting a sickly yellow light that makes the stains on the floor look black. The thick chains holding him are silver, designed for werewolves.

"Paul?" My whisper feels too loud in this place of pain.

He slowly lifts his head, and my heart breaks. His face is a map of bruises, and one eye is nearly swollen shut. They've stripped him to the waist, and I can see where claws have left deep scratches across his chest. But his eye—the one that can open—still holds that same gentle strength I remember.

"Tamara?" His voice is rough as if he hasn't used it in days. "Is it really you?"

I slip inside. "I'm here." I rush to him and kneel on the floor where he sits. My fingers find the chains, and the silver irritates my skin where Draakmar's magic touches it.

"They kept saying you forgot me." He stares at me like he thinks I might disappear on him. "They showed me things. Made me think I was imagining our time together."

"I'm so sorry, Paul." I tug at the chains, trying to free him. I ignore the pain it causes my hands. "This is all my fault. If I hadn't brought this supernatural chaos into your lives—"

"Diana?" He cuts me off, struggling to sit straighter. "Have you seen her? Is she safe? They won't tell me anything. They just keep saying the forgotten magic needs to stay pure. I don't understand what they're talking about. They keep saying ritual."

Of course, his daughter comes first. It's one of the things that made me fall for him—that absolute devotion to Diana. "I'm going to find her. I promise. But first, I need to get you out of here."

"They're going to hurt her, aren't they?" The fear in his voice makes me work faster at the chains. It gives him renewed strength as he tries to struggle free. I manage to pull a pin from his manacle to free his hand. "Whatever this ritual is, they're going to use my baby girl, aren't they?"

"No." I cup his face, making him look at me. "We won't let that happen."

"We?"

I freeze, guilt choking me. Here he is, beaten and chained, and I'm wearing another man's bite marks. "Paul, I should tell you..."

"It's true what they said?" Something flickers in his expression. "You're with a vampire now?"

I feel his words like a slap. He's been through so much, and here I am, hurting him more.

"Hey." Despite everything, his voice is gentle. "It's okay. You don't have to answer. I see it in your eyes." His unchained hand touches my face, and his thumb brushes away tears I didn't know I was shedding. "We had something real, Tamara. Something pure. But all of this is too much. This is your world, not mine. I just want my daughter safe."

The understanding in his voice breaks something in me. It was his goodness of heart that attracted me to him. Before I can stop myself, I press my lips to his in a brief, gentle, goodbye kiss that tastes of might-have-beens and regret. When I pull back, his eyes hold no judgment, only acceptance and worry for Diana.

"I loved you in our moment," I whisper. "What we had was real. Know that. I never meant any harm to come to you."

"I know." He manages to smile despite his split lip. "But you need someone who can survive in this world. I just need my daughter back."

"How delightful!" Mabel's voice slices through the darkness like a blade. "I do so enjoy a good romantic tragedy."

I spin to face her, lifting my arms to block Paul

from them, but guards are already crowding the tiny cell. She stands in the doorway, magic crackling around her fingers, looking like she's been watching us the whole time.

"Did you really think we'd make it that easy?" She steps closer, and I see genuine pleasure in her eyes. "That we wouldn't be watching? Oh, you foolish girl. Did you think we didn't know that lovesick puppy Peter was lurking around eavesdropping for sweet morsels to feed you? Sherlock Holmes, he is not. It took you long enough. We've been waiting for you. Though I had my doubts you'd show. I thought we were going to have to send you a gilded invitation with a map."

Magic crackles from her fingers, but instead of aiming at me, she turns it on Paul. He screams, body convulsing as blue energy courses over him. The sound tears through me like physical pain.

"Stop!" I lunge at her, but guards grab my arms. Even with the amulet's protection, there's nothing I can do as Paul writhes in agony. "Please! You're killing him!"

"Oh, we won't do that quite yet." Mabel's smile is cruel. "Death magic only works if he's alive for the ritual. But we can do so many things that won't quite kill him." She intensifies the spell, and Paul's scream cuts off into choking sounds.

I struggle against the guards, but there are too

many. Without the amulet, they'd have crushed me already. Even with it, they manage to force me to my knees.

"Elizabeth will be so pleased you accepted her invitation." Mabel finally releases Paul, who slumps unconscious with his one wrist still in his chains. A guard moves to refasten the manacle I had managed to get free. "She was certain you'd come for him. She said, 'Tamara's greatest weakness is that she cares about these pathetic humans.' I guess she was right. Damn. I owe twenty dollars. I hate losing bets." She steps closer, examining me like I'm a bug under glass. "How is dear Constantine? Still playing the noble protector?"

"When he finds out—"

"What? That his pet human walked right into our trap?" She laughs. "By the time he figures out what's happening, it will be too late. The ritual will be complete, the power will be ours, and you'll get to watch it all happen." Her magic wraps around my throat. The power of it takes me by surprise. She shouldn't be this strong. "That amulet might make it so I'm unable to kill you, but as I already said, there are so many things we can do that won't entirely kill you.

Black spots dance in my vision as the pressure increases. The last thing I see is Paul's limp form and Mabel's triumphant smile as consciousness fades.

TWENTY-THREE

Awareness returns before I'm able to move or open my eyes like I'm suspended in dark water. None of this is right. I should be more protected than this. With my connection to Draakmar, the amulet's magic has been getting stronger, not weaker.

My head throbs and it feels like they let my skull strike the ground when I passed out. Mabel's magic shouldn't have affected me like this. I might not know everything about the magical world, but I know Mabel isn't this powerful. She shouldn't be a threat, especially when I wear the amulet.

Unless... Have they somehow been siphoning power before the ritual?

The idea scares me.

When I'm finally able to open my eyes, the first thing I register is the moonlight. I blink to focus my vision and see an impossibly large orb magnified through a glass dome. Its light bathes everything in silver, making the circular ritual chamber feel both beautiful and terrible. Marble columns stretch up three stories to support the massive dome, their surfaces carved with classical scenes that seem to move in the shifting light.

Silver, not blood red.

The moonlight is wrong.

It has to be a good sign. If there is no blood moon, they can't perform their ritual. The idiots got the night wrong.

My hope is pointless and short-lived. A shadow brushes against the moon's edge, subtle at first. The shift is so faint that I try to convince myself I imagine it.

For the longest time, all I can do is blink and stare. It feels as if the moon looks back at me through the century-old glass, a watchful eye in the velvet-dark sky. A weight presses down on my chest. The air thickens, and it's hard to breathe. It's charged with something unseen and ancient. The end is coming. I can feel it. The eclipse has begun.

That is when I realize Draakmar is quiet. He's stopped whispering to me.

I finally manage to turn my head, only to realize we're in an abandoned bank's main hall. Moonlight spills across what was once a temple to mortal wealth and power, now transformed into a cathedral for monsters. The metal framework holding the dome's glass in place creates shadowy fingers that stretch down the marble walls. Old teller windows have been sealed with spelled iron, and through the open bank vault door, I see tunnels leading into darkness.

I should have said goodbye to Costin.

He would never have let me leave.

My failure surrounds me. Part of me believed that with Draakmar, I'd find a way through any challenge. And here I am, a failure. I never would have thought my ego would be my downfall.

The moon's glow softens as if some unseen hand is drawing a veil over it. Not dark, not yet, just dimming.

I need to fight through the residual magic clouding my head and think of my next move.

Mabel's mocking words echo in my mind, *"Did you think we didn't know that lovesick puppy Peter was lurking around eavesdropping for sweet morsels to feed you?"*

They'd played us all. They used Peter to give me exactly the information they wanted, knowing his ties to our family and Astrid would protect him. Even the timing was perfect, waiting until Costin would be trapped by daylight.

I was so sure I could rescue Paul, so confident in

Draakmar's power. I thought I was protecting Costin from having to confront his sister by coming here without him.

But they'd manipulated everything, probably even letting Peter *discover* which tunnels to use. My desperation made me an easy mark. Now, I've not only failed to save Paul, but I've also delivered the last piece they needed for their ritual.

Fuck!

I force my limbs into action as I push myself to sitting. Chains clank, and I find a manacle locked around my ankle. I wiggle my foot as I try to push it off.

I feel a draft coming from the tunnels and shiver. My throat aches where Mabel's magic choked me, but the amulet pulses steadily against my chest, its warmth the only comfort in this cold place. As the haze of Mabel's attack fades, I feel Draakmar's presence returning.

The stone floor has been polished to a mirror shine, reflecting the moonlight and making the marble seem to glow from within. They've positioned me at one point of an enormous triangle painted on the floor in red. At the triangle's center stands the altar from Thane's sanctuary, its carved words, "*Sanguis et Lūnāria,*" glowing with building power. The stains on its surface look fresh.

"Tamara?" Paul's voice breaks through my

disorientation, and I squint to find him in the shadows. They've chained him at another point of the triangle. His arms stretch wide like some twisted crucifixion. Fresh cuts cover his chest, and blood trickles down to form grotesque patterns. His expression is frantic with worry as he looks away from me.

I push to standing and follow his gaze. My heart shatters. Diana stands at the triangle's third point, wearing a white dress resembling a sacrifice from an ancient myth. Her dark curls have been braided with silver ribbons, and symbols are drawn on her bare arms in blood. She's not crying, but her eyes are huge with a terror she seems unable to voice. She stands perfectly still, unnaturally so, and a soft red glow surrounds her like a force field. There is no indication she can see us.

"It's okay, sweetheart," Paul calls to her, straining against his chains until they cut into his wrists. Blood drips onto the stone. "Daddy's here. Everything's going to be okay."

"Oh, do calm down. She can't hear you." Elizabeth emerges from between two pillars like a nightmare given form. Her leather-clad figure seems to absorb the moonlight. "The forgotten magic needs to stay pure. No corrupting influences."

Elizabeth runs a finger down Diana's cheek, activating the red force field, and I see the child shiver despite her magical paralysis.

"Don't touch her!" Paul yells, struggling harder.

"Leave her alone!" I scream. I try to lunge toward them, but the enchanted chain around my ankle holds me in place. The metal prickles where it touches my skin, despite the amulet's protection.

"Such innocent power. Do you know she still believes in magic? In good triumphing over evil? Even now, after all of this." Elizabeth's laugh echoes off stone walls. "How perfectly pure."

I hear movement from the bank vault door, and I turn to see werewolves and vampires gathering in the shadows between pillars like spectators to a gladiator match. Their eyes gleam in the darkness, which is the only way I can tell some of them apart —gold for wolves, crimson for vampires.

The three Freemonts come to stand near the altar, magic crackling between them as they prepare something in a silver bowl. Smoke rises from their concoction. The pungent smell of herbs makes me gag. Chester smiles at me. His smug look is so superior that I want to punch him in the face. I can't believe Uncle Mortimer wanted me to marry him. Francis has his eyes closed as he lifts his hands to the moon, all focus on his task. Mabel's expression mirrors her son as she looks around to make sure all eyes are on them.

As the Freemonts begin chanting, the spectators join in. I hold my thigh and pull my leg as hard as I can. The metal bites into my skin. I look around for a weapon, but nothing is within reach. I jerk my leg harder, trying to dislodge the chain from the floor.

The shadows deepen as if the chants are calling them in. I look up. What was once a faint smudge at the moon's edge now stretches across its surface, devouring the silver light piece by piece. It creeps, slow and insidious, like ink bleeding through parchment.

My heart beats faster in fear.

I had assumed this would happen at Thane's industrial palace. I doubt Costin and Astrid know about this place. We're on our own.

The chanting gains strength, the voices rising. Draakmar doesn't like it. I feel the dragon thrashing. I wonder if I could call him to me. The last time he came out of his deep hole, he'd tried to end the world. Surely that would be better than being under control of these monsters and their cult following.

The temperature dips, another chill whispering across my skin.

"The moon reaches its apex in thirty minutes, my vampire queen." Thane's voice carries across the chamber as he approaches Elizabeth. The chanting becomes quieter as if in reverence for the couple. His massive form looks huge to her slender one, and the way he looks at her makes my skin crawl. It's a combination of possession and genuine devotion. "Everything you wished for, my love. The power will be ours."

He's found someone as broken and angry as himself. A match made in hell.

Elizabeth's smile doesn't reach her eyes as she strokes his face. "Yes, my wolf king. Everything we dreamed."

Draakmar grows louder in protest. He hears the lie in her voice, and I see the calculation behind her gaze. She's playing Thane just like she plays everyone.

I know Costin cares for her, but his sister is a real evil bitch.

The amulet hums against me with an intensity I've never felt before. Since waking Draakmar, his reactions have grown stronger and more purposeful. The stone doesn't just protect me anymore. The dragon has been warning me, guiding me. I lean forward so it doesn't touch my skin as his presence becomes more insistent.

The dragon focuses my attention back on poor Diana as if he feels different with the child, less angry and more protective. I don't know what he's trying to tell me. The warning stays frustratingly out of reach. When I don't understand, I feel his growing rage, matching my own helplessness.

I look up to keep time by the changing color of the moon. There is only one thing I know for certain. We are running out of time.

Thane lifts his arms to the side, and the chanting becomes louder. The Freemonts begin circling the altar, arms lifted toward the moon. Their magic flares stronger than ever as blue fire dances around their bodies like snakes. Francis lifts the silver bowl above his head as if to help the herbal smoke rise. Chester's smug grin has become manic as if he's been possessed.

I keep pulling at my chain, falling to the floor for leverage. I don't care if I rip off the skin. I have to stop them.

"Begin," Elizabeth commands. She comes forward, arms lifted to the sides as she steps to the altar. The Freemonts stop to help lift her onto it. Chester bends over so she can step on his back as Francis and Mabel each take an arm. The move looks rehearsed for dramatic effect. Thane doesn't wait for help as he leaps up next to her, massive arms pulled toward the moon. The carved "*Sanguis et Lūnāria*" pulses beneath them.

My breath fogs in the dropping temperature. Thane howls and shifts into wolf form. Werewolves around the chamber follow his lead, their bones cracking as they transform. The ugly noises echo like gunshots off the marble walls.

"No!" Paul pulls so hard against his chains that the blood flows freely down his arms now. "Diana, baby, close your eyes!"

Diana doesn't move, doesn't even blink. The red barrier around her flares brighter as Francis begins pouring the bowl's contents in a circle around the self-anointed royalty swaying on the altar. Whatever's in it sizzles when it hits the floor, eating the marble.

Elizabeth's head snaps toward the vault door. "Right on schedule." Her smile turns cruel. "Shall we greet our guest, my wolf king?"

I turn, not hearing anything.

Thane growls, the sound more animal than human. He points an order. Half his pack moves toward the tunnels while the rest maintain their positions. The chanting never stops.

My breath catches. I don't need to hear him to feel his presence.

"Costin," I whisper. He's found us.

Elizabeth's excited smile tells me she expected this.

"Costin," I yell. "Watch out. They're coming!"

Fighting erupts in the darkness, the sounds of combat coming through the tunnels—snarls and screams, magic crackling, bodies hitting stone.

Then silence.

The chanting stops. I hold my breath.

Costin appears in the vault doorway, and my heart skitters around in my chest. He's magnificent in his fury, clothes torn and bloody, eyes blazing crimson. Behind him, I glimpse the blur of vampires engaging the wolves in battle.

"Sister." His voice carries deadly calm. "This ends now."

Elizabeth laughs, the sound wild. "Oh no, brother. This is just beginning."

"Costin," I manage, pointing across the triangle. His eyes flit to mine. "Diana."

I've already outlived my timeline. I should be dead by now. But Diana, she's just a child. She deserves a chance.

A figure darts from the shadows, ramming into Costin to engage him in a fight. The vampire attacker is joined by a werewolf, and the two double-team the master vampire. It's enough to keep him from going to Diana. I strain to get free, but my body is weakening, and the metal clamp on my ankle burns against my bloody skin.

The eclipse's reddening shadow crawls further across the moon's face, and the temperature in the chamber plummets further as life is being sucked from the air. The cultish chanting resumes and lifts, the voices taking on an otherworldly resonance that vibrates on the marble columns. Blue fire pulls from their hands, dancing toward the altar where Elizabeth and Thane stand.

Costin cracks the werewolf's neck and flies with the vampire toward the ceiling. I hear them crash in the darkness.

Paul continues to fight his chains, but he's losing strength. Blood drips down his arms in rivulets that seem to move with purpose, slithering across the floor toward the altar. The red light around Diana pulsates, and I see her small form trembling within it. Power builds in the air like static before a storm, making my skin tingle and my hair stand on end.

"You're too late to stop it," Elizabeth taunts as Costin drops to the ground. Ash from the dead vampire attacker drifts down over him like snow.

"The three magics are combining." Thane cries, bouncing in fanatical excitement.

"Witness the new era!" Elizabeth yells. The chanting stops as the crowd cheers and howls.

I see it happening. Paul's blood glows with a deep crimson light when it reaches the altar, while silvery threads of Diana's pure magic weave gently through the air like moonbeams given form. The amulet sparks as Draakmar's power is torn into the mix. Golden energy erupts from the stone, twisting and spiraling with the other magics. I feel the dragon's fury at being used this way.

Draakmar thrashes in anger. I feel him moving

from where he tries to sleep deep within the earth. He's going to surface and bring destructive lava with him.

"The moon is ready!" Francis announces, his voice carrying the same edge of madness consuming the others. The moon's face is almost covered, casting red light through the dome.

Costin's vampires surge from the tunnels, clashing with the cult around the chamber's edges, but neither side can breach the triangle of power forming between Paul, Diana, and me. The combined magics create a barrier that sizzles and sparks.

"Now!" Elizabeth commands. The Freemonts straighten their arms, channeling more energy into the ritual. The floor shakes with the force of it.

Pain rips through me as Draakmar's power is pulled harder. Paul screams as the death magic violently tears from his body, blood pooling out of his skin. Diana remains silent in her barrier, but tears stream down her face as her forgotten magic is stripped away.

"Tamara, stay strong!" Costin's screams sound far away. I see him trying to reach Diana, but the magic keeps thrusting him violently back.

That's when I hear it. Draakmar's voice is stronger now as he surfaces. The dragon's consciousness surges through me with crystal clarity. He's not fighting the ritual. He's watching Diana, trying to protect her. In her innocence, in her ability to forget and still believe in magic, he sees something the rest of us missed. A vessel pure enough to carry his power without being corrupted by it.

The moon goes dark as the eclipse reaches totality. Elizabeth throws back her head and laughs. "The power is—"

Her words cut off as Thane howls in agony. I turn to see Elizabeth has plunged her hand into his chest as if to squeeze his heart. The power he's absorbed flows up her arm.

"Did you really think I'd share?" she snarls. "All magic is mine!"

She slashes her hand across Thane's neck, cutting him with her nails.

Chaos erupts. Thane's pack surges forward as their Alpha's blood sprays across the altar over Elizabeth. They can't reach their leader.

The Freemonts' chanting falters as the ritual spins out of control. They stumble away from Elizabeth in fear. The three magics whirl faster out of us, a tornado of power with Elizabeth at its heart.

I feel my life draining.

"No!" Costin shouts, but he can't reach us through the maelstrom.

The combined magics are a force of nature now, wild and uncontrolled. Paul's chains snap as death magic pulses through him. He begins crawling across the floor to his daughter. Diana's barrier flickers and fails. And in that moment of pure chaos, I finally understand what must be done.

I reach for the amulet's chain.

My life for hers.

"Tamara, don't!" Costin's voice carries over the bedlam. He knows what removing it will mean.

The power vortex intensifies. Elizabeth absorbs the last of Thane's magic, and his massive body drops from the altar. His pack's howls of rage shake the chamber as they begin attacking the vampires in the crowd. This gives Costin's army a chance, and they gain ground. The Freemonts scramble backward in panic, looking for escape as their carefully laid plans spiral out of control. I see Elizabeth siphoning their power.

The amulet burns against my palm, but Draakmar's presence is steady now, confident.

Me for her. Everything was coming to this moment. My life for Diana's.

The dragon shows me what he knows. Diana's pure magic, untainted by darkness or power, is the perfect vessel. She will be his keeper, letting him rest while he keeps her safe. Unlike me, she won't try to use his power to fill that chasm of need to fit in with my supernatural family. She'll simply believe in it.

"Bow to me!" Elizabeth's voice screeches with manic glee. Her body contorts. "Bow to your queen!"

Paul manages to reach Diana despite his wounds, his body dragging along the floor. "Sweetheart, close your eyes!"

I'm being torn apart as Elizabeth pulls Draakmar's magic. Without the amulet's protection, I won't survive this. But Diana might.

"Brother!" Elizabeth taunts Costin as she floats above the altar. "Bear witness as I take everything!"

The marble floor cracks beneath her, fissures spreading like spider webs across the polished surface. They stretch up the walls to the glass dome. It groans and cracks in warning. The air becomes thin, making it hard to breathe. Wolves and vampires alike fall to their knees as she steals their strength.

Through the frenzy, I see Costin fighting to reach me. His eyes lock with mine, and I know he's trying to stop me. The anguish on his face nearly breaks me.

The eclipse reaches its peak. The moon hangs like a dark wound in the sky, hemorrhaging a bloody light over us. Elizabeth's form blurs, magic coursing so forcefully she's barely corporeal. The power of the three magics whips her hair around her face.

"I'm sorry," I mouth to Costin, not knowing if he sees it. I can't bring myself to say goodbye.

At this moment, all my choices narrow to one path. I could keep the amulet, keep its protection, keep Costin. But that isn't really a choice, not if I want to look myself in the mirror. Some prices are worth paying, even if they cost everything.

The chain around my bloody ankle cracks. I run toward Diana. My hands shake as I lift the amulet over my head.

Draakmar's presence wraps around me one last time—not in farewell, but in gratitude. We did what was needed. Now it's time to let go.

I trip on my wounded ankle, and as I fall, I throw the amulet toward Diana. The moment it leaves my hand, the chamber erupts in blinding light.

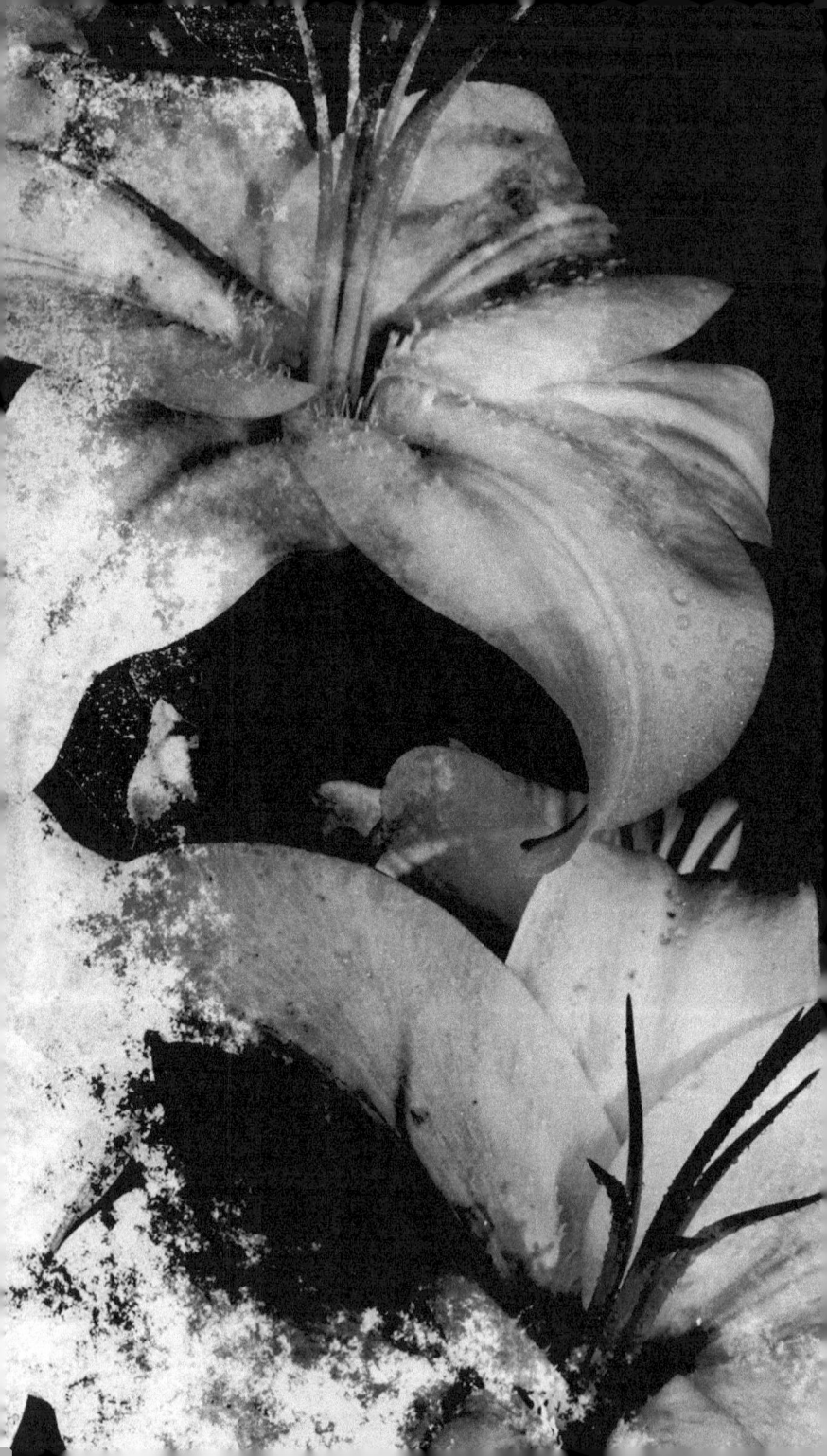

TWENTY-FOUR

The light burns away everything—sound, sensation, pain. The world ceases to exist for one endless moment, and I'm drifting into eternity.

Is this death?

Is this what I have become? An ethereal spirit with only my memories?

In this space, life feels so small. All those struggles, worries, threats... they're pointless here in this great expanse of nothingness.

It's tempting to stay in this white light, to be done with the struggle.

But then I think of those I leave behind, of Costin and Diana and Paul.

Reality crashes over like a black tidal wave, forcing me back into the abyss.

My aching body slams into the marble floor

hard. I hear an ugly crack as two of my fingers break. The taste of blood and ash is thick in my mouth. When I try to stand, my wounded ankle gives out completely.

Through tears, I see the amulet suspended in the air before Diana. It hangs, caught in an invisible current, pulsing with golden light. Paul shields his daughter with his battered body, but she reaches past him, small fingers stretching toward the stone. The look of childlike wonder on her face doesn't belong in this hellscape.

"No!" Elizabeth's scream pierces the chamber. She tries to redirect the magic, but Draakmar's power tears free from her grasp. The dragon's rageful presence fills the room, ancient and terrible. I can't see him, but I can feel the last lingering of him inside me. He's in the air, heating the cold with his internal fire.

Diana's hand closes around the amulet, and I smile. My battles are done. I can let the eternal white have me.

The Freemonts scatter like leaves in a storm. Francis pushes Mabel out of his way to save himself. Chester runs past his fallen mother.

Power surges, throwing everyone back. Wolves howl as the backlash of magic burns through them. Elizabeth is hurled from the altar.

The glass dome shatters, raining crystalline

shards that catch the moon's blood-red light. I automatically curl into a ball as they break around me. A sharp pain shoots across my leg as a piece lodges into my thigh.

I hold my leg and can't pick myself up from the floor. The last of my strength is pouring out of the wound. Without the amulet's protection, every breath is agony. That vital part has been carved out of me. My body is empty. But through the pain, I see Diana standing in a column of light.

Paul wraps his arms around his daughter. The amulet settles against the child's chest, its magic transforming from a protective barrier into something gentler. The chain shortens to fit her small frame as if it had always been meant for her. Her eyes open, and for a moment, they shine with golden fire. It's not the destructive rage I felt coming from the dragon, but the ancient finally finding peace.

"What have you done?" In a fury, Elizabeth pushes to her feet. Her perfect façade cracks, showing the terrible monster beneath. "You stupid mortal bitch!"

She launches herself at me, fangs bared. I try to roll away, but my body won't respond. This is it. This is how I die.

I'm not scared. Not anymore. Diana and Paul are safe. I did what I was meant to do.

Elizabeth comes over me, but a massive black

mass slams into her, driving her back. Blood drips from the wound in his chest and neck, but Thane isn't dead yet. His jaw snaps at her throat as they crash through a marble column.

More wolves pour in from the tunnel into the old bank, drawn by their Alpha's pain. The chamber dissolves once more into chaos as supernatural forces clash. Any alliance between the vampires and werewolves is shattered.

Through the mayhem, I see Costin fighting desperately to reach me. Elizabeth's vampires block his path, sacrificing themselves to slow him down. Even with his supernatural strength, there are too many. Each time he tears through one attacker, two more take their place. His clothes are soaked with battle as he fights his way toward me with increasing desperation.

"Tamara!" His voice carries to me. I see the horror in his eyes as he realizes he won't make it in time. He knows exactly how vulnerable I am without the amulet's protection.

A werewolf catches him from behind, massive claws tearing into his back. Costin spins with inhuman speed, but more of Elizabeth's vampires surge forward. They're not able to kill him, but they're keeping him occupied, wearing him down. Even a master vampire has limits.

Through the fray, I see Diana. The amulet's

golden light wraps around her and Paul like a cocoon. Draakmar's power protects them as the battle rages. Her innocent eyes meet mine, and in them, I see what we're all fighting for—not power or prophecies or ancient magics, but the right to choose our own fate. Diana never chose this world, just like I never chose to be born mortal into a magical family. But we can choose what we do with the hand we're dealt. Her innocence reminds me why some prices are worth paying.

I know my sacrifice is worth it. Worth everything.

I hear a deadly growl and feel hot breath on my neck. Thane towers over me with lips pulled back to reveal gleaming fangs. Without the amulet, there's nothing to stop him from—

Pain explodes through my shoulder as teeth tear into my flesh. The stories I've heard of werewolf bites have nothing on the actual feeling of the hot venom injecting into my blood. It could be I'm raw after the ritual stripped me of my protection, or maybe there's something more powerful about an Alpha's bite.

I scream, the sound raw and primal. The wolf shakes me like a rag doll, flinging me back and forth on the marble floor. I hear my muscle tear from bone. Blood streaks across the marble floor. The physical pain is beyond anything I've ever felt—

beyond the labyrinth trials, beyond having Draak-mar's power ripped away.

The wolf releases me, and I'm a crumpled mass on the floor. My blood feels like fire in my veins. The bite of a werewolf is usually fatal to humans. I've always known this. But this is worse. The magic pulled from me has left me hollow, and now wolf venom races through my empty channels, burning everything in its path.

"No!" Costin's roar shakes the chamber. He tears through the last of his attackers, leaving a trail of ash in his wake. But Elizabeth appears between us, her perfect face twisted with hate. She weaves on her feet. The magic she tried to steal has left her. The ritual was not completed.

"You can't save her, brother." She gives a cruel laugh even in her defeat. "Now you will know what it is like to lose everything. Your precious mortal who hates what we are, who's fought so hard to stay human. She's either going to turn or die. Which do you think would be worse? Loving a feral wolf the council won't let you touch, or loving a corpse? I must admit, seeing your agony either way will be delicious."

Thane pants, each breath an angry rumble. He lunges at Elizabeth, but this time she's ready. She bares her fangs, and her nails plunge into his neck. The Alpha howls in agony.

I can't focus. The werewolf venom burns through me like acid. Someone lifts my head. I know it's Costin before I see him. His cool touch is heaven against my fevered skin.

"Stay with me," he begs. "Don't leave me, Tamara. Don't leave me."

I try to speak but, instead, cough up blood. I see him eyeing his wrist and weakly shake my head, wanting him to remember what I said to him. I don't want to be a werewolf or a vampire. That brief moment floating in white light felt so safe. If that is what comes in the afterlife, I'm not scared of that fate.

The world starts to fade at the edges. This is real. Final.

"I can try to save you." His voice breaks as he lifts his wrist to his mouth. "I have to save you."

I understand what he's offering, but he can't know if it will work. I've never heard of a victim surviving both werewolf and vampire bites. Even if vampire blood could stop the transformation and keep me from dying, what would be the cost? I would not remain the same. The dark curse changes people. Young vampires are said to be the worst. They're often feral, hungry, needy creatures. They're monsters without control.

The choice I've always feared is here, and I can barely think through the pain to make it.

I lift my hand to swat his wrist away from where it hesitates next to his mouth. The effort is weak, but he knows what I'm telling him.

Behind him, Thane's body hits the floor. The remaining wolves howl in mourning for their Alpha. They begin to scatter, disappearing into the tunnel.

"It won't work, brother," Elizabeth taunts. Her eyes gleam with dark fascination. "We both know what happens when you give vampire blood to a werewolf. But maybe it will be different this time. Maybe she'll survive. Let's try it and see what happens. It'll be fun. The venom of an Alpha mixed with the blood of a master vampire..."

Costin's face twists with rage at his sister's words, but I see the desperate hope flickering behind his anger. The possibility that she might be right, that there might be a way...

My body convulses as the venom reaches my heart. Costin finally obeys and lowers his wrist. I see his face, torn between love and desperation, between his promise and his need to save me.

"You're weak." Elizabeth's voice seems to come from far away. "Always too weak to do what needs to be done."

Through the haze of pain, I see her launch herself at him. A wave of pure golden light sweeps over us. Diana stands in its center, the amulet blazing against her chest. Paul holds her hand as she lifts the other toward Elizabeth.

"Stop! No!" Diana's young voice carries ancient power. Draakmar's presence is all around us, not destructive like before, but protective. Where his power once felt like an inferno through me, through Diana, it seems to radiate like gentle warmth. The dragon appears calmer with her as if her innocence soothes his ancient rage. He has found his perfect vessel.

Paul appears next to me, ripping his shirt to bind my shoulder to stop the bleeding.

Elizabeth slams against a column. I see real fear in her eyes as she faces something she can't corrupt or control. Costin appears next to her, his hand gripping her throat. This is his chance to end her schemes, to avenge everyone she's hurt, and to finally stop her.

"Do it," she taunts through bloody lips. "Finish what you started all those centuries ago."

His grip tightens. I don't need to look into his eyes to know the war there. I see the moment his resolve breaks. He still sees a fourteen-year-old girl he unwittingly sold to a monster.

"I can't," he whispers, releasing her. "Elizabeth, please, stop this madness—"

"Coward. You've always been weak." She spits

blood at his feet. Her laugh is empty as she stumbles backward. "You can't save anyone."

Elizabeth transforms into a bat and flies out of the broken dome. Costin watches her disappear, and I fear he might follow. I don't want him to leave me.

"We have to help Tamara," Paul says hoarsely, towering over me. Diana slumps against him. The amulet's magic dims. Paul struggles to lift his daughter into his arms. He holds Diana close as if he wants to absorb all the horror she's been through into himself. "There must be something we can do to save her. Some magic potion or spell or—"

He stops as if realizing how foreign those words sound coming from him. This isn't his world. It was never meant to be.

The bank groans ominously, and the walls begin to crumble. Another spasm wracks my body.

"We have to go," Costin orders. "Follow me."

"Where?" Paul looks around, clearly not wanting to return to the supernatural tunnels. "The bank doors are welded shut."

Costin lifts me carefully. Every movement is fresh agony. "I promise we'll find a way, Tamara. We've survived impossible odds before. We're going to get you through this. I won't lose you."

I close my eyes. I hear the ceiling start to cave in and wonder if we've finally run out of miracles.

Time loses meaning. It's marked by waves of unbearable pain and glimpses of victory. I drift in and out of consciousness as Costin carries me through the darkness. I prefer oblivion over the agony of my ravaged shoulder and dying body. The wolf venom spreads like lava in my veins, and I imagine it's melting everything it touches.

"Stay with me," Costin's voice pulls me back when I start to slip away. He wants to save me. I don't think he can, but he whispers about ancient rites and possible cures if only I hold on. "Focus on my voice, Tamara."

I try, but the fever makes me see things. The past and present swirl together until I can't tell what's real. For a moment I'm in the labyrinth facing my fears. Then I'm a teenager watching Costin through the spy hole in the wall. Conrad aims a gun at Paul and shoots. A house explodes. Anthony smiles and hands me a joint as we hide in a janitor's closet at my birthday party.

Diana's small hand finds mine in the dark. "You don't have to be scared. The dragon can sleep now."

I don't have the heart, or the strength, to tell her that is not the monster that scares me. I catch a glimpse of the amulet. There is a part of me that wants to take it back so that I can end this pain.

She falls behind me, her hand dropping from mine. She's exhausted from the ritual, barely able to walk. Paul supports her with one arm while the other braces his weight on the wall to propel him forward.

"We're near the old subway tunnels," Costin says. "If we can reach the underground city, we can try to find Morvok. He can help us with the amulet so you can—"

A thunderous crash cuts him off as more of the bank collapses behind us. The ceiling groans. Dust and debris blow through the tunnel. Diana starts coughing.

"We're running out of time." Paul barely controls his panic. He lifts Diana into his arms and tries carrying her despite his weakness.

He's right. Each breath is harder than the last.

"Costin," I whisper. I'm so tired. I just want to

rest. "No more. We can't take them to the underground city."

Costin's arms tighten around me. "My home has ancient texts, healing magic. There has to be a cure. I'll find it. I promise."

This is not a promise he can keep. We both know he's lying. I see it in his eyes when another convulsion wracks my body. The wolf magic burns hotter, reshaping me from the inside out. If I am to survive, there would be time before I fully change. But my other injuries are too severe.

My injured arm is useless against my stomach, the fingers broken. Paul's ripped shirt seems to be the only thing keeping it together. I feel the shard of glass still imbedded in my leg. I grip Costin's neck. "Promise me you won't let me become a werewolf. I don't want to be a monster. Promise me you'll kill me before that happens."

He adjusts me in his arms, holding me closer. My head rests on his shoulder.

"I can feel it." My voice sounds strange to my own ears. "It's eating my insides."

"Keep walking forward," Costin orders Paul. "I'll come back for you."

"No, wait—" Paul yells, his voice drifting away as Costin speeds me through the tunnels. I become dizzy and everything blurs. I shut my eyes, fading into unconsciousness.

When I open my eyes, I'm lying on the couch in Costin's office. It's sparse from missing decorations, but someone has cleaned the debris. Diana is sitting on the floor beside me, stroking my hair. "I remember you."

Draakmar must have given her memories back. I wonder why the dragon would have done that. She's better off not knowing.

Never mind. I sound like Costin.

"Are you hurt?" I ask.

She shakes her head.

"Draakmar is a friend." I want to tell her more, maybe reassure her, and give her some motherly advice on how to survive. I'm drawn to touch the stone around her neck, its shape so familiar to my fingers. It's been with me most of my life, and it feels strange not to have it. The amulet vibrates under my touch, softer than when I wore it, more like starlight than dragon fire.

"I know." Diana rests her forehead down next to me. She doesn't fight or question its power like I always did. She simply accepts it, the way children accept magic as natural.

"I'm so sorry, Diana, I never meant..." Darkness tries to take me.

"Dad!"

I open my eyes to see Costin helping Paul. He releases the man to slump next to the doorframe. Diana rushes to her father.

"I'm okay," Paul mutters, sliding down the wall. His face is pale, and he looks like he might be sick. "That was..." He covers his mouth with his hand and shudders as if stopping himself from throwing up. "That was something else."

Supernatural travel isn't easy on mortals. I remember my first time, the disorientation and nausea. It hasn't improved, though I know what to expect now. Diana seems to have handled it better.

"Dad?" She touches his face. "Are you okay?"

He manages a weak smile. "Just need a minute, sweetheart."

Costin crosses the office in agitation. He glances at the door every few steps like he's waiting for something. The room spins when I try to track his movement, so I close my eyes.

"Costin..." I reach for him. Instantly, he's by my side. "Promise me..."

"Stop. Don't ask that of me," he denies.

"Promise me, Costin." I need him to say the words. "Promise that you won't let me become a monster. I don't want to be a werewolf or come back as a ghost. I don't want to be a creature of the night. Don't try to change me into a vampire. Let me go."

I've seen what monsters do. I don't want that eternity.

Before he can answer, Astrid sweeps into the office. She's holding her heels in one hand as if she ran to get here. Her perfect composure is cracked with worry. "I went to Thane's sanctuary but found it abandoned. They moved the ritual site—" Her gaze finds me on the couch and her eyes widen. "What happened? Where did you go?"

"Tamara needs help," he says.

Astrid comes to my side and begins peeling back the bandage on my arm to look at the damage. Her fingers trace the bite's edges, and I see recognition flash in her eyes. She glances at Costin, and some unspoken knowledge passes between them. They both know what a werewolf bite means. She presses her hands down over the wound and I feel her magic flowing into me to stop the bleeding, but there's a hesitation in the way her magic moves, like she senses something different about this wound. Like she knows what fate is coming, what choice it will force.

Through my pain-hazed vision, I want to beg them not to do it, to remind them of my wishes, but the words won't come.

"That Alpha creature bit her," Paul explains, holding Diana back. His voice shakes, not just from supernatural travel but from the weight of everything they've endured. He looks at his daughter with the amulet around her neck. I think he knows that she can never go back to being just a normal little girl. "Before the amulet—"

"Who is that speaking?" Astrid asks Costin, sounding a little annoyed to be interrupted by a mortal. She doesn't turn around.

"Paul," Costin answers. Then, as if to answer her earlier question, he adds, "There was no time to send for you. I sensed Elizabeth's presence near the old bank. When I felt her pull on our sire bond..." He looks at me. "I led my guards to them. We barely made it in time."

Astrid forces her attention back to the immediate crisis. Her hands move as if desperately trying to heal my wound. I can feel her magic is failing.

"Thane did this?" Her voice carries deadly promise. "I'll tear that flea-ridden bastard apart with my bare—"

"He's already dead," Costin interjects flatly. "One problem at a time."

Another convulsion hits me. I try to bite back my scream but fail. The sound echoes off stone walls.

"Tamara!" Diana cries in fright.

Astrid's attention snaps to Diana, focusing on the amulet. Her expression shifts from shock to understanding. "Of course. Draakmar found his perfect vessel."

I grab Astrid's hand. "Thank you."

"Of course," Astrid tries to dismiss, her hands working frantically despite her controlled tone. It's the most emotion I've seen from her probably in my entire life. "Costin, I need mandrake root, willow bark, yarrow—"

"No, thank you for raising me," I try to explain through the pain. "Thank you for being my mom." The words feel strange, given how we normally communicate, but that makes it no less true. I can feel the end coming. I need to tell her how I feel, at least once.

"Stop acting like this is the end," Astrid snaps, but there's something different in her voice. It's not just her usual stern tone, but real fear. For once, she can't manage this away or control the solution to the problem. She presses her lips tightly, choking back whatever emotion threatens to break through. "Costin, do you have Dracaena resin, fae tears, moonlit dew, unicorn horn, silver filings, anything to stop the progression?"

Costin becomes a blur, leaving and returning several times to give Astrid jars and vials. She begins mixing items in her hand and rubbing them against me in hurried desperation. I don't know how long they work to fix me, but nothing seems to help.

Pain rips through me. The wolf venom burns hotter, trying to change me.

Astrid shakes her head dumping a jar of powder on my arm in a last ditch effort. She shakes her head and slowly stands.

"What are you doing?" Costin demands. "Help her!"

"It's not working," Astrid answers, grabbing his arm to make him look at her. "If it was just the wolf venom, maybe we could stop it, but the ritual damaged something inside her. Nothing we have is working. Without the amulet, she has no protection. The residual magic from the ritual is tearing her apart. She's dying."

"She can have the amulet," Diana offers, tears in her voice. "Don't let her die."

"It doesn't work like that," Astrid's tone is firm, just like I remember it. "No one must ever wear that but you. Don't take it off or bad things will happen."

I want to tell her not to scare the child.

"Tamara." Costin kneels beside me, grabbing my hand.

"We should get her out of here. No child should see this." Astrid moves to examine Paul's wounds. "You both need healing."

"I won't leave Tamara," Diana protests.

"You must." Astrid's tone allows no argument. "Your father needs care, and you're exhausted from channeling dragon magic."

"Tamara," Paul says, but he doesn't finish whatever he's thinking.

Astrid turns to Costin, her voice dropping. "The sun rises soon. How long does she have?"

"Hours? Minutes?" Costin sounds lost.

"Then you know what must be done." Astrid helps Paul stand. Her eyes linger on where Thane bit me. "I can't force you. Whatever you choose, whatever you must do—you have the Devine family's blessing."

"We don't know what will happen if I do that," Costin answers, his voice breaking. "She made me promise not to turn her. She doesn't want this."

"She's dying," Astrid states flatly. "She doesn't understand what she's denying. Sometimes we must break promises to save those we love for their own good."

"I don't know what it will do to her," Costin hesitates, "but I can't lose her."

My eyes close, and I can't force them back open. I hear Diana crying as Astrid leads them away.

Costin's cool hand finds mine.

"Stay," I manage through the pain. I don't want to die alone. "Don't leave me."

"Never." His voice breaks. "I won't let you become a monster."

The pain comes in waves now, each one stronger

than the last. My body arches off the couch as another convulsion hits.

"I'm scared," I whisper when I can breathe again. I think of floating in that white light with no pain. I'm not frightened of dying but of becoming something I'm not. I don't want to be a predator hunting mortals, uncontrollable and feral.

"You've always been so brave." Costin's fingers trace my face, his touch achingly gentle. "From the moment I found you running through the forest after Anthony's magic burned your hand. You were so tiny, and you looked up at me and said, 'I don't want to be a snack.' You were always watching everything, questioning everything."

I try to smile, but it comes out as a grimace.

"Everything I've done..." His voice catches. "Tamara, I—"

Another spasm cuts him off. This one's different, deeper, like my bones are about to snap in two. The werewolf curse surges, but there's nothing left inside me to fight it. My body is giving up.

"I love you." The words come out in a rush. I need him to know before whatever happens next. "I think I always have, even when I was trying not to."

His forehead presses to mine, and I feel him trembling with barely contained emotion. In this moment, all his careful control, all his centuries of power mean nothing. He's as broken as I am.

"I've loved you your entire life. And I will love you for the rest of mine." His voice breaks, and I feel wetness on my cheeks. Whether they're my tears or his, I can't tell. "I can't watch you die. Not like this. Not when I've finally found the one soul in centuries who makes me feel human again."

I grip his shirt with my good hand. "Don't. You promised me."

"You could never be a monster." He pulls back just enough to meet my eyes. "You're too stubborn."

The pain rises again, and I know it's the last wave. My heart stutters in my chest. The wolf venom reaches for it, trying to stop it. I've taken too much damage. I won't survive this.

"I love you," Costin whispers against my lips. He lifts his wrist.

The choice looms between us. Honor my wishes and let me die or break his promise to save me. For centuries, he's lived with the consequences of forcing choices on others. Elizabeth's arranged marriage, the memories he's erased, the lives he's ended. Each decision has carved away another piece of his humanity. Now he faces the ultimate choice. Either way, I'm going to die tonight.

"Costin, please..." My words slur as darkness creeps in. "You... promised..."

I try to explain that it's okay to let me go, that I'm not afraid of the end, but I'm too weak to speak.

His fangs pierce his wrist.

I want to tell him to stop, but I can't form words. My body convulses one final time. I taste his blood pouring past my lips and the two ancient magics battle for dominion over what's left of my soul. The wolf venom doesn't just attack the vampire blood. They crash together like opposing storms, neither yielding. The pain is worse than before. I want to die. I can't take any more.

The darkness takes me, and I don't expect to wake up.

The last thing I hear is Costin's voice. "Don't leave me, Tamara. I love you. Don't leave me."

To be continued...

The End

NEARLY DEAD

The final installment of the spellbinding first-person POV romantic urban fantasy series by NY Times and USA Today bestselling author Michelle M. Pillow.

I was supposed to stay dead. That's the one thing everyone agreed on.

One bite. One drink. That's all it took to rip apart what was left of my humanity. Now there's a war raging under my skin-werewolf venom battling vampire blood-and I'm stuck in the middle, no longer mortal... and not quite anything else.

Costin says he saved me. That he did what he had to do. But what he really did was break his promise. He turned me into a monster.

And still, I want him.

Worse, I need him-his blood, his strength, his control. But every time I give in, I lose more of myself. The hunger is growing. So is the rage.

Everything's unraveling. My body. My past. The fragile peace holding the supernatural world together. And the only thing more dangerous than what I've become... is what I might do next.

Now, I'm out of time. If I don't figure out what I am-and fast-I'll destroy everything I've been trying to protect.

Including the master vampire willing to burn the world for me.

Merely Mortal Series

Merely Mortal
Mostly Shattered
Barely Breathing
Nearly Dead

Visit MichellePillow.com for details!

ABOUT MICHELLE M. PILLOW

New York Times & USA TODAY
Bestselling Author

Michelle loves to travel and try new things, whether it's a paranormal investigation of an old Vaudeville Theatre or climbing Mayan temples in Belize. She believes life is an adventure fueled by copious amounts of coffee.

Newly relocated to the American South, Michelle is involved in various film and documentary projects with her talented director husband. She is mom to a fantastic artist. And she's managed by a dog and cat who make sure she's meeting her deadlines.

For the most part she can be found wearing pajama pants and working in her office. There may or may not be dancing. It's all part of the creative process.

Come say hello! Michelle loves talking with readers on social media!

www.MichellePillow.com

- facebook.com/AuthorMichellePillow
- x.com/michellepillow
- instagram.com/michellempillow
- bookbub.com/authors/michelle-m-pillow
- goodreads.com/Michelle_Pillow
- amazon.com/author/michellepillow
- youtube.com/michellepillow
- pinterest.com/michellepillow
- tiktok.com/@michellempillow
- threads.net/@michellempillow

PLEASE REVIEW
THANK YOU FOR READING!

Please take a moment to share your thoughts by reviewing this book.

Thank you to all the wonderful readers who take the time to share your thoughts about the books you love. I can't begin to tell you how important you are when it comes to helping other readers discover the series!

Be sure to check out Michelle's other titles at www.MichellePillow.com